KING
REECE

Also by Shaun Sinclair

Blood Ties

The Crescent Crew Series
Street Rap
King Reece

Published by Kensington Publishing Corp.

KING
REECE

SHAUN
SINCLAIR

KENSINGTON PUBLISHING CORP.

www.kensingtonbooks.com

DAFINA BOOKS are published by

Kensington Publishing Corp.
119 West 40th Street
New York, NY 10018

All Kensington titles, imprints, and distributed lines are available at special quantity discounts for bulk purchases for sales promotion, premiums, fundraising, and educational or institutional use.

Special book excerpts or customized printings can also be created to fit specific needs. For details, write or phone the office of the Kensington Sales Manager: Kensington Publishing Corp., 119 West 40th Street, New York, NY 10018. Attn. Sales Department. Phone: 1-800-221-2647.

Dafina and the Dafina logo Reg. U.S. Pat. & TM Off.

ISBN-13: 978-1-4967-2108-2
ISBN-10: 1-4967-2108-X
First Kensington Trade Paperback Printing: July 2019

ISBN-13: 978-1-4967-2109-9 (ebook)
ISBN-10: 1-4967-2109-8 (ebook)
First Kensington Electronic Edition: July 2019

10 9 8 7 6 5 4 3 2 1

Printed in the United States of America

PROLOGUE

April 9, 2009

The man's naked, chiseled torso dripped with sweat as he pounded out a set of pushups. Headphones covered his ears, blasting raunchy rap music at ignorant levels. The song hadn't been released yet, but the man had an exclusive copy. He jammed the song so much that he knew the lyrics by heart.

He rapped, "When it come to my bars, niggas fear 'em like prison, they start squealing like pigeons, praying to God that I miss 'em! Oooooh!!!"

The last line hyped him up so much he hopped from the floor and threw a few imaginary punches at the air. He was in his zone now, doing his normal routine to break the monotony of his predicament. He lived vicariously through the music. When he bumped his tunes, he drowned out the sounds of prison. With the right song playing, he wasn't confined to a USP; he was a teenager again, roaming the halls of 71st Senior High looking for a classmate to battle. Or he was in the trenches again, putting in the work that would make him a legend in the streets. The right song dictated his mood. With the now-popular trap rap booming in his ears, he reveled in his status as a Trap Lord, and for a brief moment, he wondered what would have become of his life if he had decided to pursue a music career on his terms.

However, when the music stopped, he was forced to deal with the reality of who he was.

King Reece pushed the headphones from his head and allowed them to rest on his neck. He inhaled the stale air inside his cell and focused his attention on the wall in front of him. Taped to his wall were newspaper clippings and photos of the last four years of his life. It was his shrine of sorts, the thing that kept him going. Each portion of the collage served a purpose for him.

On the top left of the wall was the article that started it all. The headline read, "Heavy Is the Head That Wears the Crown." The article spoke of his trial and the mysterious five-year plea agreement. The article made him seem larger than life, mythic even. It detailed some uncorroborated stories of his drug empire—tales of kidnappings, murders, and lynchings. They estimated he and his gang, the Crescent Crew, had amassed more than $50 million in just two short years, and that his personal wealth was somewhere around $30 million. In the article, the writer stressed that the Crescent Crew lived their ethos—Death Before Dishonor—to the letter, in that no one from his organization turned rat in his absence. They were rumored to still be operating in his absence and stronger than ever.

King Reece had placed this article strategically first in his collage. He read the article daily to remind himself who he was and of his purpose. Being in prison was a constant battle of the mind, and even the strongest man felt weak at times. This article reminded King Reece of his stature, of his family who believed in him. This article reminded King Reece of the empire he had built from the ground up and why he couldn't fall victim to the instability of his incarcerated thoughts.

Beside the first article was another clipping. The headline read, "Music Mogul Dodges Prison." This article spoke of Qwess, King Reece's right-hand man, brother, and co-founder of the Crescent Crew. King Reece had taken his plea agreement to save Qwess from any further investigation by the feds. Qwess was on the cusp of superstardom as a rapper, producer, and label head when King Reece was apprehended and set to stand trial. Before his trial began, Reece had one of the Crew abduct one of the juror's children in exchange for a not-guilty verdict. He acted ultra-cocky at trial, and the federal prosecutor knew the fix was in. To insure a conviction, the government arrested Qwess and threatened to pin a charge on him unless Reece took a plea agreement. In the end, Reece sacrificed his life for that of his comrade.

Beside this article were numerous photos of Qwess attending industry events, photos of him on *60 Minutes*, *Forbes* listing photos, and other media clippings.

This section was important to Reece because it bore witness to the strength of their brotherhood and the results of his sacrifice. King Reece would travel out of the galaxy and fight the sun for his brother Qwess to live in peace, and he knew Qwess felt the same way. They lived, breathed, and were willing to die for each other. This was Crew Business.

A Young Jeezy song screamed from the speakers around King Reece's neck, a song about how amazing he was. Reece could relate, so he threw the headphones on, hit the floor, and got some money. After he completed his set of fifty pushups, he stood and studied his mural again.

The next section of his mural was a testament to false love, his only mistake and Achilles heel in an otherwise beautiful tapestry of the right decisions in life. The headlines read, "Disgraced FBI Agent Resigns Amidst Conspiracy Suspicions," "FBI Agent Has Lovechild from Imprisoned Kingpin." There were no fewer than ten articles surrounding a picture of the woman they spoke about: Katrina Destiny Hill.

This section of King Reece's mural was the most important for him. Although it ripped his heart like old stitches every time he looked at his wall, he forced himself to endure the pain just to remind himself to never make that mistake again. She had caught him slipping, warmed up to him, then served him on a cold platter to the federal government. King Reece—the Five Percent God-Body—adjusted his mantra to that of the Jews: never again.

The orthodox Muslims turned toward Mecca and offered their prayers every morning, the Buddhists meditated. For King Reece, this wall was his shrine, the place where he cleansed and replenished his soul every morning. His time inside was nearing its end. He had to prepare himself to reclaim his place in society and right all the wrongs inflicted upon him, beginning with Destiny.

The country had just elected a black man to the Oval Office. Surely, the world was ready for the return of King Reece.

Chapter 1

April 19, 2009

The tinted-out Suburban skated down the gritty North Carolina street en route to its destination. In back, a man clad in all black checked the rounds in a magazine then slammed it in the butt of his AR-15 assault rifle. Next, he readjusted the infrared beam mounted on the weapon's barrel and clicked it to make sure it was working. Satisfied that his weapon was ready, he radioed the two Suburbans trailing him. They reported that they were loaded and ready to go as well.

"We ready," the man said to his driver. The driver gunned the engine, and the heavy SUV rocketed forward.

Moments later, all hell broke loose as three trucks skidded to a halt in front of a duplex. Children across the street watched with mouths agape as man after man exited the trucks in all black carrying big guns. The first two men carried a battering ram, which they slammed into the front door of the duplex without warning, exploding the heavy door off its hinges. As the door crashed into the wall, the men swarmed inside like killer bees with their assault rifles leading the way. They were met with immediate resistance as the first two men to rush through the door were tagged in the chest by heavy gunfire. Their bulletproof vests prevented death, but the impact blew them back through the door for a reluctant retreat.

The army of men behind them regrouped and charged again. This time they were more careful. They rushed through the door and quickly dispatched the resisters with two shots to the chest. Then they cleared the rest of the house in under a minute, pouring into room after room until they were sure the only people inside were their victims lying on the floor gasping for breath.

The leader of the federal assault team stood over one of the men and aimed the barrel of the rifle at his melon. "Just tell us where he's at, and you can go," he said calmly. Meanwhile, the other men posted up at the windows of the home with their weapons ready.

"You wasting time, man. You gonna bleed out. Come on, what's it gonna be?" he prodded. "You gonna tell us or what? We know he was here earlier. Right here in this very damn house! Now you tell us, or we gonna toss this muthafuckin' house up while you bleed to death."

The federal agents had invaded this town on a tip. They had good reason to believe that the number one man on their Most Wanted list had just been in this very house moments ago. They had been pursuing him for nearly half a decade, and they were finally closing in on him. They refused to let him escape this time.

"What's it gonna be?" the agent asked one last time.

For a response, the man simply held out his left hand. "Listen good, because these will be the last words you hear," the man named Muhammad began. "There is nothing you can do to me that would make me feel worse than betraying *my* leader." He opened his hand to reveal a grenade.

The masked man's eyes fell on the grenade. "Whoa . . . wait a minute. Calm down," he pleaded after seeing the explosive. "Put that thing away now. Close your hand back over it real slow," he instructed, backing away. He removed his mask to reveal a pale face and striking blond hair. "We can work this out, Muhammad. Nobody has to die. All we want is your leader."

Muhammad chuckled and completely opened his left hand, revealing a full view of the grenade. Both safeties were already removed, and when he opened his hand, the spoon popped off. He looked the blond-haired leader of the assault team in his eyes and barked, "Death before dishonor! Crescent Crew to the death!" Then he tossed the grenade into the air.

The men tried to escape, but it was too late. In three seconds flat, the house exploded, taking everyone, including Muhammad, with it.

Down the street, in the woods, a lone man observed the explosion with a demented smile.

Chapter 2

The Wahid Compound was crowded with people. Visitors from all over the nation and abroad populated all three houses located on the grounds of the Wahid Compound. They had all come to welcome home a special person. A person who was dear to everyone present in one way or another at one time or another.

Qwess anxiously awaited the arrival of the guest of honor. It had been a long time coming. Four years, to be exact, since he had begun putting plans in motion to bring the guest of honor home. Now all his striving was finally coming to fruition.

Qwess walked from his house to his sister Fatimah's house, then to his mother's house, making sure everything was perfect. All kinds of foods were being served, a DJ was spinning records, and a live band was on hand to play some of the guest of honor's favorite songs.

It was mid-May, and the sweltering Carolina heat had the majority of the guests huddling by the side of the Olympic-size swimming pool located in the middle of the three houses. As Qwess made his rounds he saw various people whom he had personally invited to this little shindig. As he passed through Fatimah's house a second time, he saw just the brother he needed to speak with: his brother-in-law Raheem. He had been searching for him all afternoon, and he'd finally stumbled upon him. Qwess slipped into the room and gently pushed the door closed behind him.

"*As-salaam alaykum!* You just the man I need to see," Qwess said.

"*Wa alaykum salaam.* What's up, Qwess?"

"I need to holla at you about something," Qwess said.

"What's on your brain, brother?" Raheem asked, although he already assumed where the conversation was going.

Qwess sat on the bed and weighed his words carefully before he spoke. "Listen, I spoke to Fatimah. She told me what happened."

"And?"

"And," Qwess replied. He stood to look in the mirror beside Raheem where he was getting dressed. "She told me about you coming home late. She told me about the argument y'all had. She told me about finding the lipstick on your collar and the number in your pocket."

Raheem was visibly embarrassed and more than a little perturbed. He knew Qwess could be about that action, but he also knew Qwess was one to mind his own business. Raheem didn't know which Qwess was coming at him.

"So, what's this got to do with you?" Raheem asked.

Qwess allowed himself a chuckle before he answered, "It has everything to do with me," he said. "Number one, that's my sister and your wife! Number two, you got kids—four, to be exact—that don't need to see this kind of shit. And number three . . ." Qwess placed both of his hands on Raheem's shoulders and squeezed them tight. "You put your hands on her again and I'm going to put mine on you!"

Raheem felt more offended than threatened. "Qwess, you know me better than that, yo. I mean, all couples have problems, but I would never do anything to hurt your sister. I guess I'm just nervous about today."

Qwess could tell Raheem was truly being sincere, so he relented in his aggression. "Yo, I understand where you coming from, bro. I imagine it could be stressful for you. All I'm saying is, treat your wife right. What kind of man would I be to let somebody just manhandle my sister? You know what I'm saying?"

Raheem nodded.

"Cool. Now stop worrying and come on out. He should be here any minute. In fact, that's them pulling up now. Come pay your respects."

"All right, I'll be out."

Qwess left Raheem and went to meet the limo that had pulled onto the compound. There was already a crowd surrounding the car, so Qwess fell back and played his part.

His mother emerged from the limo first. She was garbed down in an exquisite gown with matching hijab. She was beaming from ear to ear, for she was extremely happy. Fatimah, and her three boys and one girl, crowded the limo, preventing the other occupant from exiting. Aminah Wahid quickly ushered them out the way and reached inside to give the last occupant a hand. Seconds later, Khalid Ali Wahid, the patriarch of the Wahid Clan, emerged from the back of the limo wearing a cream linen suit. He stood to his full six foot, three inches and took in the whole scene before him.

Throngs of people rushed to congratulate him on his freedom. Some people he knew by face, others by name only. Khalid had been gone for almost fifteen years. Most of the people present, he had seen grow up through pictures only.

He hugged his dear daughter Fatimah tightly. She had

been nineteen years old when he left the streets for his state-sponsored vacation. Now the teenager he had left was a grown woman with a family of her own. Of course, he had seen her on the many visits over the years, but that was in the element created by the government. It was different seeing her in the free cipher, in her element. She had grown to be a beautiful woman. She had also made him a grandfather—four times over.

Khalid bent to hug his grandsons. The two twins and the youngest boy all returned his hug. The youngest child, a two-year-old girl, appeared frightened. She had never seen him in person, only through pictures. She couldn't accurately discern the difference between a picture and reality; therefore it scared her.

Khalid picked her up and attempted to break the ice. Naturally, she wailed out in terror. Then, suddenly, she became quiet as her gaze extended beyond her grandfather. Khalid hadn't noticed the little girl's father walk up until Fatimah introduced him.

"Daddy, this is my husband, Raheem," Fatimah said. Khalid passed the baby off to Fatimah and issued Raheem a firm handshake. This was their first time meeting.

"Nice to meet you, son," Khalid offered, pumping Raheem's hand like a piston. Raheem almost buckled from the grip. Khalid was fifty-three years old, but looked to be only thirty-five, thanks to the regimented workout he had accustomed himself to while in the federal penitentiary. He looked thirty-five but had the strength of a man ten years younger than that.

"Nice to meet you, sir. I've heard a lot of good things about you," Raheem offered, forgetting his Muslim etiquette. Khalid was Muslim in theory, as was Raheem, which would make the proper greeting *As-salaam alaykum*. However, due to Raheem's nervousness, his etiquette went out the window.

"I hope so. Are you taking care of my little girl?"

"Yes, sir."

"Good, good. Because that's still my heart. I would hate to see her unhappy," Khalid said, boring his gaze into Raheem. The statement was made with clear underlying implications. The twinkle in his eye and the smirk on his dark cheek made it clear that Khalid Ali Wahid was still gangsta at heart.

"No, sir. You don't have to worry about that," Raheem assured him.

"Good. Now where's my boy—Qwess, as he's called nowadays?" Khalid asked, looking around the compound.

Everyone in front of him parted like the Red Sea until there was a clear line of sight between father and son. Both men froze as they took each other in, Khalid in his heavenly white and Qwess in his royal cream attire. As Khalid stared at his son, a lone tear slid down his cheek.

Khalid was so proud of his son. Not because he was responsible for bringing him home, but for all his accomplishments thus far. His son had become a legal millionaire, an international superstar, a Grammy Award–winning artist, a philanthropist, and a serial entrepreneur. The most important accomplishment to Khalid was that his son hadn't forgotten the most important thing in life: He had taken care of his family. He had done the right thing by assuming the role of the head of his family. Now, Khalid could return to his rightful role and reassume his rightful place as head of the family.

"Come here, son!" Khalid beckoned. Qwess gently sauntered over. "*¿Como está mijo?*"

Qwess was surprised to hear his father speaking Spanish, but he returned the greeting.

"*Yo soy bien.*" I am well. "*¿Tu hablas español, sí?*"

"*Sí. Muchas gracias a tu.*" Yes. Thanks to you.

For a moment, it was just the two giants and no one else. A

special moment shared between father and son. A rendering of mutual respect.

"Well, father, when you're finished here, meet me at my house. I have something for you," Qwess requested.

There were a lot of guests that had come a long way— some from as far as Cuba—to pay homage. Qwess didn't want to prevent a happy homecoming in any way. So he excused himself to his mansion, while his father reacquainted himself with friends and family. They would have plenty of time to catch up. Plus, he had business to attend to. So, as he retreated to his mansion, he made sure Doe and Hulk were in tow.

Hulk was Qwess's personal security. Qwess's stature in the entertainment industry required that he roll with security now. He couldn't go anywhere without being mobbed by fans. It was only fitting that Hulk be his security since he was a chiseled three hundred and twenty pounds of muscle and stood six foot six barefoot. He had also been with Qwess for almost ten years in one capacity or another. First in the streets, then in the music industry. Through it all, Hulk had been there. He had seen the good, the bad, and the ugly, and kept his mouth shut. He possessed secrets that could bury Qwess in a box forever. He had done things for Qwess that could give him the needle. The two men were bound by blood.

Doe was vice president at Atlantic Beach Productions and had completely bossed up. He and Qwess went back even further. Both were only fifteen years old when Qwess had moved to North Carolina after Qwess's father was convicted and subsequently sent to prison. Qwess and Doe had clicked immediately. They bonded over their mutual love of music. Qwess rapped, and Doe's cousin Reece rapped also. In fact, Doe's cousin Reece had already secured a record deal when Qwess met Doe. Doe introduced Qwess to Reece inside of a rap cipher in which Reece was dominating. Qwess flowed and displayed his skills, and although Reece emerged the victor of the cipher, he was impressed by Qwess's skills. From that day the men became inseparable. That is, until Reece had caught his bid almost four years ago.

"Yo, man, what that house nigga John Meyers say?" Qwess asked Doe, referring to his point-of-contact at AMG Records, ABP's parent label.

"Same ole shit. '*Come on, please stay. We can sweeten the pot,*'" Doe mocked.

Qwess chuckled as he logged onto his computer in his home office. Hulk grabbed an energy drink from the miniature refrigerator while absently listening in on the conversation.

"Yeah, I bet that they do wish they could sweeten the pot. Fuckin' vultures! We gonna give 'em this last album and that's it. Ya dig?" Qwess promised.

"No doubt. When you scheduled to do the magazine interview?" Doe asked.

"I believe it's next week."

"Word?"

"Yeah."

"So, have you decided who you gonna take to be Mysterio yet?" Doe wondered, more than a little concerned.

Qwess sighed, "I haven't decided yet. I'll probably just take Flame and fudge it. Ya dig? We gotta get just the right person to play the part," he explained. "What's up wit' ole girl? She ready to come on over to ABP yet?"

Doe scratched his head, buying time. He hated to be a disappointment, but it was what it was. "Yo, man, she definitely ready to leave AMG, but they ain't trying to let her go."

"What you mean, they ain't trying to let her go?"

"She still under obligation for another album because of that extension she signed. And AMG not budging."

"Oh, we can make 'em budge!" Hulk interjected. "It

wouldn't be the first time we had to give someone a little motivation."

"Yeah, I know we can, but we not trying to go that route. Not yet anyway," Qwess decided. He stood to answer the knock at the door. "We'll see how she handles things. After all, that is your broad, Doe."

Qwess opened the door and let his father in. Khalid oozed into the room. He'd always had a smooth yet powerful presence, but since his release he was practically floating.

"*Salaam alaykum*, brothers." Khalid checked out the spacious office with marble floors. "This is a nice spot you got yourself here, son."

"Thanks. Pop, this is Rolando and Hulk," Qwess introduced.

Khalid waved his hand in dismissal. "Between what you told me and what I've read in those magazines, I feel like I already know them." Khalid looked Hulk up and down. "Damn, son, I didn't realize you were *this* big! What are you, six-five?"

"Six-six."

"So, Rolando, Reece is your cousin, right?

"Yes, sir."

"Um-hmm." Khalid shook his head. "Damn shame what happened. I wish Salim would've come to me a week before. Just one week and it probably wouldn't have happened like that."

Khalid was referring to Reece's bust. Qwess was visiting his father the very day Reece was busted. Turned out Khalid knew all about Reece's girlfriend being a federal agent. He had been trying to speak to his son, but Qwess had been unable to pay his father a visit due to the demanding schedule the music business heaped on him. Ironically, the day Qwess did come was the day it was too late.

"Yeah, I know."

Qwess's mood changed from festive to somber. He always wondered what if . . . What if he had put his family first?

"You can't blame yourself, son," Khalid said as if reading Qwess's mind. "None of you can. Besides, he came off good. What he got, like a few months left?"

"Nah. Like a few weeks," Qwess corrected. He quickly changed the subject and suggested everyone return downstairs to enjoy the party.

As they wandered back out to the party, Qwess tugged at his father's arm, and the two of them took a detour to Qwess's garage. Inside was Qwess's green Lamborghini Murciélago, platinum Bentley GT, and black Hummer H2. At the end of the fleet was a car with a cover over it. It was evident that it was a convertible as the cover seeped into the car's interior. Qwess guided his father to the end of the fleet and removed the tarp to reveal a shiny maroon Cadillac XLR with the top reclined. It was complete with twenty-inch chrome factory rims. He passed the keys to his father.

"You bought me a Cadillac!" Khalid said, astonished. "You remembered?"

"Of course. I know you love your Cadillacs."

Khalid frowned. "But it's a convertible. What's up with that?"

"I know you don't like convertibles, Dad. Check this out." Qwess pushed a button on the keyless remote and the hardtop slowly ascended from the trunk. "I'm the same way about 'verts, but this ain't that old El-dog you had. Technology has improved."

Qwess and his father shared a laugh at the thought of Khalid's old '79 Eldorado. Khalid marveled at how far things had come since he had been gone. During sentencing, the judge told him cars would be flying before he came home. The judge was being sarcastic, but he wasn't far off. Convertible hardtops and shit. Khalid hugged his son again.

"I'm proud of you, son. You've come a long way on your own. Now I'm ready to help you with all you got going on."

"Nope," Qwess interrupted, shaking his head. "You've been gone for a while. You deserve a vacation that's not government-sponsored. I remember how you used to say you regret not taking care of yourself and going to see other parts of the world when you was making all that money. Well, Mom expressed the same sentiment over the years. So, for the next six months, you both are officially on vacation at my expense. When you come back you can start as counsel for the label."

Khalid was beyond word. "I don't know what to say."

"How about thanks? I know you; you gonna try to get out of it, but, Pop, I want to do this. You more than deserve it."

Khalid knew his son was as strong-willed as he was and wasn't taking no for an answer. Therefore, resistance was futile. He simply agreed.

The band could be heard playing Isaac Hayes outside the garage. Neither Qwess nor his father wanted to be rude, so they decided to return to the party.

As Qwess walked back to the party, he was truly happy. He had amassed a substantial fortune in the past four years doing what he loved. He had four artists—excluding himself—that sold well their first time out. (In fact, his female rapper, Saigon, had gone platinum.) His last album was completed, and it was expected to go at least triple-platinum. After the album, he was retiring to concentrate more on the business side of Atlantic Beach Productions. He planned to sign more artists and groom them to take over the industry. The good thing was he was severing his ties with AMG, so he would reap full benefits from however many albums he sold. Qwess also had an ace in the hole.

On his last album, Qwess had introduced the world to an artist named Mysterio. Mysterio had guest-appeared on a whole song on the album. The song was so true to the heart and precise, record labels had hounded Qwess for months, offering unprecedented deals just to get Mysterio to spit a verse on one of their artists' records. Of course, Qwess declined. He knew Mysterio had the potential to change the game if he played his cards right. However, when it came to Mysterio, things were a little more complicated than people knew.

For now, he would just revel in his happiness. His father was home, business was good, and in a few weeks, he was going to shock the world, for the last piece in a long-awaited puzzle was about to be added.

Chapter 3

FCI Petersburg, Virginia

> *Reece,*
> *I don't know what to say anymore. It's obvious you
> don't wish to see me when you are released soon.
> Truthfully, I don't know if I should want to see you
> after all you've put me through. At least you did call off
> the dogs. For that, I am thankful. Yet I really don't care
> anymore. I'd rather die before I let my son not know
> who his father is. My son—no, our son—asks me
> about you daily. Where is his father, he asks. He's get-
> ting so big now! He looks just like you!*
> *I know you're thinking about how bad you want
> me dead. Well, know that sometimes I wish the same
> thing for myself. I never realized how much I loved you
> until now. It seems I have a way of running off loved
> ones (my mom and dad). For this one time, I want to
> make things right.*
> *So, I've quit the Bureau. I'm moving back to*

North Carolina, and I will bring you your son. One
way or another you will deal with me. Our son, Prince,
deserves it.
    Love,
    Destiny

Reece crumbled the letter in his hands. He could not believe the audacity of this broad. *She's talking tough like she run*
shit! Reece thought. He knew he should have killed her when
he had her in his sights that day at the hangar. Hell, he had
even saved her life from behind the wall.

Samson had had one of the Crew members track her down.
He was sitting right outside her house waiting for her to return home when Reece placed the call to abort the mission.
The woman just didn't know how close she had come to ex-
piring that day. She didn't realize he was solely responsible for
her continuing to breathe this fresh air. Now she was insisting
on seeing him? Reece still didn't know what made him abort
the mission. It just didn't seem right at the time, but if she insisted on "seeing" him, he would make sure she saw something
all right.

Reece took the picture from the envelope and scrutinized
it closely. The little boy definitely looked just like him. He was
getting big, too. Destiny had been sending him pictures for the
last four years he had been incarcerated. He suspected it was to
receive his mercy and soften his heart into sparing her life. She
had named the baby Prince Reece Kirkson. Her logic was that
kings birthed princes. She even locked li'l man's hair up so he
sported long dreadlocks just like his father used to. It was refreshing to see a miniature version of himself. He couldn't help
but feel a sense of pride, even under the circumstances.

"Kirkson, you ready to go to your appointment?"

Reece looked out his cell door. Officer Robinson was
waiting with his back to the door. This was a sign of respect.

In the beginning, Reece and Officer Robinson bumped

heads daily. Officer Robinson felt that Reece, being an inmate, was subject to his whims. He also felt that Reece had to take any shit he spewed out. Officer Robinson soon found out the hard way that Reece wasn't going to be anyone's punk.

The tension had bubbled to a head one day in the mess hall. Officer Robinson told Reece the time was up for him to eat. Reece tried to inform him that he was barking up the wrong tree. Still Officer Robinson refused to back down. He proceeded to get in Reece's face and called him a boy. Then he committed the ultimate violation: He spat in Reece's food.

The whole mess hall waited with bated breath, waiting for the infamous King Reece to flex his muscle. Everyone on the yard knew all about King Reece. His street wars were legendary. Everyone knew how he dealt with adversaries, and Virginia was Crescent Crew turf, especially inside.

Yet in this case, nothing happened. Reece simply smiled at Officer Robinson and said, "Remember, you did this. Know it when it comes to you."

Officer Robinson smiled in exaggerated arrogance. "No, shithead, *you* did this to yourself. *You* came here," he snarled.

Reece smiled and nodded his head. No one in the mess hall could believe what they were witnessing. Prison had zapped the gangsta out of King Reece. Or so they thought.

A week later when Officer Robinson returned to work, he rushed into Reece's solo cell (being a crime lord had its perks). Once the two were alone in the room, Officer Robinson literally got on his knees and begged Reece for his life.

"I'm sorry, sir! I'm *so* sorry!" Officer Robinson whined. "I didn't mean any harm." He dropped his head and offered Reece a cell phone. "Please call them off. *Please?*"

With a smirk, Reece placed a call to Bone, Samson's right-hand man, whom Reece had personally promoted before he went away to prison. Reece turned his back and spoke briefly, then ended the call.

"You're clear—for now," Reece said. "There will be no

more mercy, though. If you offend me again, you will be dead before you even know what the offense was. So, if I were you, I'd walk real light around here," he advised. King Reece spat in his face, then kicked him in the ass. Then he kicked him out of his room and kept the phone.

Officer Robinson obtained a new sense of fear and respect for King Reece after leaving work early one day shortly after the incident in the mess hall. Upon walking into his home, he discovered his wife's chihuahua's head in his bed. Inside the detached head's mouth was a note with instructions on how to save their lives.

After that day, Officer Robinson became one of King Reece's biggest "do-boys" behind the wall.

"Officer Rob, let me freshen up," King Reece requested.

A moment later King Reece emerged in a pressed uniform and greeted Robinson. They walked in step along the tier en route to King Reece's doctor's appointment.

"So, man, you going to do the right thing this time or what?" Officer Robinson asked, attempting to make small talk.

King Reece could sense Robinson's uneasiness around him so he obliged him with idle chatter, "Yeah, ya know it," he said dryly.

"Hey, I'm serious, man. You have a lot of potential, man. You could do a lot of good for your community. A lot of people look up to you."

King Reece just listened, not really committing to the conversation. As they passed other inmates along the way, several inmates greeted King Reece with, "*Uhuru Sase!*"

This was the customary salutation for the Black Guerilla Family set. King Reece now sported a shiny bald head with a goatee. This was the uniform for the BGF, so he was commonly mistaken as a member. The BGF was a notorious Black Nationalist gang that strived for peace but wreaked pure havoc when crossed. They were also very politically oriented with a primary focus on black liberation by any means necessary. Inside the federal penal system, one normally had to mob down with some type of organization or another to prevent being preyed upon. FCI Petersburg, Virginia was no different. There were Aryan Brotherhood, Nation of Islam and Orthodox Muslims, Latin Kings, Mexican Mafia, MS-13, Folk Nation, Crips, and Bloods. Just about every gang was represented inside, and they all played for keeps. Crossing any of the various gangs was an almost immediate death sentence—unless one of the other gangs took up the debt.

King Reece did the majority of his time in Petersburg and was subject to the same law of the land. However, Reece had no intention of joining a gang. He *was* the gang, Crescent Crew to the death. Other than Crew business, he was about his paper. Shit, if he didn't make dollars, it didn't make sense!

However, doing time, there were numerous activities to indulge in. Education in some sort of way was the focal point of the majority of the activities. King Reece, never being dumb, participated in numerous study groups. He had been striving as a Five Percenter for quite some time. He had mastered his 120—the prerequisite lessons that a Five Percenter was obligated to learn—a long time ago, and thus had a lot to contribute to any conversation. There were other Five Percenters on the compound, but Reece had sworn his allegiance to another "cosa," The Crescent Crew, and although the Crew was comprised of Muslims or Five Percenters, their ties ran a whole lot deeper than just mathematics. Reece *built* with the other Fives, but he kept his distance. He was done recruiting members for the Crescent Crew, so he saw no need to engage.

King Reece and Officer Robinson finally made it to dental. He was signed in and took his seat waiting his turn to be seen.

Among the other changes King Reece made to his appearance while inside the joint—which included chopping off his locks—he had also customized his grill. He had two-carat diamonds placed in the center of all his teeth, including his molars. Now when he smiled in the sun, a bright rainbow graced his smile. He literally talked money. He was here to get his last dental exam before he maxed out.

An inmate worker sweeping the floor noticed King Reece and ran over to pay his respects.

"Peace, King Reece! Are you straight? Ya need something?"

King Reece recognized the skinny brother as the only other Crescent Crew member on the compound. He didn't know him from the street. In fact, the only way King Reece knew he was part of the Crew was because of his tattoo.

A few months back, inside the exercise room, the brother had been working out. He took off his shirt to flex his tatted muscles, and King Reece peeped the Crescent Crew logo sprawled across his back. In the center of the words, there was a crescent and star with the initials "C.C." bisecting it. Initially, King Reece suspected the cat was an imposter, because ever since *Don Diva Magazine* did a story on the Crescent Crew, a lot of imitators had been springing up all over the country. King Reece confronted the dude and questioned him. He name-dropped Bone as his sponsor then confirmed his oath and allegiance. King Reece wasn't surprised. Since the day he had deputized Bone, Bone had been a major asset. In fact, Bone was running most of North Carolina with Samson in exile in Mexico. King Reece had never questioned Bone's loyalty or intentions before, because Bone himself had been inducted into the Crescent Crew after a spectacular hit on a police officer. Reprisal for one of the comrades killed by that same officer. Yet King Reece couldn't help but wonder what the Crew was coming to. The brother in front of him didn't even look as if he was tough enough to be part of his Family! He didn't have the look of fortitude in his eyes, that fiery inferno that emanated from the depths of a man's soul. It accompanied a man used to making life-and-death decisions in the blink of an eye. King Reece knew it well. It was the look that stared back at him when he looked in the mirror.

"Nah, brother, I don't need anything. What's your name again?"

"Power." He looked offended that the boss of all bosses didn't remember his name. "Ya remember me, right?"

"Yeah, yeah, I'm just not too good with names. Don't worry, though, I always know my brethren when I see them," King Reece assured him, attempting to placate the young solider. Apparently, it worked, since Power's eyes lit up.

"Yeah, I know what you mean. I know you got a lot on your mind, especially since you 'bout to hit the bricks," Power said.

He doesn't know the half of it, thought Reece. "No doubt."

"I know when you touch down, the Crew gon' be tight again! Boy, I can't wait!"

"Shit, what's wrong with the Crew now?" King Reece had heard some rumblings about things, but he had never spoken to someone who was fresh off the bricks like Power was. He had only been in for a year.

"Well, you know. We still straight, but we took a few hits. A few soldiers got killed. Some got knocked."

"Yeah, that come with the life. They all holding strong, right?" King Reece was on edge waiting for the answer. Last thing he needed was a new indictment.

"No doubt!" Power gushed. "You know you set the example of how to handle the system. Take one for the team. Them crackers don't know how to deal with us. Everybody knows you had that trial beat. They didn't know how, but they knew you had it in the bag."

King Reece chuckled, thinking about his master plan for trial.

Power continued, "Kidnapping that juror's child was genius. Then the fact you took a plea after that! Man . . ." He shook his head in disbelief and gave King Reece some dap. Then he raised his hands in surrender. "All hail the king."

Power and King Reece enjoyed a brief laugh. Then Reece cut it short. People were starting to stare.

Suddenly, Power leaned in and whispered something in Reece's ear.

"You heard about Monstruoso?" Power whispered.

"Who?"

"Monstr—ohhhh you know him as Samson."

"Samson?"

"Yeah. Word is, he's back in the States."

Reece shook his head, not believing the info. "Nah, yo, can't be." Samson wasn't that crazy. Him being back in the States could have drastic implications. Reece knew Samson had to be smarter than this. Then another thought crossed his mind . . . What if Samson was back in the States to roll over on him? What if he was drunk with power and wasn't ready to relinquish the mantle to King Reece? What if he was going to pull a Sammy the Bull?

"How you know Samson back in the States?" King Reece demanded, his paranoia kicking in. When playing the game on his level, he could never be at ease.

Power told King Reece what he had heard. "Well, the other night Muhammad's house got raided by the FBI. Now, dig this . . . usually, it's the DEA running up in spots. Never the FBI. So, with the Mexican cartel connection that Samson has, they had to be looking for him."

"So, what happened? Did they get him?" King Reece asked eagerly.

Power shook his head with a smile. "Nah. The house was blown up and everybody inside got killed. Took out four FBI agents, but Muhammad killed himself, too." Power shrugged, "Hey, death before dishonor."

"Death before dishonor," King Reece repeated. This was the Crescent Crew's ethos; they lived by the code and died by the code. He shook his head at the thought of another soldier returning to the essence.

"Well, after the explosion, some brothers went down to holler at some Crew members. Turned out some detectives were shaking everybody down asking questions about a tall black guy the week before," Power explained.

"Where at, Lumberton?" Reece knew that Muhammad was strong in Lumberton.

"Nah, Wilmington. He expanded. Anyway, last I heard somebody told on the dude who told the police about seeing something at the house."

"So, what happened to the snitch?'

"Nothing, last I heard."

Reece quietly exhaled. "Oh, good then."

"Good?" Power asked, confused.

"Yeah, that means Samson is not here."

"How you figure?"

"Well, put it like this: If Samson was here and he knew about the snitch, you'd know it. Trust me. I trained him myself."

That put an end to that conversation.

"So, you gonna crush shit when you touch down, huh?" Power was suddenly amped again. Reece grinned mischievously. He liked to play his cards close to the breast.

"We'll see, li'l brother. We'll see."

Chapter 4

It was a cool Carolina night. There were very few people on the back street that the two plowed down. Both men were clad in black, and one man was substantially shorter than the other. Both were massive in weight. They marched with a sense of purpose. They both knew they were in hostile territory, but this piece of business had to be done.

The men cut down a side street leading to one of the most notorious housing projects in Wilmington, North Carolina. Just before they reached the center of the courtyard, they were startled as someone stumbled into the alley beside them, nearly knocking the shorter of the duo over.

With blinding quickness, the shorter man swept the feet from under the unsuspecting man, causing his head to slam into the concrete. Simultaneously, the bigger man of the duo drew his pistol and aimed it at the unlucky victim's head. The victim never knew it, because he was unconscious the second his head hit the pavement. The duo thought about killing him but decided against it. Someone would need to tell the locals about this visit. Plus, he was not their target. This was business.

The two men moved on into the courtyard. There were

more people out than anticipated. Being that it was late May, everyone was expected to be in Myrtle Beach at the Bike Fest, showing off the spoils of the drug game to impressionable females. Yes, there were a lot of people out, but that didn't stop the show. They knew the person they were looking for was on the grounds, and these two men refused to be denied.

It took only a few more moments of prowling the grounds before the person they were looking for materialized. With no hesitation they approached him, showing no regard for the person he was talking to.

The man noticed the duo, but it was too late. The little one smacked the person he was talking to, knocking him down. The big one smacked their target upside the head with a heavy pistol. The gun exploded into the night air.

BOOM!!!

The man's legs collapsed out of fear, but before he could sink to the ground, a huge hand clasped his shirt, keeping him up. Then the big man smacked him again and again with the pistol. Each time he landed a blow, the gun fired off into the air. The people who had been in the courtyard earlier sought refuge in the shadows of the gothic buildings yet still looked on in fear and curiosity.

Soon the big man grew weary of beating his target and hemmed him up by his collar. Looking him in his eyes, the big man snarled, "I'll teach you about that telling shit!"

He pushed the man's head between his legs and bent over to pick him up. The big man held the snitch raised high into the air and paused. He swung him around slowly for the hood to see then came down with all his might, power bombing the snitch into the pavement! The snitch's neck and back cracked simultaneously, silencing his screams. The back of his head cracked opened like an egg, displaying his skull and some brain matter for the world to see. A foul odor seeped out into the air: a combination of bloody guts and fecal matter as the snitch took his last shit posthumously.

The smaller of the duo finally released his powerful mana-
cles from around the snitch's friend's neck, and the two rose to
leave unencumbered. The onlookers still didn't leave the comfort of the shadows, but the incident was etched firmly into
their mental Rolodexes—as was the description of the assailants. However, neither of the assailants cared, and none of
the spectators dared reveal themselves. The street general of
their hood was down at the beach getting his freak on, therefore no one was around to protect them. Even the few dealers
who remained behind didn't dare come out. One reason was
because they knew what this assault was perpetrated for. More
important, they knew who it was perpetrated by, and no
one—no one—wanted the type of drama that messing with
them brought on.

Chapter 5

Flame lay in amazement at his good fortune. I mean, sure, this wasn't the first threesome he had had, but it was definitely the most memorable. Just the way Roxanne was moaning had him rock. And oh, that skin! That beautiful red skin! He normally went for redbones, so this wasn't new. Still, he rarely saw skin so beautiful.

And how could he forget—*damn, what's her name? Shit!* The way she was sucking his dick, he could think of a few names she deserved. Damn, did she kiss her mother with that mouth? Free! That was her name. She was one of those Bohemian types. *Def Poetry Jam* and shit. If they only knew how freaky she was. *She need to write a poem about that,* thought Flame.

From the sunlight cascading through the glass picture window, Free's hair appeared to be red. It also looked like shampoo was sprinkled loosely inside of it. In actuality, it was Flame's jizm. When Free sucked him to climax the first time she insisted he shoot his load in her hair. Said it turned her on. And damn if she didn't cum herself as she rubbed it in. The things broads do for gratification!

Flame wasn't surprised. For the last three years, he had been an international star. He had seen and experienced all types of perversities throughout his world travels. Nothing surprised him anymore. Usually, the finer the woman, the freakier.

"Oooh, Flame, put it in my hair again," Free begged, momentarily interrupting the exquisite fellatio. She could sense Flame about to climax.

"Ooh, wait! I wanna taste it, too!" Roxanne stopped licking his ass and crawled to the front to drink from the flesh fountain.

Just as Flame was about to bust, he heard the sound of a loud motorcycle. Being that this was Bike Week, he wouldn't have been surprised normally. However, this wasn't normal. Flame was inside Qwess's mini-mansion right on the beach in an exclusive gated community. The house was so far removed from any city street that you couldn't tell it was Bike Week unless you left the gates, which were about five miles away.

Flame mentally tried to rush his orgasm. He recognized Qwess's chopper out front. He knew he had to hurry up. It was bad enough he had these tricks up in Qwess's house! He really would be fucked up if he wasn't ready to roll. They had business and business was *always* first.

Flame released his juices in Free's hair and ushered the naked women downstairs and through the door into the adjacent pool house. He told them to get dressed and stay put.

Qwess was entering the great room just as Flame returned through the back door.

"What's up, Flame. You ready?" Flame had a guilty look on his face. He didn't know if Qwess knew why. He attempted to divert the attention.

"What's up with that funny-ass helmet, yo?" He was alluding to the German-style, chrome open-faced helmet still on Qwess's head. Qwess scoffed and took it off.

"Aw, nigga, this the shit. You don't know nuthin' 'bout dis."

He buffed the helmet affectionately. "Plus it match the bike, ya dig?"

Qwess started up the stairs, but Flame tried to distract him.

"Yo, what time the reporters from the magazine coming?"

"They should be here by now." Qwess started back up the stairs. He wasn't even halfway up the stairs before the smell accosted him.

"Flame! What you been doing?"

"Nothing."

"That's bullshit! It smell like pure pussy in here."

Flame couldn't hold it in. He burst out laughing. "Yo, my bad, but, damn, you missed it. I had these two bad bitches in here."

"I don't mind you funking up the crib. That's why I got it. It's a playhouse. But make sure business come first," Qwess reminded him.

"Business is first."

"Then why you ain't ready?"

"I, uh, was getting ready."

"No excuses. Just results. Now get dressed."

Flame did as he was instructed, but he had one more question. "Why we getting dressed anyway? Ain't we doing the interview here? Let's just keep it real."

Qwess came into the guest room where Flame was dressing. "First of all, we not doing the interview here. I told you that a thousand times. You forgot our basketball team competing in the three-on-three tournament?"

Flame slapped his forehead. He had completely forgot.

"See, how you gonna be ready to take over the label and you can't remember crucial shit like appointments. I'm telling you, this my last album. You gotta hold us down, Flame. This is your spot. I groomed you for it. At least I thought I did. Don't tell me I was wrong.

"Nah, Qwess, I got you, man. Just wait. You'll see."

The doorbell rang. Qwess let the reporter, photographer, and an assistant in. He offered them something to eat or drink, which they declined.

The reporter from the hottest magazine in hip-hop was attractive. She wore capris with a tank top. The male photographer looked eccentric with his curly hair, tattered jeans, and Vans. Judging from his skin tone he was obviously of mixed heritage. The assistant was very cute. Everything about her read "intern," from the shabby clothing to the inquisitive look in her eyes.

After seating them on the supple bone-white leather couch in the great room, Qwess excused himself. While he was gone, they openly admired the huge home. The Italian marble floors, ornate granite pillars framing the front door, and African artifacts elegantly decorating the walls spoke of conscious opulence. This was just how they expected Qwess to live.

"Damn, boyfriend shit is tight!" the reporter acceded. Moments later Qwess rejoined them.

"So, Qwess, are you ready to start?"

"No, Qima, we aren't doing it here."

Qima was surprised Qwess knew her name. She openly blushed, turning her light face a deep red. She'd had a light crush on him for years, but she knew he was probably out of her league. "So, where are we doing it?'

Qwess smiled. "Everywhere."

"Everywhere?"

"Yeah. We hitting the road. It is Bike Week. I'd be shirking my duties as Beach Ambassador if I didn't show you some sights in my city." He spread his arms expansively.

"Thanks, Qwess, but I've seen more ass than Atlanta strip clubs. I wouldn't exactly be mad if we chilled here."

Qwess smiled. He liked Qima's pizzazz. "Don't worry, we do have a destination. We're going to a three-on-three tournament at Broadway at the Beach. We have a team competing. We can do the interview on the way. As soon as Flame is ready."

"Oh, Flame is here?" Qima perked up.

"Of course."

"Well, what about Mysterio?" She peeped Qwess's reluctance. "Come on now, Qwess. You've been promising the hip-hop world for months now that you going to introduce us to Mysterio."

Qwess pumped his hands. "Calm down. I will, I will. Just when the time is right."

Flame glided downstairs in a white T-shirt, cargo shorts, and wheat Timbs. His diamond-encrusted ABP pendant sparkled on his chest. He and Qwess posed for a few pictures inside the house. Then outside by the pool. Next in front of Qwess's white Mercedes Maybach.

After the photographer was content with his shots for the magazine, they all climbed into the Maybach with Flame at the wheel. The photographer rode shotgun while Qwess, Qima, and her assistant, Andrea, sat in the luxurious back seats. Everything about the Mercedes was opulent.

Qima got settled as they drove up the long, winding road to civilization. Once comfortable, she took out her tape recorder and began firing away.

"So, Qwess: First off, is it true you're retiring?" She thrust the tape recorder in his face. Qwess couldn't help himself.

"Damn, baby girl, you cool as hell, but you don't play no games when it comes to getting that story, huh?" Qima caught on to his point and moved the recorder out of his face. Just a little. Then she patiently waited on an answer.

"Yes," was all she got.

"Just yes?" she repeated. Qwess nodded. "Why?"

"Well, you know, I'm burnt out. It's like the game ain't the same . . ." He hesitated. "Truthfully, I had only planned to do one album. Ya know, you spend your whole life making your first album. Your experiences and whatnot. Shit, I had material for days in the beginning."

"So, what happened?" Qima asked. When Qwess talked she was enthralled—as was her assistant.

Qwess continued. "Well, it's like it wasn't how I expected it to be. Don't get me wrong. I'm thankful, but I just don't feel comfortable anymore. I feel like the public is unappreciative."

"Unappreciative?" Qima repeated. "Come on now! You changed the game. You were one of the few rappers actually talking about something of substance. When everyone else was talking about how much cash they spending or how much ass they bending, you offered a different perspective. Hell, personally, I'm a fan."

Qima's assistant, Andrea, nodded her agreement as well. Qwess tried to hide his blushing. After all his years of success he was still apprehensive about receiving praise for his work.

"Thank you. I'm glad—"

His speech was interrupted mid-sentence when a Suzuki motorcycle shrieked past the car with pipes on full blast. Qwess rolled the window up tightly, and the car became like a tomb.

"Like I was saying, I'm glad someone appreciates my work."

Qima nodded. "Look, Qwess, this is off the record." She held up her stopped tape recorder to prove her point. "The game needs you. I'm twenty-six. I'm still a hip-hop fan, but the majority of the music coming out of the matrix I can't get with. I mean, I admit I may be a bitch sometimes, but my momma ain't raised no hoe, slut, trick, et cetera. And I ain't bending over and shaking my beautiful ass for nobody unless they are worthy!"

Qwess gave a hearty laugh for that one. She had used the term "the matrix." Qwess hadn't coined the term, but he damn sure made it famous. It referred to the music being played on the radio as not being real. A fantasy world. A place where anybody could be anything, yet only a few really controlled what was going on. Qwess also had to give her props on her other comment. She did have a beautiful ass.

"So, my question is," Qima continued, "what are the mature adults going to listen to? Hip-hop used to be about addressing social injustice, and other plights plaguing the black community. Not about making a sound track for the strip club. For Christ's sake, what are our little girls going to grow up to be."

On cue, a shiny motorcycle pulled up beside them at the stoplight. A female looking no older than fifteen was on the back of the bike shaking what little rump she possessed seductively, all the while trying to see into the Benz.

Qwess saw the disgust on Qima's face and pulled the suede blinds shut over the rear window. Andrea did the same on her side. Qwess pushed another button, and the translucent roof went through three different phases before he found the setting desired. It allowed just enough light to pass through so as not to be uncomfortable.

Qwess didn't appreciate the fact that Qima had turned the interview into her own personal soapbox. She was supposed to be a professional, so this was unbecoming of her. She was in the company of a man who had done wonders for the world that was her livelihood. A man who was contemplating retirement. Yet she was waxing poetic. Qwess didn't like it one bit.

"So, Qwess, if you retire, what are you going to do with the label, ABP?"

Qwess half turned, facing her. "See, that's part of the reason why I'm retiring. I want to focus more on the business side. You know we got Flame tearing the game up. We got the hot R and B duo Desire. Not to mention Saigon. She always reps for the ladies. Plus we got another prospect we trying to sign. Someone you're already familiar with."

"And of course, Mysterio," interjected Qima.

"Yeah, and, uh, we're also trying to make a movie out of this screenplay my man wrote. So, I'll have plenty to do."

"Uh huh."

"Ultimately, I have done what I set out to do as a recording artist. Now it's time for me to conquer something else."

"Speaking of conquests," Qima jibed, switching gears, "word is you're quite the ladies' man. You've been linked with quite a few models and actresses since your broken engagement to . . . What's her name?"

"Hope."

"Yeah, that's it! What happened with that anyway?"

Qwess was reluctant to answer. He was never big on putting his real personal business out. The actresses he drilled were fair game. They were already in the spotlight, but Hope wasn't. And even though their relationship had gone all to shit, he still wanted to preserve her honor.

But he always gained favor in press circles because he never pulled punches. All questions were game with him. Nothing was off limits. So he decided to do both.

"We just grew apart. We grew older and in different directions." Shit, that was the least of it, he thought.

"All right, Qwess. The ladies wanna know. Are you and the model Allysin an item?"

Flame could barely contain his laughter in the front.

"An item? No," Qwess answered with a straight face.

"The actress Melinda Wolf?"

"No." Still with a straight face.

Qima smiled. She knew where this was going.

"Okay, Qwess. I get the point. You're not married, right?"

Qwess held up his left hand. A big square-cut diamond ring draped his ring finger, but it was not to be confused for a wedding band.

For the remainder of the drive she asked Qwess numerous questions ranging from his association with the infamous Crescent Crew—which he evaded like a seasoned politician—to what his favorite color was. By the time the Maybach reached Broadway at the Beach, Qima's tape was just as exhausted as she was, but she was pleased. Qwess had answered every question she had thrown at him. Even Flame was briefly interviewed.

Flame wheeled the big car into a reserved parking spot beside a Maserati with the top still dropped. Qwess paused a moment to throw on his trademark designer glasses before exiting the comfy confines of the Maybach. Normally he wore a pair of wood-grained Versaces with rose tint. Today he wore a pair of Cazals that looked like they were stolen from the late eighties.

"You all are my guests, so stay close to me," he informed Qima and her crew. When Qwess extended his hand to help Qima, he could've sworn she gave him "the eye." However, she plastered her glasses over her eyes too quickly for him to tell for sure. What couldn't be missed, though, were her nipples. They were rock hard and threatened to puncture her flimsy tank top.

There were an assload of people out at the celebrity basketball tournament. Security was just as thick to accommodate the diverse groups participating in the tournament.

Record Label versus Record Label; Hood versus Hood; State versus State; Models versus Actors, etc.

ABP sponsored its own team of five: Doe, Hulk, Amin (the business manager for ABP), Raheem (Qwess's brother-in-law), and Yusef (the head of PR for ABP). Doe, Hulk, and Amin were the starting three for the ABP Powerhouse squad. They were playing on court six, all the way at the back.

As Qwess and his entourage made their way through the thick crowd, they couldn't help but notice the scantily clad women all crying for the rappers' attention. Some of them thought Qwess was with Qima, and Andrea was with Flame, possibly because both ladies clung to each man's shirt so as not to be lost in the crowd.

"I'm not blocking you, am I, Qwess?" Qima asked sarcastically.

"Nah, I'm already in the company of enough beauty," he shot back.

"Cute."

When they finally reached the bleachers at court six, Qima was relieved.

"Whew, I don't know how you men do it. I've seen more butts than a jailhouse ashtray."

Qwess issued her a sideways glance. "What's up with your fascination with butts?" he joked.

"Oh, cut it out." She pinched his arm.

Doe and the crew were suiting up to play next. When Doe saw Qwess and company, he swaggered over.

"Yo, man, what took you so long? Who is shorty?" he asked, pointing to Qima. He gave Qwess that look. Qwess hurriedly dismissed the thought. "Nah, bruh. She's the reporter."

"Damn, she cute," Doe offered.

Qima blushed. "Damn, y'all just trying to butter me up so you can get good press." She tried unsuccessfully to feign indifference. It was no use. She was obviously impressed.

"You guys keep up the flattery, and you just might get the cover," Qima insinuated.

"That's the plan," whispered Qwess.

"Ah, yo, you see your boy over there?" Doe pointed to the other side of the court at another rapper/CEO named Maserati.

Qwess shot his eyes to the sky dismissively. "I swear homie just trying to compete wit' us in everything. Hell, if he take a little more pride in his work, he might be all right," he said.

"Ya know," Doe cosigned. He got Qima's attention. "Hey, the only quote you need from me is this: The takeover continues. Atlantic Beach Productions will still reign supreme in the face of Qwess's retirement. Why? Because Doe said so. You got that?"

Qima laughed.

"I'm serious." Doe wasn't smiling at all. "Now watch us wreck shop on the court."

With that the starting three for the ABP Powerhouse took the court. On the opposing side was none other than Maserati and his group The Gangstas.

Maserati mean-mugged the ABP crew the entire time. Like he was tough or something.

When he looked at Qwess, Qwess winked through his Cazals.

Things hadn't started out this way between the two. In fact, Qwess tried to get along with the cat in the beginning. Five years ago, when Qwess accepted his Promotion & Distribution (also known as a P&D) deal through AMG Records, Maserati was the hottest artist in the world. Period. He had smashed the game with his debut album, *Dying to Get Rich*. When Qwess re-released his debut album, *Janus*, nationwide, it gained steam immediately. Qwess (and possibly Maserati) knew it was only a matter of time before he blew up worldwide. Inevitably, this proved to be true.

Then at Bike Week four years ago, Qwess outshined Maserati during a performance. After all, Qwess was from the beach, and this was in front of the home crowd. Maserati took this as a snub, and ever since had been trying to create some type of beef between the two of them. Everyone knew that was Maserati's schtick. He got on by a diss record.

Qwess knew the plan, so he ignored Maserati. Maserati in return became more embittered. The height of the fiasco was when Qwess took home best album honors at the Source Awards later that year. Of course, he beat out Maserati for the award. Then, to add injury to insult, Flame also beat out The Gangstas for best new artist.

That defeat planted a seed of hate in Maserati. He focused all his attention on his record label called Gangsta Life in hopes of one-upping Qwess sometime down the line. So far his plans had been unsuccessful. Qwess and ABP had broken the mold and put the music industry in a stranglehold. Yet at every major event, you could bet that Maserati would be present, trying to best Qwess or anyone affiliated with him. This was no different.

The referee blew the whistle and threw the ball up. Hulk tipped the ball to Amin. Amin set the play up. Hulk went down low to post up. At six foot six and 320 chiseled pounds, no one could stop him down low. The closest man to his size was Roy Bangs of The Gangstas. Roy was six foot three, 240.

Amin dropped the ball to Hulk on a bounce pass. Hulk spun and threw the ball down so hard the pole shook. The ball hit the pavement and stayed planted where it landed. One to nothing.

"Arrrgh!" Hulk screamed. The ref picked the ball out of the pavement and gave it to Maserati to take out. For fear of a slaughter, the rules were alternate possessions.

Maserati inbounded the ball to Young B of The Gangstas. The ball was nearly stolen by Doe, but Young B had mad handles. He regained control and tossed an alley up to Roy Bangs. Bangs caught the ball and was in midair just inches from the rim. Out of nowhere, Hulk came and swatted the ball—with force. Bangs slammed to the ground. The ball flew to court five, interrupting their game. Hulk snatched his jersey off.

"Get that shit out of here! This my house!" The sidelines erupted. The spectators from court five shifted to court six. On the sideline, Flame collected his bets.

"I told you, dawg. These nigga can't see my big homies!"

On the court, the game was reset. Bangs demanded the ball.

"Give me the rock. This nigga can't see me."

Maserati gave him the ball out to Young B. Young B pulled up a two-pointer in Amin's face.

"Swish!!!"

Two to one Gangstas.

Bangs and Young B connected on the same play two more times, making the score six to two.

ABP Powerhouse called a timeout. Amin was subbed with Raheem. The game resumed.

Raheem inbounded the ball to Doe on a backdoor pass. Doe went to lay the ball up when Roy Bangs caught him with an elbow, knocking him to the ground. Hulk ran over to his aid immediately. He pushed Bangs out of the way. Bangs just smirked and joined his teammates on the sideline.

"You all right?" Hulk asked.

"Yeah, I'm straight," Doe wheezed. "Now let's punish these cats. No holds barred."

Just then the ref ran over.

"Fellas, come on. Let's keep the peace. Just shoot the tech shots, and keep the game clean."

Doe, Hulk, and Raheem told him okay, but their thoughts were different.

After Doe made the charity shots, the game resumed. Hulk posted up and slid one off the glass. Maserati fumbled the in-bound pass. Doe retrieved it and fired a two that banked off the glass into the net.

Seven to six. The game went to twelve.

Roy Bangs attempted to commandeer the game again. He gave Maserati the eye. Maserati returned it. Roy Bangs pushed off Hulk and shot to the basket. When he got there the ball awaited him. He caught it and threw it down with a reverse dunk.

The sidelines erupted. Gangsta Life supporters stood and crowded the side of the court.

Qwess threw a towel down in disgust. Flame smacked his forehead. "Damn homies!" Roy Bangs dapped Maserati up. .

"Told you. This nigga can't see me!"

Maserati shot Qwess a glance. The point was clear.

Qwess called a timeout.

"You brothas, listen up! This can't be happening. Naw, man! These cats can't see y'all. Look, we can't lose. Do I need to suit up?" Qwess acted like he was changing out of his clothes. Hulk stopped him. "Quit tripping. I got this. Just give me the ball." He looked at each team member. "Give me the ball!"

When the game resumed, Qwess gave Maserati a knowing smirk. Hulk put on a show.

He threw one down on Bangs and Young B. Doe stole the ball and gave it to Hulk again. Hulk shot the ten-foot jumper. Swish!

Maserati scored on a layup.

Raheem reciprocated.

Maserati scored again.

Ten to nine.

Doe passed the ball in to Raheem. Raheem set it up. Hulk posed up outside the arc. Raheem passed Hulk the ball. Hulk closed his eyes and hoisted up the two-pointer.

Swish! Game over.

Qwess, Flame, and other ABP supporters rushed the court to congratulate the winners.

Qima instructed her photographer to snap multiple shots. This would make for good press.

Maserati stormed off the court in disappointment. Again, Qwess had beaten him. His team was eliminated from the tournament. There was no need to hang around. Yet he still had to get the last word.

He noticed Qwess had brought along an entourage. From his numerous dealings with the press, Maserati recognized Qwess's guests as magazine reporters. In fact, the same curly-haired photographer had shot him numerous times for the magazine. Maybe this was what he needed.

Maserati walked back to where the crowd had congregated. He strolled right up to Qwess unimpeded and shoved him in the chest.

"You can't beat me yourself, so you had to send your do-boys!" spat Maserati.

Before Qwess could retaliate, a few referees as well as spectators intervened, creating a wall between the two rappers.

Qwess was genuinely surprised. The shock was apparent on his face when he snarled. "You punk muthafu—Ooh! Get out the way. Get out the way!" The wall didn't budge. Instead they tried to placate him.

Qwess wasn't trying to hear none of that shit they were talking. Only when Hulk gently slid his arm around his neck did he calm down.

"Not now. Not now. We'll see him again," Hulk whispered in his ear. Qwess was reluctant, but he conceded. This time.

Qwess nodded in agreement, all the while starting at Maserati with murderous thoughts.

Maserati saw that he was going to get away with his bull-shit and started talking noise.

"Yeah. I told you the niggas was pussy!" he assured anyone who would listen. He took special care to say it within earshot of the reps from the magazine. Qima shot him a contemptuous glare and grabbed Qwess's arm.

"Could you take me back to our truck? I'm ready to go. I've had enough of this."

Qima snatched Qwess back to reality. He'd almost forgot she was there. Here he was about to smack this nigga up in front of reps from the hottest magazine in hip-hop. That'd be real good for business, he thought.

"Yeah. Let's go." He signaled to Flame, who was still trying to get an angle on Maserati and his crew.

Flame reluctantly withdrew and joined Qwess. Together they navigated through the crowd of *oohs* and *ahs* back to the Maybach. Before they climbed in, Qwess looked to Hulk. "I'm dead serious. I refuse to let that shit slide. Ya dig?"

Hulk nodded. "You don't have to. Just pick a better time, all right."

"No doubt.

Qwess climbed into the driver's seat and burned rubber peeling out of the reserved parking space.

When they arrived back at Qwess's house, Qima came inside to talk to Qwess while the rest of her crew loaded the equipment into their Expedition.

"I just want you to know that I'm proud of you for not showing your ass. Most brothers would've thought that they had something to prove."

Qwess nodded. If she only knew the thoughts that were raging through his mind at the present moment.

"Yeah, tell me about it," he agreed.

Qima extended her hand. "Well, I guess this is it. Thank you for showing me a good time."

Qwess feigned a smile while shaking her hand.

"Don't mention it. I hope I gave you enough info to go with the cover story."

Qima chuckled. "Now you know it's not up to me who gets the cover. Nice try, though."

Qwess grinned. Qima continued, "I will do everything in my power to see that you do, though. You deserve it."

With that Qima turned to leave. Qwess watched her switch with a little more authority than usual. Under different circumstances he would've had to tap it. But for now his plate was just too full. Qima was cute, but she couldn't hold a candle to the other chicks he was knocking off. He was on his fourth model, third actress, and still hit one of his old chicks, an R & B singer, from time to time.

Qima was cute, but his plate was most definitely too full right now. Yeah, most definitely.

Chapter 6

Reece walked through the double doors into the visitation room. He saw a lot of familiar faces on his way to the officer's booth and greeted them with a slight head nod. He showed the officer his identification. The officer told him his visitor was at table H7. Normally Reece would've spotted his visitor right away, but due to the crowded visitation room he could barely see three feet ahead. Now that he knew the table, he spotted his visitor right away.

Vanilla sat patiently at the table. When Reece approached the table she stood to greet him.

"What's up, boo?" She hugged Reece tightly.

"Nothing much. How was the drive up? You have any problems?" Even incarcerated Reece was still trying to control things. He asked about her journey as if he could change things.

"Nah, it was uneventful," Vanilla replied.

Reece's eyes roamed over Vanilla in appreciation. She was still gorgeous. She had put on a few pounds in all the right places since Reece had made her stop stripping. Her creamy skin was smooth and soft. Her long hair was pulled up into a ponytail on top of her head. Diamond earrings dripped from her ears, and a huge rock weighed her right ring finger down.

"You look good, girl," Reece complimented. "You put on a few pounds, didn't you?"

"Yeah. You like?" Vanilla asked. She whirled around to let Reece see all of her curves. Her small waist made her ass seem larger than it actually was.

Reece nodded with a smirk. "No doubt." He scanned the visitation room, looking at the room in the corner where they usually had their me-time. "What's up with what you got on, though?"

Vanilla was wearing skin-tight jeans. She usually wore a dress of some kind so that she and Reece would have easy access for sex. When the urge arose, Reece would set it up with a guard so they could go to a private room when Vanilla visited. Looking at her now, all sexy and thick, he was ready for some action.

Vanilla frowned. "My aunt Flo in town," she explained.

"Word?"

"Word."

Reece licked his lips. "Is it *on* on, or just on?"

Vanilla playfully punched Reece in the arm. "It's enough, nigga. You ain't getting no pussy today," she said. "But don't worry, I'll be back next week, and you can knock the bottom out of it. Promise."

Reece smiled, and they sat down. "That's what I'm talking about," he mumbled.

Vanilla came to visit Reece three times out of the month. Reece even paid for her apartment in Richmond so that when he needed her she wouldn't be far away. Throughout his whole bid Vanilla had been a permanent fixture, holding him down like an anchor. When Reece needed money, she brought it. When he needed drugs, she brought them. When he needed sex, she came. Literally and figuratively. When he needed to convey a message to the streets, she was his female

Hermes. No matter how minimal or major the task, when Reece called, Vanilla answered.

It seemed like just yesterday to Reece that Vanilla and her stripping cohort, Cretia, had enjoyed their first threesome with him. In reality, it was more like five years and change. During their numerous encounters, Vanilla had hinted that she was down to put in work for Reece, but he couldn't see himself putting trust in a woman for anything other than his sexual pleasures. However, Vanilla was persistent. It wasn't long before King Reece put her to work. During the now-infamous Crescent Crew War, which had cemented his status in the underworld, Reece had used Vanilla to set up a rival. Testing her loyalty, Reece killed the adversary right in front of her to see how she would respond. To his surprise, Vanilla's heart seemed to be just as cold as his. He actually saw her smile when he killed the man.

Still, his comrades urged him to murk her, too. She had witnessed Crew business, and only Crew members lived to tell that tale. However, Reece vetoed their suggestions. For some reason he felt that she wouldn't betray him. So, against the behest of his comrades, he spared Vanilla's life. So far, Vanilla had proved him right.

Vanilla played her position better than some of those same comrades who had advised him to dispose of her. She had become his trusty ride-or-die throughout his whole bid! Even before he came to prison Vanilla had shown her loyalty to Reece. The whole time he was with Destiny, Vanilla was in the background doing things for Reece that he had felt Destiny was above doing. She was Reece's personal freakazoid. In return, Reece took care of her just as he did anyone who was on his team.

Vanilla reached across the table and caressed Reece's hand. She gazed into his eyes. "So, are you ready or what?"

"Ready? Hell, yeah. I'm ready!"

Vanilla chuckled. "I know that's right."

"Damn right. So, what's going on out there?"

Vanilla exhaled. "Same ole shit. Ain't much changed."

"Oh, yeah?"

"Yeah."

"So, how's the club?"

"Don't worry. The club is fine," Vanilla assured him. "Qwess comes by to get the money every week. Your money is fine, Reece."

Reece mocked surprise. "What? I ain't say nothing about the money. I ain't worrying about that," he said, lying through his teeth. He knew damn well if something happened to his money, he was going to flip.

Vanilla pursed her lips in disbelief. "Yeah, right. Anyway, I got a message for you from Samson. He sent word by some Mexican that he is dealing with now."

This was what Reece was waiting to hear. Vanilla had taken the four-hour journey to deliver this news in person. Reece knew the government was monitoring all of his communication.

"Is Samson back in the States?" Reece whispered. "What is it?"

"Well, he said he has a surprise for you, but he couldn't tell you until you get out."

"Oh, yeah? You seen him?"

"Nah. How would I see him all the way in Mexico?"

Reece paused for a moment, contemplating whether he wanted to let Vanilla in on all the goings-on. He needed to know, so he asked, "Well, the way I hear it, he is not in Mexico."

"What?!" Vanilla exclaimed. "That's crazy."

"Yeah. No shit, but that's the word I'm getting."

"Hold up, Reece. That's crazy. Why would Samson come back? He's still wanted on murder charges and everything else. I know he doesn't think just because you locked up, the feds ain't gonna still want his ass?"

"Nah, like I said, it may not even be true. Ya know what I'm saying? But just keep your ears and eyes open."

Samson was Hulk's twin brother and Reece's bodyguard in the free world. He had been with Reece at the hangar the day he was arrested. When the feds were attempting to bust onto the tarmac, it was Samson who cleared the way for Reece and his woman, Destiny, to board their flight to Mexico. Reece murdered an FBI agent in cold blood so Samson could catch their flight. Reece and Destiny never made it to Mexico; Samson did. He was calling the shots for the Crew now from exile in Mexico. His only line of direct contact to Reece was Vanilla.

"Reece, king, if he was in the States I would know. Trust me."

"Okay. Just keep your ear to the streets."

With the finality of that statement, Vanilla moved on. "I'll be so glad to see you free," she said, stroking Reece's goatee.

"Oh, yeah? Why is that?"

"Because this is not the place for a king." Reece didn't know how to take her compliment. The last thing he wanted was a serious relationship, especially with Vanilla. She was cool, but she was not the relationship type, not for someone like Reece. After the ordeal with Destiny, his trust in women was shattered and nonexistent. He would need an angel from the heavens to restore his trust.

Vanilla already knew Reece's feelings when it came to relationships, so she put his fears to rest.

"Reece, don't get sentimental on me. I'm not looking for anything or expecting nothing. I play my part because you're a genuine person. Nothing like the monster everyone perceives you to be. Besides, it's not like I'm not profiting from our arrangement." Vanilla tried to sound opportunistic so as not to give Reece a true indication of how she felt. However, there was no way to disguise her love for him. It was evident when she looked at him.

"Yeah, I know that's right," Reece agreed. He knew how

she felt, but it just could not be. "But listen, Vee," he told her. "When I walk out these gates next week a free man, I'm going to remember this. All that you've done. It means a lot to me. Hell, I thought I would have had to kill you by now." He said this with such ease that it seemed he was joking. Yet Vanilla knew he was dead serious. "You surprised me, though. I plan on changing the game. Only a few cats know what I plan to do when I touch down—"

"Reece, you know you can't jump back out there right in the trap," Vanilla interrupted.

"Calm down. Calm down," Reece soothed, motioning with his hands. "Have you ever known me to be stupid?"

"No."

"A'ight then."

"But everybody keep talking 'bout how when you come home it's gonna be on, and yada yada yada."

Reece chuckled. "I feel ya, but I control my circumference. What Reece want, Reece get. A'ight?" Vanilla nodded.

"Good. Now I need you to tell Qwess to be here at eight a.m. sharp, and no matter what he say . . . no parties."

"All right, I'll tell him. Anything else?"

"Yeah. What's up with the lease on the apartment?"

"It's up next month. You want me to go ahead and start moving?"

"No. I want you to renew the lease, all right?"

Vanilla was confused.

"Just do it. Trust me." Reece stood. Vanilla followed suit. As they walked around to the vending machine Vanilla asked, "You ain't get no more letters from that bitch Destiny, did you?"

Reece didn't answer, so Vanilla continued.

"I hope not. How that cop bitch gon' shoot you, send you to jail, and then try to act like everything is straight. I better not ever see her. I'll kill her myself."

Reece knew she'd have to get in a long line along with everyone else before she could do that. It was hard enough calling off the dogs before. Destiny was a marked woman. She had managed to become the only person to ever infiltrate the infamous Crescent Crew. She had seduced their leader, claimed his heart, then revealed herself to be an undercover federal agent. She had even shot him in order to arrest him. While he was down, Destiny had written him letters every week, proclaiming her love for him, and sending him photos of their child. Reece never responded.

"You don't have to worry about her. She'll get hers," Reece told Vanilla.

Destiny was begging to see Reece. Once he got out, it was going to be impossible to protect her if she insisted on seeing him.

Destiny was only one problem Reece had to deal with upon his release. He actually had a more pressing problem upon release. One he had to play by ear. He knew the Crew wasn't going to let this other decision stand uncontested, but what choice did they have? Reece was his own man. Reece called his own shots.

Chapter 7

Flame cruised down Murchison Road in his hometown Fayetteville, North Carolina, better known as Fayettenam. He was in his Mercedes SL with his best friend 8-Ball riding shotgun. The top was dropped, letting the beautiful June sun shine on them while they bumped music from Flame's new unreleased album.

"Damn that beat bumping," commented 8-Ball. "Who did it?"

"Qwess. I told you he stepped his game up. The nigga retiring from rapping, but he still doing the beats. Shit, nigga getting a quarter mil per track," Flame explained.

8-Ball nodded his head, then turned the music down. "Yo, man, I been meaning to ask you something, too. It seem like you be kissing that nigga Qwess ass. What's up with that?"

"Qwess ass? What you mean?" Flame challenged.

"You know what I mean! Qwess tells you not to come to the hood too much, and you don't. Qwess tell you to cut off childhood friends, and you do it. Hell, you only even fuck wit' me half the time. It's like this nigga yo' daddy or something."

Flame was partially offended, so he held no punches. He

turned onto the campus of Fayetteville State University and pulled into a parking spot. He turned the car off but kept the music on. He looked 8-Ball right in the eye.

"See, it's like this," he began. "Ever since I met the cat he showed me love. Improved my situation. And he never broke his word with me. He told me he was going to make me a millionaire. I am—a few times over. He told me to watch out for old friends because they become new enemies. Look at J.D. and them. They got beef because I ain't get them out of jail for their bullshit. Hell, so far everything he told me has been true. So, until he's wrong I'ma listen to him."

8-Ball pondered for a moment, but came right back. "So, you saying fuck the hood. Fuck the niggas that had your back?"

"Had my back!" Flame exploded. "J.D., they was ready to send me to jail over a piece of pussy I ain't even hit! And they the OGs of the hood. So, imagine what the li'l niggas will do."

8-Ball was confused. For all his wit, he still wasn't too bright. "So, what you saying?"

"I'm saying, the niggas that show me love, I got love for them. Otherwise, I can't fuck wit 'em. I got too much to lose. Know what I mean?"

"Yeah," 8-Ball whispered. He really didn't understand. He actually thought Flame was selling out, but since he shared his riches with him he didn't want to rock the boat. Instead 8-Ball suddenly turned the music up.

"Man, fuck all this soft shit. Let's go over to the park and see what kind of hoes out here. I know we ain't come over here for nothing."

"No doubt." Flame cranked the Benz up, and they rode over to the park.

Broads of all kinds were out around the basketball court watching students and civilians ball. When Flame and 8-Ball rolled up, several heads turned to see the source of the music. Everyone who looked nodded in appreciation of the wide-bodied Benz sitting on twenty-two-inch Lorinser rims. The candy silver matched perfectly with the chrome rims, making the whole car look like it was aluminum.

Flame stepped out with 8-Ball right behind him. They walked to the edge of the court and observed the game. It wasn't long before girls surrounded them, obviously local college girls.

"Ooh, this is nice. Are those diamonds?" a slim, cornrowed coed asked. *Fuck kind of question is that?* Flame thought.

"I never seen silver shine so hard," another female stated.

"Silver?" Flame scoffed. *And these are supposed to be the educated broads? Damn,* thought Flame. "Naw, baby. This is platinum," he corrected.

It was apparent these chicks had seen him on videos by the way they were jocking him. Flame had never had problems getting girls before, but since his music career had blasted off it was senseless the way broads threw pussy at him.

He put these chicks in the gold-digging category and treated them as such. A half hour later he and 8-Ball were leaving the park with a sexcapade scheduled for later that night.

Later, Flame and 8-Ball were reminiscing about a previous escapade as they waited for their food at a mom-and-pop rib shack.

"Yo, man, I'm telling you, ball, shit was tight as fuck. Remember the time we was in Japan and the room-service chick freaked us?"

"Yeah! How could I forget!?"

"It was like that."

"Damn!"

The conversation from earlier was still fresh in Flame's mind. 8-Ball had been his best friend since the sandbox. Flame desperately wanted him to understand his new status. He couldn't soar like an eagle by hanging with penguins in the hood. Flame was a millionaire; he was *supposed* to act different! He didn't hone his craft and work nonstop to remain the same. Flame wanted to be the same ole G from the hood, but the truth was, he was so big he had become a prisoner of his own fame.

The attendant brought their food, and they left the diner in Flame's Benz. They pulled up to a light, and 8-Ball was complaining about his order.

"Damn, these mu'fuckas can't never get an order right," he griped. Flame tuned him out and just bobbed his head to the music.

Suddenly, a burgundy van screeched up beside them, partially blocking them off. A masked man jumped from the back of the van with a shotgun.

"Yeah, nigga! You know what it is! Get the fuck out!" He thrust the shotgun in Flame's face. Another masked man was sticking a shotgun in 8-Ball's open door. 8-Ball fell out onto the pavement. Meanwhile Flame still gripped the steering wheel, refusing to move.

The man poked the barrel into Flame's face, and blood spurted from his mouth "Nigga, move now!" Shaken, Flame reluctantly crawled out of the window, not even bothering to open the door.

The man with the shotgun butt stroked him in the back of the head and knocked him down. Behind them, a car blared its horn in protest. The jackers were oblivious to it. One of them hopped in on the passenger side while the other one stepped over Flame and commandeered the car. The van peeled off with Flame's Benz right behind it. Flame lay on the pavement reeling in agony. He clutched his face, and blood oozed through his hands.

"Shiiiiit!" he cried out. Flame looked over to 8-Ball, still lying facedown in the street cowering like a bitch. He rubbed his neck where he felt pain. More blood came back on his hands. That's when he realized his necklace was gone.

Damn, he didn't even feel them snatch that off. That was $40,000!

Flame picked himself up off the ground when spectators

rushed to his aid and realized who he was. In the distance he could hear sirens wailing. Moments later, the paramedics arrived and treated him on the spot. He was too embarrassed to allow them to take him to the hospital.

After they treated him, he took a cab to his home in Kings Grant—sans 8-Ball.

Flame stumbled into his home shaken. *I could've been killed,* he said to himself. He shook his head repeatedly, reliving the scene in his head. He kept seeing the van pull up and screech to a halt. He smelled the burned rubber and felt the cold steel in his mouth as if it were happening right now. Flame shook off the memories and collected himself. He didn't know what to do next. One thing for sure, the booty call for later was off. He was in no condition to entertain. He had pissed on himself, and he still couldn't stop shaking. He was in no condition to chase ass. He only wanted to chase justice.

Rolando walked into his palatial Carolina home. As he walked through his marble foyer he noticed dim light emanating from the grand room. Once he entered it, he discovered the source of the light. His wife, R & B sensation Niya, awaited him at the top of the spiral staircase. She wore a see-though teddy that partially covered her ample breasts, and underneath it a crotchless thong. In her hand was a bottle of Dom Pérignon accompanied with two long-stem glasses.

"Hmm, you're home early," Niya cooed. Doe dropped his briefcase where he stood and began his ascent upstairs.

"Shit, if I would've known this was waiting on me, I would've been home a lot sooner."

"Boy, you crazy." Niya laughed. She greeted Doe with an embrace once he reached her.

"Word, though. What's up with this?" Doe questioned between kisses.

"Well, I know the great King Reece will be home tomorrow, so I'm going to get me now because I know you have a lot of catching up to do when he gets home." She led him by the hand. "Now come on."

Doe loved an assertive woman. Niya led them to the bedroom and stood Doe before the bed to undress him. Niya avoided eye contact the entire time. Doe didn't want to disrupt the moment, but he knew something was wrong with his wife. A part of marriage was compromising, so he had no choice but to address the issue.

"Hold up, hold up." Doe stopped Niya from unclothing him. "What's wrong, Sunshine? Tell Daddy what's wrong."

Niya looked away. "Nothing,"

Doe cupped her chin in his hands. "Come on now. You know I know better than that."

Niya was persistent, "No, Boobie. Not now. Tonight is about us. We'll discuss it later."

Doe was not to be denied. "No, Sunshine. Something's on your mind, so let's discuss it."

It didn't take much more prodding.

"Okay, if you insist," Niya surrendered, blowing out her nose. She plopped down on the bed and garnered Doe's full attention.

"Are you sure you want Reece in on your company? I mean are you sure he is done with the streets? If not, he could bring you down. I know he's your cousin, but—"

"Calm down. Calm down," Doe whispered. He kissed Niya on the forehead to placate her. "Everything is under control. One thing my cousin is and has always been is a businessman. He has money tied into the company now, so he is going to protect his investment. He finally allowed us to use his money. That's why we don't need AMG anymore. We can afford to go fully independent again. And once we release you from your obligations at AMG, the money will pour in." He spread his hands. "So, he'll do right."

Niya was still unsure. "You think those vultures will release me?"

"I have no doubt they will," assured Doe. "Now stop worrying so much. I got you."

Doe kissed her deeply on the lips. She reciprocated. He placed long, wet kisses on her neck. Niya moaned in pleasure and scooted farther up on the bed. Doe removed her lace teddy, unleashing her soft mounds of flesh. All that remained was her crotchless thong. Doe took each breast into his mouth and sucked them gently and deeply, taking a moment to nibble on each nipple that extended a full inch due to her arousal. Niya wrapped both hands around his neck and pulled him in. She dug her nails in to his neck as the passion intensified. Doe moved from Niya's breast down to her navel, then to the inside of her thighs, where he plunged two fingers inside her hot wetness. He strummed her insides as if he were playing a guitar.

"Oooooh, baby . . . just like that," Niya hissed.

Doe stopped pleasuring Niya to pleasure himself with admiration of her beauty. Looking at his wife was like experiencing a visual orgasm. Her perfect 36Cs heaved from desire. Her six-pack abs flexing was like human art. The short hairs on her tight pussy were trimmed into a perfect heart as if done by a barber. Even her muscular thighs were feminine. Niya was sexy personified.

Doe licked his thumb and ran it over Niya's swollen clitoris; then he plunged his head between her legs and took it into his mouth. At the same time, he slid his middle finger inside of her wet slit. He sucked Niya's clit while twirling his finger inside and sent Niya vacationing on the winds of ecstasy. While Niya bucked wildly, Doe penetrated her back door with another finger. At first, she jumped more out of surprise than pain, but once Doe established a rhythm between his sucking and plucking, Niya came again and again. Her juices were so sweet to Doe. He could've pleased her this way all night, but he was ready to feel her.

He swiftly removed the remainder of his clothes and prepared to penetrate her. Just as he guided his penis to Niya's entrance . . . the phone rang.

Doe never interrupted his drive or missed a beat. Nothing was going to prevent him from pleasing his wife. Nothing except the message echoing on his machine from Flame.

Doe snatched the phone from the cradle. "You were what?!!"

On the other end Flame was distraught. "I got carjacked."

"When? Where?"

"Earlier. By *Payettebille* State."

"Are you all right?"

"Yeah."

"Where you at anyway?"

"I'm at home."

"Did you get hurt or anything? Have you been to the hospital or filed a report?" Doe had a million and one questions.

"Nah, man."

"Why not? And why are you talking like that?"

Behind Doe, Niya was just recovering from her numerous climaxes and was demanding to know what was going on.

"My lip swollen. The *mu'puckas* hit me in the mouth with the gun. My puckin' tooth knocked out!"

"What?!"

"Yeah!!!"

"All right, calm down. Calm down," ordered Doe. He had to keep himself calm as well. "Go downtown and I'll meet you there in an hour."

"Okay. Is Qwess coming, too?" For the last few years, Qwess had been a big brother to Flame. So he wanted him there through this ordeal.

"Nah. He in VA picking up Reece in the morning, but I'll let him know. Get ready. I'll see you in a few."

"Okay."

"All right. Peace."

Doe replaced the phone in its cradle.

Niya stroked his back.

"We're not going to be able to finish, are we?" Doe shook his head as he explained to Niya what had happened. Niya rolled off the bed to get dressed. She was visibly deflated. She knew that once Reece came home she would have limited time to spend with her husband. She just wanted this last night with him. This last night of calm before the storm. Yet it was not to be. Destiny could only be controlled in a perfect world. And this was not it.

Chapter 8

Reece placed his legal box onto the counter in the control room. The control room officer greeted him with a smile.

"Going home today, huh?"

"Yep."

"Good. I hope you stay out of trouble. Is it true you won't be needing a transportation arrangement?"

"Yep."

"Okay. Sign here and here." He motioned to the appropriate places on the paper. "Oh, yeah! You have some mail that just came in for you today. Hold up a sec and I'll get it."

He disappeared and emerged moments later with a letter in hand. Reece read the address and started to tear it up. However, he thought better of it. He could use this information later. So he pocketed the letter.

"You got some clothes up here, too. You can go in there to change." The officer motioned to a small room beside the control room and passed Reece a garment bag. Reece stepped into the room, bag in hand. He unzipped the bag to reveal a cream velour jogging suit. In the bottom of the bag neatly lay a pair of brown Giuseppe Zanotti sneakers with silver metal

straps. Hanging on the end of the hanger was a leather acces-
sory bag. Reece opened it to find a Rolex watch, diamond
pinky ring, two diamond stud earrings, and deodorant with a
vial of Egyptian musk oil. Reece dressed quickly and exited
the room.

"Okay, son, you ready to roll?" the officer inquired.

"No doubt."

"Hold up. Someone wants to escort you to the gate."

The officer made a phone call, and in no time Officer
Robinson arrived.

"Ready for the big day?" Officer Robinson asked Reece.

"Yep." Reece was short on words this day. He had a lot on
his mind and was ready to get back to the world.

"Good. Allow me to walk you out."

Officer Robinson walked side by side with Reece to the
gate. When they arrived at the gate, Officer Robinson paused
and thrust his hand out. The two unlikely allies shook hands.

"Reece, you're a brilliant man, much too smart to be in a
place like this," Officer Robinson said. He tilted his head toward the street. "You have a lot of power out there in those
streets. You have the ability to influence a lot of people's lives.
Imagine what would happen if you used that power for
good?" Officer Robinson allowed his words to linger for a few
seconds. "Anyway, let me know if there's something I can do
for you." Recce thought about the offer for a moment. He
wasn't one to align himself with authority, but there was something he felt he could entrust Officer Robinson with and still
remain true to the code.

"Matter fact, there is something you can do for me,"
Reece said. "You know Jenkins? The little brother that works
in medical?" Robinson nodded. "Okay. Make sure he gets
everything he needs while he's here. Take care of him and I'll
take care of you."

"Sure thing," Officer Robinson promised. "Now are you
sure you straight on transportation?"

"Yeah. That's my ride right there." Reece pointed to the platinum colored Bentley parked in the back of the parking lot. Qwess was sitting on the hood.

Officer Robinson squinted to look at the Bentley. "Say, is that who I think it is?" he asked.

"Don't know. Depends on who you think it is," Reece retorted.

"Man, I know that's not Qwess, is it?"

"Yeah. That's my brother," Reece said casually.

"Are you serious? He came all the way up here by himself with no bodyguards?"

Reece chuckled at Officer Robinson as if he were silly. "Yeah. I told you I'm kind of a big deal out there. That's my brother, so why wouldn't he come up here? You want me to introduce you to him?"

"Would you? My niece loves this guy!"

"Sure, come on."

The gate opened and Reece led the way. Qwess saw the officer coming and met them halfway. Reece introduced them, and Qwess shook his hand.

"Pleasure to meet you," Qwess said. "I hope you took care of my brother while he was in there."

"Me and Kirkson got along great," Officer Robinson claimed, giving Reece the eye. He was geeked. "Aww, man. That song on your last album about the penitentiary, I was feeling it. I took the advice on it, too."

"Oh, yeah?"

"Absolutely. I mean, we all have a job to do in life, but we are all brothers."

Qwess smiled. "Well, it sounds like I did my job then." He tapped Reece on the shoulder. "Ready, bro?"

Qwess wrapped things up and gave Officer Robinson an autograph. Then the two brothers walked over to the Bentley in silence. Neither of them spoke a word for a full two minutes. Then they both burst out in laughter and surrendered to a tight embrace.

"Yo, what the fuck you did to your head, man?" Qwess smacked Reece on his bald dome.

"Yo, cut that shit out, man!"

"And what is that shit in your mouth?"

Reece flashed a smile, and a rainbow lit up his face as each diamond-encrusted tooth reflected in the sun.

"Yo, you like this shit, right?"

"It's straight," Qwess admitted.

Reece walked around the Bentley, inspecting the luxury vehicle. "What's this, a Continental R?" Reece asked.

"Nah, it's a Bentley GT. It replaced the Continentals."

Reece stroked his chin and nodded, "Nice, nice . . ." He pointed to the rims. "Are those dubs?"

Qwess laughed. "Yeah you have been gone awhile. Niggas ain't riding dubs no more. If you ain't sitting on dub-deuces or better, you ain't sitting on shit."

Before Reece caught his case, he had a fleet of Bentleys, a Maserati, Ferraris, and a McLaren F1.

Qwess leaned against the Bentley and pointed behind Reece. "Like this right here pulling up, it's on twenty-twos."

Reece turned around just in time to see a beautiful two-toned Mercedes Maybach 62 gliding into the parking lot. The car was emerald green on the top and bottom with a cream center. The twenty-twos sported a cream chrome lip with an emerald-green center. The car coasted to a halt right in front of Qwess's Bentley.

"Yoooo, I know you didn't." Reece said, smiling hard. The diamonds in his teeth flashed like paparazzi.

Qwess shook his head. "I didn't; *she* did."

The back door of the Maybach opened, and Vanilla stepped out wearing a skintight white skirt with green Christian Louboutins. She ran, hopped into Reece's arms, and wrapped her thick legs around his waist.

"Heeeey, my king!!!!" Vanilla planted kisses all over Reece's body. "I can't believe this day has finally come!"

Reece hugged Vanilla tight, his muscular arms sinking into her soft flesh. He snuggled his nose into the crease of her neck and inhaled her scent. She smelled wonderful!

"I knew you wouldn't miss this day," Reece said.

"Wouldn't have missed it for the world."

Reece turned to Qwess. "Did you know about this?"

"Not until the last minute. I helped her with the car, but it was all her idea."

"Baby, please hurry up so we can go to the condo," Vanilla pleaded.

Reece set Vanilla down and watched her sashay back to the limo. Then he gave Qwess some dap. "What time we pulling out?" he asked.

Qwess shrugged. "Whenever you finish handling your business. Tomorrow morning?"

"Sounds good to me."

Reece joined Vanilla in the back of the Maybach. She had already stripped down to just her thong and awaited him with the seat reclined. "Driver, put up the partition, please?" Vanilla called to the front of the Maybach. "Don't want him to see me on my knees," she said to Reece.

Reece grinned and sat down checking out the confines of the car. He felt as if he was in a forest with all the wood and hide.

"Lean back, baby. Let me give you the respect you deserve," Vanilla said, crawling to her knees.

As the car pulled from the parking lot, Vanilla pulled on Reece. Although they had had sex while Reece was inside, this was different. They didn't have to listen for the guards or rush before their move was interrupted. Reece didn't have to concentrate on busting his nut quickly. This he could enjoy. So, in the back of a three-hundred-thousand-dollar vehicle, Reece laid his head back on the pillow in the headrest and enjoyed his freedom as Vanilla praised him.

As Vanilla took him deep into her mouth, Reece allowed himself the luxury of dropping the guard on his mind.

Being incarcerated was an exercise in restraint. He was forced to restrain his natural desires. He was forced to restrain his movements. He was forced to bite his tongue. He was forced to restrain his mind from processing his emotions because he had to be on guard. All the time. He was forced to restrain his memory because daydreaming about things outside the walls was the quickest way to get killed.

Today, Reece freed himself of everything. He allowed his mind to drift back to the times he was on top. Through his mind's eye he saw the mountains of drugs he had peddled, he saw the blood of the adversaries he had crushed beneath his feet, he saw the millions of dollars he had amassed. The visions made him smile. He was a made man who had beaten the system.

Vanilla slurped loudly on his dick and snatched Reece from his thoughts. She tightened her jaws on his erection, and Reece almost lost his mind. He ran his hands through her long blond hair affectionately, then coiled her tresses around his hand. He used his hand to guide her warm mouth to where he wanted it. Unconsciously, he gently pushed his pulsating erection into Vanilla's mouth. Vanilla wrapped her hand around the base of his dick and jacked him off while she sucked him harder. Reece pumped in her mouth. Vanilla sucked harder. Reece felt electricity zipping through his balls. He pumped Vanilla's face furiously. She sucked him harder. Reece wailed in amazement.

"Ahhhhhhhh!!!"

In the back of the Maybach with his beautiful ride-or-die bitch, King Reece found his freedom.

The following morning, Reece and Qwess left Virginia in Qwess's Bentley. They were driving the four-hour trip back to

Fayetteville so the brothers could catch up on things and Reece could acclimate himself to the free world before he was thrust back into his persona as King Reece. Vanilla was flying home and leaving the Maybach in Virginia.

As they careened down the Virginia backroads at high speed, Reece fired away questions like a prosecutor.

"So, your old man home now, huh?" Reece asked.

"Yeah. Him and my mom in the islands somewhere right and now living it up, ya dig?"

"That's what's up. I'm trying to hit me an island somewhere, but after we take care of business."

"Yo, don't even sweat that. My pops took care of all the paperwork before he left. Him and Amin linked up and squared everything away. The distribution contracts, the manufacturing contracts, everything. I'ma tell you, too. They didn't want to do it. Talking 'bout 'who's your parent company?' Like we need a parent company to deal with them. Ultimately their greed won out."

"So, your pops is pretty good at law, huh?" wondered Reece.

"Hell, yeah! I mean think about it. He had fifteen years to do nothing but study law. All types of law. Shit, pops was so tight they was calling him Hammurabi up in that joint!" Qwess joked, referring to the so-called father of modern law.

"Yeah, I know. His name was still ringing back there. I couldn't believe they shipped him as soon as I got there. Your uncle still maintaining, though."

"Word?" This was a sore subject for Qwess. Through all his finagling he still hadn't been able to bring his uncle home. Partly because of what his uncle's own hands brought forth: He was still dealing drugs behind bars and consequently had accumulated an expensive prison record.

"Yeah. He rolling with the BGF. Those niggas be wildin', too! They sharp, though."

"I bet they are. Unc was always sharp. He just like getting that bread, ya dig?"

"I can feel him. So, those dickheads hot, huh?" Reece asked, changing the subject.

Qwess scoffed. "You know it. But I fulfilled my obligations, so it ain't shit they can do. They tried to offer me an ass of money. I'm talking unprecedented shit."

"Word? How much?" Reece smirked.

"Nah, negro, don't even think about it."

Reece shrugged his shoulders. "I'm just saying, though."

"Saying my ass. We already rich. What's another few mil? Plus if we get Niya on our label, that's a major bread. She guaranteed triple-platinum this time. Independently that's big-boy cake."

Reece could see dollar signs already. "So, what's the hold up? She ready to get out, ain't she? I know she better be. Hell, family come first!"

"Yeah, but it's a little more complicated than that."

"Don't worry about it. We'll see what's up. Yo, isn't that a Shoney's up there? Let's stop. I'm ready to eat some real food."

They entered the Shoney's, and Recce ate what seemed like everything on the menu. Qwess repeatedly joked about his voracious appetite. When they exited the restaurant an hour later, they were both stuffed. They piled into the Bentley amidst stares. They were still in Virginia, and black people didn't drive 150-thousand-dollar cars in this neck of the woods, especially young black males.

"Yo, man, you don't have any smoke?" Reece asked once they were on the highway. "I'm ready to get my head bad."

"No, man. We in the wrong place for that. These are some racist mu'fuckas." Qwess had already been checking his rearview constantly the whole trip. "Don't worry. All that and more is waiting when we get home."

Reece cut his eyes at Qwess. There was a lull in the conversation, so Qwess turned on the radio. There was a time when his cars didn't even have radios because he simply didn't do them. Being a CEO, however, one had to monitor the radio to see where his artists charted. A song by Maserati pumped through the JL Audios, which got Reece amped.

"Man, what's this shit I hear about that nigga punking you at Bike Week," inquired Reece, turning down the radio. "That shit was all over the radio. Don't tell me you getting soft. I know this nigga ain't push you and you did nothing!" Reece was practically squirming in his seat.

Just as Qwess was about to explain, a blue light flashed in his rearview.

"There these mu'fuckas go," Qwess swore. He instinctively checked his speed. He was doing seventy miles an hour. Not exactly the speed the speed limit, but not exactly speeding. In this neck of the woods, in a Bentley, he might as well have been doing two hundred miles an hour. He debated whether to pull over or not, then decided it would be best. After all, he could outrun the cop on his tail, but he couldn't outrun those roadblocks. So he slowly pulled over. He looked into the mirror as the highway patrolman exited his cruiser. When the patrolman traced the contours of his brown round and spat a huge wad of tobacco in the road, Qwess just knew they were in trouble.

The patrolman strolled to the car and ducked his head into the window. "Son, do you know what I'm stopping you for?"

"'Cause I'm young and black, and my hat is low. Do I look like a mind reader? Sir, I don't know," Qwess retorted, not missing a beat. He read his name tag: Officer Ropes. Shit.

"Okay, smartass. You mind stepping out your vehicle," Officer Ropes twanged. "And gimme dat der licenses and registration."

"Like I ain't stepping outta shit. All my papers are straight." Qwess passed Ropes the paperwork. Reece was tapping

Qwess on the leg, signaling him to comply. Qwess was oblivious to it.

Officer Ropes looked over Qwess's paperwork. "Son, you baahs long way from home to be actin' dumb. We don't like yo' kind 'round dees parts nohow. Now if I tell you to step out yo' vehicle, den dat's what you do."

Qwess didn't realize the seriousness of the situation and remained defiant. "Look, I know my rights. It's not necessary for me to step out my car to complete a traffic stop."

"Oh, you some type of lawyer ur somethin', somebody impo'ent ur somethin'? We'll see when the dogs come."

With that, Officer Ropes radioed for help. Inside the car Reece chastised Qwess.

"Yo, you just had to show your ass, didn't you? You just had to!"

"Man, fuck these Keeblers. They ain't searching my shit. What you acting scared for anyway? You already did the bid now."

"Damn right!" Reece exploded. "And I ain't trying to go back!"

"Well, just chill. I got this. Don't even panic."

Officer Ropes came back to the car. "Now look, baahs, I'mon gib you one mo chance to ac' right. If you still pussyfooting when my back up get chea—" He removed his dark sunglasses and looked hard at Qwess. "Ooh, boay, you gon' 'gret it."

That was all the prodding they needed. Qwess exited the vehicle, submitted to a pat-down, and paid the ticket on the spot. Officer Ropes called off his backup, and Qwess reentered the car, but before he left Officer Ropes had one more thing to say.

He ducked his head into the car and said, "Boays, I s'gest you take it easy 'cause all we do 'round dees parts is hunt and fuck. If we ain't hunting or fucking, we hunting sumthin' to fuck or fuck up. Don't let it be you."

With those parting shots, he returned to his cruiser and peeled off in the other direction.

For the next hour, Reece and Qwess cracked up over the officer as the Virginia countryside whizzed by. Once upon a time, Reece would have had the officer tracked down and handled for playing them like that. It didn't matter that the officer had no idea who King Reece was; Reece's ego was bigger than the East Coast and all violations were met with violent force—and police weren't exempt from their wrath. A lot had changed since then, though. The year was 2009, not 2003, and reinvention was the word of the day for Reece.

Hours later when Qwess and Reece pulled into the driveway of Reece's mansion, they were still tripping off the traffic stop.

During Reece's incarceration he had liquidated a lot of his assets because he knew the government would be after him like nothing changed. They couldn't get him on criminal charges, so he knew they would try to hit him in the pocket. He had already paid some back taxes as part of his plea agreement, but that was only a drop in the bucket. He knew it. They knew. He knew that they knew it. So to combat the problem, he sold a lot of his property. His five-star car lot, some of his luxury apartments, and his mansion. (He sold the mansion to Qwess, who promptly sold it back to him for a dollar.) In addition to that, he had sold his whole luxury fleet of automobiles. The only things he owned now were his funeral homes, club, and mansion. Only good thing was he now had part in ABP. It was guaranteed to make him more millions over the next few years.

Reece and Qwess exited the Bentley and stretched, then made the trek up the granite stairs. No lights were on inside the mansion.

"I've been maintaining your house for you. Shit, really I've been staying in here. This shit is plush," Qwess was explaining to Reece while he fumbled over the electronic keypad to unlock the door. Reece was surprised, but glad that Qwess had obeyed his requests not to have a homecoming party. This was Reece's thinking when they entered the mansion; of course, it went quickly because as soon as they walked through the foyer, the lights came on, and a room full of people yelled, "Welcome home!"

Reece saw a lot of familiar faces, mostly original members of the Crew. A lot of women were present, too. Some were from his club. Others were from Fatimah's, Qwess's sister's, salon. They all chanted, "Hail King Reece!" Reece felt a little embarrassed, so he asked them to stop. As Reece made his way through the crowd he spotted Hulk, Muhammad, Born, and other members of the original Crescent Crew. They all wore either green or cream, the colors of the Crescent Crew, to pay homage. Reece dapped each of them up individually. Reece noticed that Hulk looked like he was the one who finished a bid, because he was brolic now. Hulk had always been huge, but now he was chiseled, similar to a statue. Muscles bulged underneath his linen shirt without mercy.

After all of the salutations were rendered, everyone took the party out back to the pool. Draped around the deck were decorations of all sorts. On the table just aft of the Jacuzzi was a huge red velvet (Reece's favorite) cake with the words "Welcome Home" scribbled on it. Beside the table stood Doe, his wife, Niya, and Vanilla. Doe beckoned Reece over.

"What's up, cuz-o?" The two cousins hugged. "You too cuz-o." Reece hugged Niya as well. She giggled heartily. Vanilla then grabbed Reece and stuck her tongue in his mouth, to the jeers of the crowd. Reece played it smooth, though he was pissed. He didn't do no kissing.

They cut the cake and commenced to party. Reece stood by the table accepting greetings from the numerous people who came by to pay respect.

As Reece looked over the grounds of his home, he analyzed things to see how they had changed since he had been gone. Right off the bat he could sense some tension among the crew.

It seemed that there were two factions of the crew now: one part that was still in the streets, and another part that wasn't. It was apparent by the way they moved.

Muhammad, for instance, observed any and everybody with a watchful eye. He looked in Reece's direction a couple times each minute to make sure no harm came his way from "off brands" attending the party. This was supposed to be his movement, as he was a captain in the ranks of the Crescent Crew—street side.

Now, Amin, he played in the water with the ladies. He openly got intoxicated with a blunt in one hand and a bottle of Cristal in the other. He never even shot Reece a glance. It was like he didn't have a care in the world. Reece wasn't surprised. He was Qwess's business manager and thus a Crescent Crew member—legit side.

Reece had heard some ruminations of just this type of thing from Vanilla a while back, but so far, so good. However, he knew that if things weren't done right, this could potentially be a volatile situation. Ideally, the street side was supposed to hold the other side down. Reece had expressed this to Bone via numerous messages from Vanilla.

"Here, sweets. Eat some cake." Vanilla interrupted Reece's thoughts, passing him a piece of cake. He bit a chunk and passed it back.

"You don't seem too happy. What's up?" Vanilla wondered.

"Nothing. Just got a little something on my mind," replied Reece. He was thinking about the letter in his pocket. As of yet, he hadn't read it, but the suspense was killing him. He couldn't take it anymore. "Yo, excuse me for a minute."

Reece left the poolside area and walked to his bedroom. When he entered, all kinds of memories flooded his mind. He vividly remembered how he and Destiny used to have fun in this very room. Playing naked tag, wrestling naked. The numerous role-playing episodes. They would lie in the bed for hours sharing stories from their childhood and expressing dreams of a future together. She had told him how she wanted their wedding day to be. She spoke of lilacs and diamonds and pearls. She spoke of family being flown in from Jamaica. They were so deep in love. So deep . . .

Or was it all a lie?

Reece had so many questions. Reece closed his eyes, and a vivid memory of them making love replayed across the theater of his mind. He could hear Destiny panting in his ear telling him she was about to climax. Reece smiled. He found so much comfort in the vision. In his mind, he looked into her eyes to see her face do that thing that he loved when she came.

Instead, he saw her face on the tarmac that day, the day she pointed a Glock at him and toppled him from his throne. The memory buckled his knees, and his leg throbbed where Destiny had blown a hole through it.

Reece grimaced and walked over to the balcony. He pulled out the letter and ran his fingers over the envelope. He had so many questions, so many holes he needed filled in.

Reece had committed murders and didn't lose a wink of sleep. He tortured men—cut their balls from their scrotums— with a smile on his face. He tossed adversaries from rooftops and couldn't even remember their names or the violations that caused their deaths. He had reigned as a king over men, and a god over kings, yet the one thing he couldn't conquer was his feelings for Destiny.

He was torn beyond measure. Mixed feelings paralyzed him. One part of him wanted to see her bleed to death . . . slowly. Another part of him wanted to see her head chopped off and thrown in the depths of the sea for her treason. Yet another part of him longed for her. He desired her stimulating conversation and craved her touch. Her scent, like lavender and love, lay inside his nostrils. He couldn't help but think about her. She had been a permanent fixture in his mind every day that he was in prison, each day brought on a different angle. One day he wanted her dead, the next day he craved her presence. Then there was the issue of his son.

Hence the complexities of the man called Reece.

Reece looked at the letter again. It was dated two days ago, which meant it had come from the East Coast. Reece was more than a little reluctant to open the letter. Maybe the letter would fill in some of the blanks. Maybe it would lead to more questions. The only way to find out was to risk reading the letter he held. Reece opened the letter and began to read:

> Reece,
> Congratulations on your release. I pray that you do the right thing. God has spared you your life for a reason, so please take advantage of it.
> Like I told you before, I've moved back to North Carolina now. I won't give you my address, but I will give you my number so we can coordinate a meeting with our son, Prince. He is so excited to see you. Until then, take care.
> Love Always
> K. D. Hill

There was a number at the bottom. Reece filed it away in his memory then closed the letter. He had expected more. He didn't know what he expected, exactly; he just knew he expected more than that. The more he marinated on the letter, the more he became incensed.

Suddenly, he shredded the letter. "Bitch! What the fuck she talking 'bout God spared my life? We gon' see if that motherfucker spare *her* life!"

Reece had always talked to himself from time to time, but since he had gone to prison, it had gotten out of hand. Plenty of times his roommate had thought another person was in the room with them. Then he realized Reece was just off his rocker.

Reece paced back and forth in deep thought, volleying scenarios of how he was going to deal with Destiny. The number was pinned in his head like a billboard. He pulled his phone out. He dialed the number but didn't push send.

A loud commotion downstairs ripped his attention from the phone in his hand. Reece quickly exited his bedroom and rushed down the long hallway. He slowed down before he reached the balcony that looked over the great room. Reece paused a moment then took a peek around the corner. What he saw surprised him.

Standing in the middle of the room towering over everyone like a god was a bald-headed black man. On each side of him were Latino men. They were huge also, but nowhere near the size of the central figure. This guy had to be every bit of 350, 375 pounds and stood no less than six foot seven. Upon closer inspection, he looked familiar to Reece. Hell, he resembled Hulk, but their faces were almost the exact opposite.

Suddenly, like a ton of bricks, it hit Reece.

"Samson!"

The huge figure looked up at Reece running down the stairs and broke out in a huge smile, immediately setting the room at ease. All other guests outside of the Crescent Crew were clueless as to who this individual was. However, those inside the Crew knew their comrade very well.

Samson greeted Reece with a powerful hug, lifting him up. When he put him down, Reece inspected him closely. "Yo, what did you do to your face?" Reece asked.

"Ha ha, the miracles of medicine," Samson replied, enthused. One of the Latinos asked Samson a question in Spanish. Samson answered in Spanish, never missing a beat. The Latino man leaned in to hug Reece. "A friend to Monstruoso is a brother to me," he told Reece in broken English.

Reece gave the man his hand instead of a hug. He didn't know this cat, or no Monstruoso either. Muhammad saw Reece's tension and pulled up beside him. Then Samson spoke.

"Oh, you don't have no love for your brother now?" he asked, looking at Muhammad.

Muhammad scowled. "Nigga, I don't know you!"

Reece halted him with a hand on his chest. "Hold up, homie. Look closely."

Muhammad scrutinized the giant in silence. Then he caught it, too. "Oh, shit!! My nigga!"

No one recognized Samson because he had gotten plastic surgery on his face as well as his hands. It was done out of necessity, since he was wanted dead or alive in the United States. He was a regular feature on *America's Most Wanted*. Samson, never one to be daunted, continued to venture in and out of the States, if only for the surprise effect alone. When the Crescent Crew saw him coming to make moves despite the bounty on his head, it garnered him tremendous respect. He would pop up on blocks one minute, and be gone the next. His selective absence increased fear. The thought that the de facto leader of the Crescent Crew was liable to appear anytime anywhere, unannounced, kept allies in check and adversaries on the run.

But his bold moves came with risks. One time in particular, the police got behind Samson and made him pull over, no doubt for DWB (Driving While Black). The patrolman just knew he had hit the jackpot. He just knew he had caught the big fish when he saw the giant driving the Mercedes. Luckily for Samson, he had a copy of his twin brother Hulk's driver's license. He played the part of the pissed-off industry bigwig so ceremoniously that the patrolman let him go to avoid embarrassment for the department, as well as a big-boy lawsuit. The move was too close for comfort, though. Soon after, Samson decided not to take any more chances. He went back to Mexico and paid one of the top surgeons in the world to alter his appearance. Sure, he would miss being able to assume his brother's identity, but chances were something he couldn't take. If captured, he was guaranteed never to see the light of day. Therefore, the ends definitely justified the means. It would take some time to get used to, especially with his former twin brother eyeing him like he was.

"What's up, li'l bro?" Samson asked Hulk, making a point to remind him that he was his senior by a few minutes.

Hulk didn't say anything as he walked up in Samson's face. He walked around his whole body sizing him up before returning to his face. Suddenly, he hugged him tightly. "I knew you'd be here."

"No doubt. Wouldn't miss it for the world," Samson replied.

"Didn't I tell you they was gonna trip out about your face?" Hulk laughed.

"Yep," Samson said and nodded.

Reece interrupted the brotherly reunion. "Yo, nigga. You better take off them gators before they get wet 'cause we having a party out back!" Everyone was ushered back to the pool area.

A half hour later the party was interrupted again when Bone rolled in. He was wearing a platinum-and-diamond-encrusted ABP chain and eagerly looking for Qwess. Qwess came over to holla at him by the pool with a puzzled look on his face.

"What's the deal, dawg?" Qwess asked, looking at Bone's neck.

"Yo, where's the homie, Flame?" Bone asked. "I got something for him." Bone was smirking something fierce.

The conversation was cut short. Reece tossed a ball from the pool and hit Bone smack in the head.

"Oh, you can't pay no homage to a nigga?" Reece asked, walking over out of the pool. What's up, Boney Roney?"

Bone was dumbfounded. "N-nah, yo. It ain't like that. I didn't see you."

"Shit, I can' tell," Reece cut him off. "I just get out the joint and you ask for this nigga?" He pointed at Qwess. "Before you ask for me? What's really going on?"

Bone didn't know how to take Reece because Reece wasn't smiling. Bone definitely didn't want to get on Reece's bad side. He knew shit was about to change now that he was home.

"Yo, I got something good for the li'l homie Flame. You told me to hold the label down, right?"

"Yeah."

"Well, you'll dig this, then. Come on." Bone knew Reece would love this. Qwess called Flame and Hulk. Samson followed behind Reece.

Bone led them to the front of the round driveway where all the cars were parked. Flame was surprised to see his brand-new Mercedes SL sitting out front.

Flame couldn't contain his excitement. "Oh, shit! My baby. How did you get her?" he asked Bone.

"Don't worry about that. Just be careful from now on." Bone extended the keys to Flame. Flame rushed over to the driver's side then circled the whole car inspecting it. There were bloodstains by the driver's side mirror and on the front quarter panel.

"Yo, what's this?" Flame asked, too wrapped up in amazement to know better than to ask certain questions.

Bone quickly rushed over. "Where!?"

"Right here." Flame pointed to the spots.

"Oh, shit. My bad." Bone managed a weak smile before wiping the spots off with a mischievous grin. By now everyone had gathered around the car.

"Is that what I think it is?" Reece asked.

Bone was a little hesitant about spilling the beans in front of Flame, so he nodded but cut his eyes toward Flame, signaling secrecy.

Reece caught the hint and promptly dismissed Flame, but before Flame made it to the house, Bone called him back. "Here, li'l homie." He passed Flame his necklace. "You shouldn't have no more problems in the 'Nam. The word is out now that you with us out here in these streets, so don't even sweat it. Go where you wanna go, however you wanna get there. A'ight?"

"A'ight. Cool." Flame gave him dap and peeled back inside to the party. He wasn't inside two seconds before the questions started being shot at Bone.

"How'd you get it back?"

"Where the blood came from?"

"Did you murk this nigga?"

"Where he at now?"

Bone silenced all the queries when he proceeded to tell the story of how a local fence had come to one of his spots wanting to unload some hot stuff. He insisted that he came to see Bone because Bone was the only one who could afford to pay what he demanded for the merchandise. Bone, already getting the word about Flame's misfortune, figured the fence would know something about it. So, at the very least, he decided to talk to him. He couldn't believe the jewel that was dropped his lap when (as Bone so eloquently put it) the stupid mu'fucka drove the Benz right up in the joint. He even had the stupidity to be wearing the diamond chain.

Bone pretended everything was copacetic in order to get the dude to tell him how he came upon the goods. Of course, the fence narrated everything. After all, wasn't Bone a straight murderer? Bone made the fence lead him to the jackers and leave them alone.

Bone intentionally left out the other details.

"So, where they at now?" asked Reece. He was about to jump out of his skin! He loved to hear about his soldiers putting in work.

Bone just smiled. "We can go check 'em out now. When I heard you were home, I decided to hold off and let you handle things. Figured it would be a perfect way to get your feet back wet."

Reece didn't know who this cat thought he was, trying to force him back into shit. He started to check him, but then decided he'd go along to see how Bone was putting it down.

"A'ight. Where they at?" asked Reece.

"If you ready, we can roll on out."

Reece sensed Qwess ice grilling him hard, so he told Bone and Samson to meet him in the truck.

When it was just Qwess and Reece, Qwess wasted no time rebuking Reece.

"Yo, what's up? Fuck you trying to do? Don't lose focus. Like you told me a long time ago: If you out, stay out!"

Reece was half listening. He was already salivating at being around some action. "I got you, bruh. I'm just going to ride and get the scoop on things. See where they mind at," he said, looking far-off.

Qwess was still unsure. "All right, you your own man, but know that it's bigger than you. A lot more people got a lot more to lose, ya dig?"

"Relax, Qwess. I ain't in no hurry to get back to no cage. I said I'm going to just check things out," Reece assured him. "Now be easy. I'll be back soon."

Reece strolled off to the waiting Infiniti truck, climbed into the back, and they drove off into the night.

Inside the truck, Bone drove, one of the Mexicans, Gil, rode shotgun, and Samson, Reece, and the other Mexican sat in back. Samson made formal introductions, and Reece found out Gil's name as well as the name of the Mexican on the other side of him with the long ponytail. His name was Chabo. According to Samson, the two Mexicans were his soldiers in his "new" business venture. He didn't divulge exactly what that venture was.

When Bone turned onto Raeford Road, Reece knew exactly where they were going. His old torture rack. He sat back to enjoy the long ride.

"Yo, what you got planned for the weeks ahead?" Samson

asked. "Heading down to Mexico kicking it on the yacht for old times' sake?" Samson offered with a chuckle.

"Naw, I'm heading out to L.A. to do the Soul Train Awards show with Flame and Saigon. You know I bought into the label now."

"I know that, but that don't mean you can't roll with the Crew. You are still Crescent Crew, ain't ya? You ain't pulling a Qwess on us, are you?"

Samson was referring to the way Qwess had practically abandoned the Crescent Crew when he got out of prison to do the music thing.

"Nah, I'm just heading out west for a few days. That's not a crime, is it?"

The question was loaded. Reece was taking the temperature of things. Based on Samson's answer, Reece would decide how deep to delve into his plans.

Samson caught the tone in Reece's voice and knew something was amiss, so he played his part. "Nah, no problems, King."

"Okay, cool then," Reece said with an icy tone. "I really ain't trying to fuck wit' no broads like that, nah'mean. Fuck all them bitches! I'm on some new shit right now."

By the tone of the conversation, Reece was making it apparent that he was top dog. He asserted his dominance with his tone. He had been gone for a few years, and like the leader of a pack of wolves, Reece had to reassert his authority. Gil and Chabo had never seen anyone trump Samson. Samson always controlled situations in their eyes. Seeing Samson bow down to Reece raised his stature in their eyes—and lowered Samson's.

Samson conceded his point. "Yo, I feel you, God. After all that bullshit ole girl put you through I wouldn't love them hoes either. Take it back to Snoop '93 and shit." He chuckled to lighten the mood.

Samson's statement took Reece back to his original thoughts.

What to do with Destiny? The chick just didn't know who she was dealing with.

The fact that she was his son's mother could only ice the stinging pain of betrayal for so long. Couldn't she see that? Oh, well, Reece thought, she'll see before it's over with.

After traveling for about an hour, Bone finally turned off onto a side road. He maneuvered the huge luxury SUV through narrow dirt roads until they came to a cabin. Situated at hundred-foot intervals were huge pit bulls. They were chained to stakes driven into the ground, which permitted the seven dogs to cover every square inch of the grounds freely.

One by one, each passenger exited the vehicle and stretched from the long ride. Gil and Chabo were unfamiliar with their surroundings, thus overly observant and jittery. Bone, Samson, and Reece were all too familiar with this place. Prior to Reece's incarceration, during the Crescent Crew wars, this had been Reece's personal torture chamber. Bone wasn't part of the Crescent Crew during the wars, but he had heard numerous stories of Reece's exploits. In fact, on occasion Bone had used the cabin himself, most of the time to get a point across to a stubborn adversary. Sort of like now.

The group entered the cabin, and they were immediately assaulted by the smell of urine and feces. It was no secret where the smell emanated from as everyone observed two hood men tied up in the center of the room. The cabin itself wasn't big. It consisted of a central room with two smaller rooms adjacent to each other. The ceiling was lined with beams running across the entire room. The two men were seated directly under a beam. Both had already soiled their pants.

Bone walked over to them and removed their masks. It took a few seconds for their eyes to adjust to the light. When they did, both men wished they would've remained closed.

"Aw, shit!!" they both exclaimed in unison. They recognized well who two of the men in front of them were. They knew Reece from his reputation and recognized him from his mug shot picture in *Don Diva* magazine. Samson they recognized from the few times he had come to the block to collect personally.

"Don't 'aw shit' now," Bone taunted. "Time to pay the piper, muthafuckas." Bone backhanded them both for good measure.

They started bitching immediately. "Man, we didn't know! I swear we didn't know!"

Bone knew he was being watched by the big dog, so he had to play extra hard.

"You didn't know? Oh, well. You will know now!" Bone retrieved his gun from his waistband and commenced to pistol-whip the unlucky jacker on the left till blood spewed from his mouth and oozed openly from his head.

"You know who this is?" Bone asked the jacker on the left while pointing at Reece. Jacker number two was a little more firm than his partner. He maintained eye contact as he nodded his head.

"Oh, yeah?" Bone continued. "Well, you know this is the wrong nigga to fuck wit'!

"I didn't fuck wit' him!" the jacker spat at him.

"Yes, you did. When you fuck with one of the Crescent Crew you fuck wit' all of 'em," Bone explained. He was obviously enjoying his position as a Crescent Crew captain. "Fuck you wanna jack a nigga for anyway? You should be running up in them white people banks. Yeah, but you don't wanna do that, huh? You hard in the hood, but scared to go where the real money at."

As Bone chastised and toyed with the victim, Reece and Samson calmly observed. Reece was thinking about how he really didn't need to be here. Qwess's warning echoed around his head, *"If you out stay out!"* He remembered telling Qwess the exact same thing when his fiancée was murdered by the

Blood Team some six years ago. Qwess eventually relented and let Reece handle retribution. Now would Reece be able to leave the streets alone and go legit?

Samson was observing Bone and Reece. Bone wasn't surprising to him. He already knew Bone was gangsta. After all, he did shoot a police officer multiple times to earn his spot in the Crescent Crew. Nah, Samson was watching Reece carefully. Something wasn't right with him. Normally in these types of situations Reece would've been a lot more amped. Instead he just looked on detached, sort of like he didn't want to be there. A part of him wanted to attribute Reece's uneasiness to him just coming home. Yet, in reality Samson knew better. Reece was a stone-cold killer. He was jaded when it came to extinguishing life's fire. Samson decided to try something.

He walked over to where Bone was taunting the victims, and in a move that surprised everyone . . . he untied them.

"Stand up." They obeyed, though one was shaky. "If you want to live, fight for your life," Samson told them. In the moment's hesitation that occurred, Samson punched one of them in the stomach. The strike echoed off the walls. The man blew blood from his mouth, his yelp sounding off like a trumpet. No further prodding needed, the other man rushed Samson. Samson feigned capture purposely. He acted like he couldn't get away.

When it was assumed he couldn't get away, Chabo stepped up. He grabbed the man by the neck, and he quickly spun out of Chabo's grip. He tried to rush Chabo, but Chabo spun around quickly, sweeping him and hitting him in the neck with the end of the razors discreetly tucked into Chabo's ponytail. The man attempted to scream, but nothing came out except air.

His already wounded partner saw this and wailed like a banshee. Samson gut-shot him to silence him. The man buckled, and Samson commenced to pummel him mercilessly. He rained blow after powerful blow. His gigantic arms pumped like pistons. All the while Samson sneered at Reece from an angle.

Reece returned the glance, but it was crystal clear that he was uncomfortable.

"Get you, nigga!" Samson ordered. "Gil, come get some." Gil moved up to his place but with a bat that he had retrieved from the corner. He swung the bat, and the unlucky jacker's knees cracked with a sickening crunch. His ear-splitting screams claimed the room. Gil stabilized himself to swing again, but Reece stopped him.

"All right, man. You made your point," Reece stated to Samson. "Go ahead and finish it." Samson chuckled knowingly and scooped the victim up from behind. He wedged one of his massive arms underneath his chin and grabbed the back of his head with the other hand. Samson pulled up with his arm and pushed out with his hand simultaneously. There was a loud popping sound. Samson released the now lifeless body to let it slump to the ground.

"Good, now take me home. I got an early morning," Reece demanded.

Hours after the incident in the cabin, Samson, Chabo, and Gil sat in one of Samson's many Carolina hideouts smoking weeds and sniffing raw cocaine.

"Ju know, man, I don't know 'bout ju friend," Gil was saying to Samson. "Him no seem like him ready for 'dis. Are ju sure he can handle dis? Are ju sure he can handle dis pressure?"

Samson inhaled a huge cloud of powder into his nose. "Man, listen, King Reece is as thorough as they come. So, hell yeah, he can handle the pressure." Samson punctuated his sentence with another deep snort.

It was Chabo's turn to speak up. "Hey, man, maybe ju should slow down on the cocaine. Powder and juice no mix, vato."

Chabo was referring to the steroids Samson was taking.

Ever since his plastic surgery, Samson had been taking huge doses of steroids, partly to enhance his looks, partly to assist him in his other trade. He was required to lift heavy loads and do plenty of manual labor. Not to mention look imposing (like that was ever hard). All of this was part of his new occupation.

"Vato, you loco. I feel *mas fuerte* than ever," Samson retorted, flexing his muscles to illustrate his point. Everyone chuckled, but Chabo remained firm.

"*Sí, vato. Tú eres fuerte.* But if ju man is like ju say. Him no want no weakness. Sí?"

Now Samson was offended. "Look, vato, I said I'm straight. I'm six-foot-five barefoot. Three hundred eighty-five pounds! How the fuck am I weak, anywhere?!" Samson snatched off his shirt to reveal bulging muscles and entrenched veins. It appeared that his heart was in each individual vein the way they pulsated. Samson's voice raised a couple of octaves. "I AM A MUTHAFUCKIN' MACHINE!!! I bow to no man, okay, vato!" He spat the words out like a vile cuss.

Chabo was used to the mood swings, although they were becoming more and more frequent lately. Yet Samson was his comrade. He wished him no harm or ill intent. Therefore, he only wanted to ease the tension.

"Calm down, *amigo.* I only want the best for ju. Just be careful wid ju *amigo.* Him no seem like forgiving type, *de accuerdo?*"

Samson calmed down just like that. "Of course, *mi amigo.* I got things under control. Now that King Reece is home, we can finally put the pieces together. Just like I've been telling you."

Everyone resumed their cordiality for the rest of the night. They got high and became immersed in their own thoughts. Each one was thinking about the future of their crew. Gil and Chabo were never official members of the Crescent Crew. They were more like honorary members. Still, as went Samson, so went Gil and Chabo. Everyone wanted to succeed.

They were all wealthy beyond their wildest dreams. In Samson's case, he was filthy rich. He had come a long way from his humble beginnings in Mobile, Alabama, through the ranks of the U.S. Army, and now the second-in-command of one of the largest, longest-going criminal enterprises in the nation.

Yes, Samson had come a long way, and he refused to turn back. No matter the cost.

Chapter 9

Los Angeles, California

Qwess maneuvered the Impala through traffic on the freeway. Reece rode shotgun with Doe and Amin in the back. They were in California and loving it. Earlier in the day, Flame and Saigon had taped a very well lip-synched performance on *Soul Train*. They were now separated and doing their thing with some handlers from the label in tow, while Qwess, Doe, Reece, and Amin did their thing. They were *supposed* to be going to check out an A & R to submit some tracks for a hot new Cali artist. However, simple was never the case when they got together.

Reece sat in the tricked-out drop, real cool-like taking in the scenes of L.A. When Qwess finally hit the strip, Reece couldn't believe his eyes. The women were drop-dead gorgeous! Women that made Halle Berry look like a duck. And damn if it didn't seem like everybody was in shape. This wasn't Reece's first time in Cali. He had been out here a few times on business, and a few times with Destiny; therefore he had never paid any attention to anything else except what he came to do or who he did while he was here.

Qwess observed Reece out the corner of his eye with a sly smirk on his face. Qwess was no stranger to L.A. He had become a regular fixture in the lives of a few L.A. actresses and models. As he was a connoisseur of all things beautiful, it was only fitting that he regularly visit the land of beautiful people. He even had a cozy little loft up the coast. After spending thousands of dollars on hotel rooms monthly due to his pleasure and business trips, he deemed it cheaper to lease a place. Qwess wasn't thrifty by any means, just practical. He'd figured like this since he was going to be doing the damn thing real big in Cali, he might as well cut corners other ways. Oh, and he *was* going to be in Cali. Qwess had grown up on a beach, but Myrtle Beach couldn't hold a candle to L.A. It was like the difference between a Hyundai and a Rolls-Royce.

Even Allah-fearing Amin and old-faithful Doe were catching hell trying to abstain. Their heads were snapping so vigorously, it was only mercy that prevented whiplash.

"Man, goddamn!" Reece finally unleashed. "Now I see why your ass stayed out in Cali so much. These bitches finer than a muthafucka!"

"Reece, could you please stop disrespecting these sistahs, brother?" Amin piped from the back seat.

Reece looked behind him in pure disgust. "Man, for the last time, I told you this my fuckin' mouth. I don't know why you trying to save these hoes—or acting like it, anyway. You trying to cut just like every other nigga out here. You ain't different 'cause you know how to put bullshit in a pretty package."

The car erupted in laughter. Amin wasn't laughing. "I mean, yeah, I get mine, but I don't disrespect the sistahs." Qwess scoffed at him. Amin clarified. "Or at least not until they disrespect themselves."

"Negro, who you think you talking to?" Reece wasn't

convinced. "I saw you at my party grabbing ass like you was Mike Tyson and shit. Now you all holier than thou? Negro, please!

"Check it. You go through the shit I been through or see the shit I've seen, then we can talk, Mr. Sheltered. You forget I own a strip club. I seen the best at work, and I'm here to tell you. Ain't none of them shit. Sooner or later they show they true colors. All those bitches!"

Reece turned the music up louder. That was that with that. *How is a dude who never left the house as a kid gon' tell a certified don something about women?* thought Reece.

Reece felt that, when it came to women, Amin was the dumbest rich dude he had ever seen.

Surprisingly, Doe spoke up in Reece's defense.

"You, Ock, I used to feel the same way you did. Me and this brother used to go at it all the time, but I have to tell you. In the end he was right. Over the last few years I done seen broads that you'd never expect do things you'd never believe." Reece was vigorously nodding his head in the front seat. Doe continued.

"Bottom line: Ninety-nine percent of them hoes ain't shit."

"Oh, so Niya's a hoe?"

Silence enveloped the car. Even the music stopped.

"N-now see, my wife's different," stuttered Doe after a while. "She's that one percent."

"Is she?" Amin pressed on. "I mean do you really know? After all, you are out here right now. For all you know a brother could—"

"You, stop playing!" Doe interrupted. Just the thought of someone laying pipe to his angel made his stomach turn and his blood boil.

Up front, Reece was silent, but behind his huge square designer shades, his eyes were slits. He was thinking the same thing. One never knew with a woman.

"Seriously, though, Ock. What makes your woman so special? I'm sure there are a lot of dudes who thought their women would never be backstage giving 'professionals,' but they do."

"Yeah, but that's different." Agitation was evident in Doe's response.

"Oh, so you telling me that out of all the women in the world—millions—you lucked up and got the one faithful one? I mean, that is if your assessment is true."

Mild-tempered Doe was getting heated. His cheeks were now red, courtesy of his light complexion.

Qwess observed the whole exchange through the rearview. It was entertaining at first, but things were getting out of hand. "Yo, man, chill out with that shit. Word up!" said Qwess, attempting to defuse the situation.

"Nah, brother. He defending this Neanderthal!" He pointed at Reece.

"Man, I done told you about playing with me!"

"'Cause he right!"

"Man, chill out!"

The whole car was up in confusion with both Reece and Qwess turned facing the back. In the fracas, Qwess never saw the red light.

A horn blared and caught his attention. He slammed on the brakes desperately. The Impala skidded through the light with a loud screech, coming bumper-to-bumper with a maroon Cadillac truck. The truck had screeched to a halt as well.

Qwess did an appraisal before exiting the vehicle. Doe had hit his head on the back of the seat. Other than that, everything was cool. First thing Qwess checked was his bumper. It was mere centimeters from the Cadillac. The driver of the truck had yet to exit the vehicle. All types of people began to crowd the intersection, pointing with their hands covering their mouths.

"Shit, just what I need!" fumed Qwess. He bent over to inspect the bumper of the truck. He was still bent over when the driver approached.

Qwess abruptly stood and looked eye-to-eye with Lisa Ivory. Slasher extraordinaire. Model-actress-singer-producer. Lisa was only twenty-two years old and had conquered the entertainment industry already. She had begun her career as a model at the ripe age of fourteen. Over the years she had evolved to be every bigwig's dream and every man's nightmare. Raised in the Bronx, New York, by an Italian mother and Jamaican father, she was a devout Catholic and rumored to be a virgin, in the sense that a man had never touched her. There were numerous rumors that she was gay.

On this particular day Lisa wore white spandex pants and a matching sports bra with Nike cross-trainers. Her hair was done in her trademark cornrows. Nothing fancy. Just straight to the back. Still, she was gorgeous, and Qwess couldn't peel his eyes away from the beauty.

"Ohhh, I apologize," offered Qwess. "I don't know what I was thinking. I guess I got preoccupied for a minute, and . . . and . . ."

Lisa Ivory put her hand up to silence him. "Don't worry about it. It looks like no harm was done except maybe spilling my juice."

Qwess did a double take and noticed the damp spots on her bare stomach and sports bra. He had been busy checking her out the first time so he didn't notice. Now he did. Juice glistened off her smooth, cream-colored skin. She hadn't bothered to wipe it off. She let it stay glistening under the California sun.

"Oh, that's my fault. I feel so bad. Here I am, almost took out an icon in a traffic stop! Not the way to go out."

Lisa smiled. "What you talking about? I almost sent a musical genius into early retirement."

Now it was Qwess's turn to smile. "No, no, it was clearly my fault."

Lisa shook her head. "I'm not talking about a car crash. I'm talking about road rage. When my drink spilled on my new workout suit I just knew I was gonna flip on somebody."

They both laughed. Qwess checked out her accent. Despite living out in Cali for a long time, she still maintained a pure New York accent with a hint of Jamaican patois. Qwess dug it in a big way. She sized him up with her eyes lingering in certain places.

Before they could indulge in the conversation, police arrived on the scene. After all, they were clogging the intersection of a busy strip. The patrolmen assessed the lack of damage, requested autographs from both, and suggested they take their convo out of the busy street, before leaving to direct traffic.

"Well, I guess that's our cue," Lisa joked.

"Yeah, I guess so. Hey, look, I'm in town for a couple of days. Won't you let me take you out to dinner or something? You know . . . to make up for this," Qwess added.

"Hmmm, I don't know."

"Come on, what's a meal between friends?" he insinuated.

Lisa laughed. "Oh, so we're friends now?"

"Hey, I'm an optimist."

"Okay, Mr. Optimist." Qwess flashed the smile. Diamonds lit up the day. His whole bottom grill was iced out.

"Sure. Why not?" Lisa decided. She had heard enough about him to know that at the least she'd have fun. Plus, his southern accent tripped her out. It would be entertaining enough just to sit and hear him talk for a couple of hours.

She went back to her truck to retrieve a business card. While she was gone, one of the patrolmen shot Qwess a rebuke. It was obviously time to go. Lisa returned just in time. Qwess slid her his card as well and promised to call her.

When Qwess returned to the Impala, Reece was in a deep trance on his c-phone. Doe and Amin had, thankfully, changed the subject from the topic that caused the accident, but were still debating. That was just their thing: Amin couldn't see the glass paradox he lived in, and Doe couldn't see his naïveté when it came to women. And the world kept turning.

"Say, wasn't that ole girl Lisa, Ebony or something like that?" Amin asked as they continued down the strip.

"Ivory," corrected Qwess.

Doe bust out laughing. "Oh, shit. Qwess almost slumped Lisa Ivory!"

"She looks smaller in person, though," Amin commented.

"Hmm-mmm," Doe cosigned.

"She got a nice ass, though. I ain't know she was holding like that," Amin added as an afterthought. That put more fuel on the fire. The debate started back up.

Qwess wanted no part of it. "Who dat?" He tapped Reece on the arm. Reece put up his hand and mouthed, "Chill nigga." His face was all scrunched up. A few minutes later he wrapped the call up.

"Who was dat?" repeated Qwess.

"Destiny." The word rolled off effortlessly.

"Who!"

"Destiny." He had everyone's full attention.

"What she calling you for? What she talking about?" Doe demanded.

Reece was real calm. "Nothing really, except giving me my little man."

"Word?" Qwess was shocked. "For good?"

"Yep. Pretty much."

"When?"

"ASAP."

"Get the fuck outta here! You serious?"

"Yep. Pretty much."

This news was too much to handle. First, Destiny contacting Reece. Reece actually talking to her for a change. Then the bit about the son? This was too much. Everyone in the car grew silent and watched Reece. Reece sat idly with a far-off look behind his huge shades. His bald head shone. He stroked his goatee in deep thought.

"Wait. So you telling me Destiny is going to *give* you your son?" Doe persisted.

"Yep. Pretty much."

"Why would she do that?" Amin piped. Even he knew about their tumultuous history.

Reece removed his shades and stared into Amin's face with the most penetrating gaze. "Brother, I told you. You'll never know what goes on in the head of a woman. They're crazy." He said it in slow, measured tones, then put his shades back over his eyes. Leaned back in the seat. Zoned out. Only Qwess knew from the conversation that Reece wasn't quite telling the truth. He had an ulterior motive. Qwess knew Reece better than anyone. He only prayed that Reece's ulterior motive wouldn't jeopardize their investment.

"Yo, man, this stack here is not coming up right! What's up with this?" Samson spoke to Phil.

Samson was in the main office of Club Flesh, seated at the head of a huge green marble conference table. Club Flesh was Reece's strip club, but it doubled as headquarters for the Crescent Crew. This was where business was conducted for the Crew. The office was soundproof and contained all of the state-of-the art accoutrements: video monitors, stereo equipment, communication devices. It even contained a small cache of weapons.

A meeting was being held with all of the Crescent Crew captains. It was time for all of the captains to turn their money in.

Once a month all twelve captains took the journey from their respective cities to Club Flesh for the sit-down. Present this day were Phil Black, who ran Columbia, South Carolina; Ant Live, who had a stronghold on Myrtle Beach; AB, who controlled Charlotte; Roy Rogers of Wilmington, North Carolina; Damien the Don, who repped Greensboro; DT, who held down Greenville, South Carolina; Eye Born, who ran Florence, South Carolina; Love, who weighed in for Newberry, South Carolina; Naseem, who checked in for northern Georgia; Jihad, who was present for Tennessee; Wadu, in for Virginia; and of course Bone repping Fayettenam and all surrounding cities. Bone had much clout in the Crescent Crew, so he occupied the opposite end of the huge table.

"Yo, what you mean it's not coming up right?" Phil Black inquired.

Samson pulled the money machine closer to him and slipped the money stack inside again to illustrate his point. The machine wheezed briefly then beeped twice, totaling up the exact same sum.

"It says $9,900. The other stacks had an even ten—like they're supposed to." Samson pointed to the remainder of the stacks of Phil's pile that cluttered the table. "Now is this just a problem with this one, or are the rest short, too?"

"None of them should be short," Phil insisted.

"My thoughts exactly." Samson grabbed another stack of money, inserted it into the machine. Ten thousand showed up on the machine. The remainder were on point also, so after Samson counted them all, Phil reached into his pocket and gave Samson a hundred dollars.

"Yo, that's my fault," Phil confessed. Phil took a silent consensus of the rest of his brethren. Their faces were all poker, so he couldn't tell if he had lost face in their eyes.

Samson tossed Phil's final money stack in a duffel bag, where he put Phil's other nineteen stack as well as everyone else's twenty stacks. He placed the duffel bag in an adjacent room and returned to the table to address the brothers.

"All right, listen up. I know everybody's tripping wondering what's going to happen now that me and King Reece are back. Well, for those of you who don't know or weren't a part of this organization when he was home, he's a fair person. As long as everyone keeps performing and don't try to get slick, everything will be a'ight."

Everyone nodded.

"Now you know some heat is going to come down on us since he's home, but don't worry. Everything's cool. As long as we pay these greedy fucks we'll be all right," Samson said this very condescendingly. DT had fucked up and missed payment more than once.

"Ah, yeah, man. Kip handling it."

"Kip?! Muthafucka, I told you to handle it!" His massive hand smashed the table, shocking no one and everyone. "Fuckin' Kip was supposed to pay him last time and forgot. Is Kip a fuckin' captain? Do you want to give him your spot at the table? Don't leave something so important to no one else. Ya got that?"

He looked around at everyone, letting them know this was meant for them also.

"Something small as this can bring us all down. Y'all niggas been slipping!" Samson spat disgustedly. He focused his wrathful stare on Bone. Bone buckled under the steely gaze and looked away.

"We didn't come this far to—"

His phone rang, interrupting his tirade. He saw the 213 area code on the screen and answered. It was Reece.

Samson excused himself from the table, spoke a few minutes and returned. He overheard one of the brothers complaining about Reece not being present, as he sat back down. Ant Live decided to clear the air by voicing what was on everyone's mind.

"The brothers want to know why King Reece isn't here at the meeting. *We* feel like we staying true bringing the money without fail. The least he could do is show us some respect by being here. These meetings are important. As you said yourself, no ranking member is exempt from these meetings." Most of the brothers nodded in agreement.

Samson felt a little like that himself deep down, but after all he and Reece had been through, he tried to suppress his ill feelings.

He responded, "Well, brothers, King Reece is exempt. Obviously the heat is still on him. The man murdered a federal agent in broad daylight so I could go free. He was never charged with that crime. Just because he's free doesn't mean they don't want him. Would you all want him to lead them right to us?" The brothers shook their heads. They hadn't thought about it like that.

"Okay then." Samson had made his point. "One thing about King Reece, he's Crescent Crew to the death. He birthed it, and he'll die it."

The brothers weren't finished. Ant Live continued on. Obviously he felt someone had appointed him spokesman.

"We also concerned about the two Mexicans you kick it with. How you gon' mob down wit' some wetbacks? That goes against everything we stand on." Ant Live was referring to the fact that the majority of the captains were die-hard Five Percenters. Thus if it wasn't black, it wasn't right and exact.

"Ho, ho, ho. There are sixteen shades of black. Mexicans are half original. You need to study your lessons," Samson corrected. All the brothers loved a good debate or cipher. That was the contradiction. The Crescent Crew were all extremely enlightened individuals. In fact, that was the basis of their bond. Yet in the name of the dollar, they could all get as savage as the Dark Ages of Europe. Despite their squabbles, they were all carved from the same mold. Outcasts, rebels, geniuses.

Samson continued his speech. "Furthermore, these two helped me hold it down in Mexico. That's why I fucks with them. Nuff said. Now if we can get back to business, and stop worrying about small shit."

That was that with that. Samson wasn't the type to sugar-coat anything. Unlike Reece, who operated like a stiletto, Samson operated like a butcher knife. Reece used tact to keep the soldiers on point. Samson was just brutal. The soldiers understood this. That was just his way. No one took offense. As far as the Crew was concerned, as long as everyone was eating, thriving, and staying loyal to the Crew, they could not give a fuck how Samson talked to them. Proof was in the pudding.

"Roy, are you sure you need a hundred of them thangs?" Samson inquired.

"Yeah."

Samson went around the table giving out tickets. "Tickets" were the *work* that the Crew transported back to their cities. An hour later, the meeting was adjourned. After everyone had left to return to their respective cities, Samson sat at the marble table brooding. His heart was heavy.

He retrieved a bag of cocaine from his front pocket and threw it on the table. He pushed a button to reveal the bank of video monitors facing him. He sprinkled some cocaine directly on the marble table, separated it into thin lines, then filled both nostrils to capacity. The potent powder pushed him to the back of the high-backed plush leather chair. The springs in the chair creaked, threatening to crumble under the enormous weight it held. Samson tilted his head back and looked at the television screens. The women were shaking their moneymakers for the patrons. Samson stared absently at the screens and analyzed his problems.

He had returned to the States eager to see his leader. He had always been loyal to King Reece, as Reece had been loyal to him and the Crew. However, Reece seemed torn. Shaken. Samson couldn't help wondering if he was going to remain loyal to his endeavors with Qwess or his endeavors with the Crew.

The Crescent Crew sensed a slight shift in Reece's priorities, but prior to today no one had voiced their concerns.

Now it was on the table. Samson had quelled the concerns for today. He put his word on the line. He had to speak with Reece ASAP about this. It could become a problem.

Samson's second dilemma was what Reece had told him on the phone. He couldn't believe Reece was talking with Destiny again! Sure, she had his son, but she had crossed not only him but the Crew also. She deserved to die, just like the only fool who testified against Reece at trial.

During the call Reece had instructed Samson to track Destiny down and keep an eye on her for him when she came to town in two days. Samson didn't know what he had planned. All he knew was Reece forbade any harm from coming near her way.

Oh, well, thought Samson. He'd respect Reece's wishes . . . for now.

Chapter 10

AMG, parent label of Atlantic Beach Productions as well as numerous other minority-owned record labels, had business offices throughout the world. Their southern division's headquarters were located in Bank of America Towers in Charlotte, North Carolina. The entire twenty-eighth floor belonged to AMG. A beautiful, petite administrative assistant greeted visitors the moment they stepped off the elevator. The waiting area boasted fine Italian leather sofas the color of money. The ivory walls were lined with gold and platinum plaques of AMG's artists. Qwess, Doe, Amin, and Niya bypassed all of this and went straight into the main conference room, which contained a glass wall that spanned the entire room and gave occupants a breathtaking view of Charlotte's business district.

Inside the room with the others were John Meyers, token Negro and head of AMG's Black Music Division; Lansky, the top corporate attorney for AMG; and Linda Swansen, VP of AMG, tenacious SOB.

"Salim, you're being unreasonable!" Linda was relaying to Qwess. "We've already given you your masters just to sign you.

Now you're asking us to relinquish control of the master recordings of all of your artists. This is unreal."

"Well, if that's unreal, I'll tell you what's very real. Me walking. It's either that or nothing."

Qwess was having a ball! He enjoyed having all the cards in his hand. He knew AMG would never meet the requirements he was demanding in order for him to re-sign with AMG. His demands were meant to deter them. He had no intention of re-signing. He had all the capital needed to go fully independent and cover distribution expenses. Unlike other artists with their "own" record labels, Qwess fiercely embraced independence. He loved the autonomy it brought him. For the past five years he'd played the compromise game. "Make a song about girls." "Make a song about clubs." "Make this . . ." "Make that . . ." No more. There was no new Bentley, house, or anything else they offered going to make him change his mind.

"Wait a minute, Salim. Let's be rational here. Now we've made you a very rich man over the years . . ." Qwess scoffed at Linda while she spoke. "Now we can continue to enrich your lifestyle. You need the continued exposure AMG can provide for you. As I understand it, you're about to break a new artist. Mysterio, correct?"

Qwess nodded.

"Good! Just re-sign with us for another five albums—a three-sixty deal—and we'll give him the same guarantee of exposure as we gave your other artist . . ." She fumbled for the name.

"Flame," John Meyers assisted.

"Yes, Flame. With our resources, we can make Mysterio a household name, just like we did Flame."

Three-sixty deals were taking root in the entertainment industry. A 360 deal was a deal that allowed record labels to receive a percentage of any money an artist generated, from concerts to merchandise to movie deals. Typically, an artist didn't make much money off record sales, and they rarely recouped their advances. In the past, performance and merchandising was where they made up for the difference. Savvy artists could make more money from merch and concerts than they would record sales. The industry caught on to how much money they were missing out on and arbitrarily changed their business model. The 360 deal was the result of this change.

Qwess raised his hand to silence her. "Linda, I have to respectfully decline. You asked me to hear your offer with an open mind. I did, and my answer remains the same. ABP is officially done doing business with AMG. Now could you please pass me the paperwork?"

Linda Swansen grudgingly accepted defeat. She gestured for Lansky to supply Qwess the paperwork. Qwess slid the paper to Amin, who briefly perused the packet and gave Qwess a stern nod as he passed it to him. Qwess signed the paperwork, leaned back in his seat. He steepled his hands waiting on the next issue to be brought up.

Amin took the floor. He stood up, smoothed out his shirt, stroked his long beard, and commenced his pitch.

"As you know, I represent Mrs. Diaz here, and frankly my client is very unhappy . . ." Amin went on to explain how AMG had reneged on numerous promises to Niya. How they made unrecoupable expenses recoupable, how they garnished wages for her advance without her knowledge. All because her manager was a do-boy for AMG. He proceeded to explain how Niya was on the verge of bankruptcy because of the overpriced producers and big-budget videos AMG insisted she needed in order to be a star. He summed up his speech by letting them know that he had been retained as new management to either reconcile the situation or get her out of the deal altogether.

Linda, John, and even Lansky were livid when Amin completed his speech.

Linda spoke first. "Excuse me, what did you say your name was again—Ramen?"

"No. Amin."

"No. You must've said Ramen 'cause surely you have soup for brains if you think you can walk in here and make demands for someone we already own."

Amin was aghast. *Own?* Linda wasn't finished. She hadn't made it to the number two spot in her profession by being docile.

"See, what you fail to realize is no matter who her management is, we own her. We have her under contract for at least two more albums and an option for two more. So, Mr. Amin, if you'd be so kind as to spare us your scathing review of our infractions toward Mrs. Diaz, it would be greatly appreciated." Linda's nostrils were flared, her pale face now pink. She leaned back in her seat. Amin stole a glance at Doe and Niya. Doe was on the verge of exploding. Nobody talked to or about his wife like a piece of property! If it weren't for the tremendous amount of respect he carried for Amin's business acumen, he would've disobeyed his explicit instructions to stay calm and let him handle things. However, he did stay calm and let Amin handle things.

"Ms. Swansen—"

"Mrs."

"Okay. *Mrs.* Swansen. You and I both know there are legal approaches to take to rectify a faulty contract. I was sincerely hoping we could at least act like civilized individuals to bring about the best solution."

The words were barely out of his mouth before she responded. "There aren't any laws broken here. This is how business is done."

"No! Don't do that! You know Niya is entitled to an increase in points determined by the amount of records sold."

Linda tilted her head to the side, sizing up her opponent again. Then she smugly responded, "Entitled, my dear. Not guaranteed. If you look closely at the contract you'll see she waived that right to the company when she signed for her advance."

Amin looked at John Meyers, who nodded agreement.

"You shysty sons of . . ." Amin whispered. He was now shocked and upset. He didn't realize the game was played so dirty. It was then that he realized just how fortunate he was to be dealing with Qwess.

"Don't be upset, dear. I realize that you're close to your . . . client, but in the business world nepotism works best if it's practiced from the start. You can't change horses in the middle of a race." She gave Qwess the coldest look, as if to insinuate if he rode with the team, Niya would get shown some love. "Okay, now that that's settled, is there anything else?"

Qwess returned her stare as he got up from the table.

"Nah. That's it. Have a nice life," he shot over his shoulder while leaving with his Crew in tow.

Reece was in Charlotte as well. Only he was there for unfinished business. He had been playing phone tag with Destiny for the past few weeks and finally built up enough trust that she allowed him to come visit her. More importantly, he was finally going to meet his son, Prince, for the first time.

When Destiny had visited Fayetteville a couple weeks prior, she was all alone. She had returned to the city to give a deposition on an unrelated case and hoped to see Reece. Unfortunately, he was in Cali on business, but he did provide a crew to protect her. Destiny's life had been threatened. Certain members from the department held a grudge against Destiny because she had refused to go hard against Reece at his trial. They felt she had defected and crossed the blue line. She had received death threats and at one point really feared for her safety. She expressed this to Reece when they talked while he was in Cali. Because of their child, Reece enlisted a security detail to guard her while she was in town. After that gesture, she gained a little more trust in him and they arranged for Reece to come visit in Charlotte.

Reece parallel-parked his Cadillac STS in a vacant spot in front of the single-family home. The 'Lac had no rims, no system. Just dark tint. Reece had balled out of control enough to last two lifetimes before his incarceration. Though he still had a penchant for nice cars and things, and still had a beast or two tucked away in the cut (like his new Maybach), he no longer drove them on a daily basis. The stock-trim Cadillac fit his new modus operandi.

While in prison he had learned an important lesson about perception just by studying people. He understood that the way people perceive you dictates how they treat you. That being the case, Reece didn't want to raise any eyebrows. He was flying beneath the radar until he regained his footing. He had lynched more niggas in the Carolinas than the KKK. He didn't wish to be remembered by any family of his victims.

There was also the matter of the police. National news outlets had reported his release. One never knew what they were capable of with their shiny badges and happy trigger fingers. So Reece figured out of sight, out of mind. The lower profile he kept, the safer he would be.

Reece climbed from the Cadillac and smoothed over his simple white T-shirt and jeans. He stole a glance at his Movado: 11:35 a.m. Still early.

Reece walked through the small gate up the steps and rang the doorbell. His heart thundered in his chest, and for some reason his hands felt clammy. He took deep breaths to calm his emotions and puffed his chest out defiantly.

Inside, he heard a kid yell, "Mommy, someone's at the door!"

Reece heard someone fumbling with the locks on the door, then it opened slowly. Reece peered through the glass and saw a miniature version of himself. His son, Prince, placed his hands on the glass door and stared at Reece.

"You look like my daddy," the five-year-old observed.

Reece exhaled a ball of stress and stared at his son. He couldn't believe his eyes. Prince was a carbon copy of him. His long locks dangled past his shoulders, and his dark brown skin looked pure. Large, inquisitive eyes beamed from his head in curiosity.

Reece bent down to his son's eye level and placed an open palm on the glass door. "Hey, little guy. What's up?"

Prince placed his hand on the door and smiled.

"Prince, what did I tell you about opening that door!" Destiny yelled as she came around the corner. "Who is it any—"

Her words stuck in her throat when she saw Reece at the door. She had been aware of him coming to town, but he was early by a few hours. In the quickening silence that ensued, Destiny sized Reece up. She admired the way his bald head glistened in the midday sun. The way his T-shirt grooved in and out of the cuts in his shoulders. Even with a loose T-shirt on, it was clear Reece followed a workout regimen religiously.

Reece's breath was stolen the moment he laid eyes on her. Destiny was wearing powder blue velour gym shorts and a tank top. The shorts hugged her curvy hips while the tank top gripped her 38Cs like an eager lover. Her shoulder-length hair was dyed brown and hung loosely framing her face in perfect contrast with her smooth peanut-butter skin. His pulse quickened as a roller coaster of emotion careened through his brain. He stood frozen in place as he stared at the love of his life and the person who had broken him.

"Mama, don't he look like my daddy?"

"That's because he is your daddy," Destiny said. She unlocked the glass door to let Reece in. Reece stepped over the threshold and scooped Prince in his arms.

"What's up, li'l man?" Reece nuzzled Prince on the neck. Prince wailed out in a mixture of confusion and fear. Who was this man that resembled him so much? "Calm down, li'l man. I'm your daddy; I'm not going to hurt you. You don't have love for your daddy?"

Prince stopped kicking and screaming long enough to examine Reece more closely. "You said you're my daddy?"

"Yeah! I'm your daddy."

Just saying the words filled Reece with pride. *A daddy . . . I have a son . . .* The moment was surreal for Reece. It was one thing to see his child through photos. This was different, this was . . . real. He was actually holding an heir to his throne.

"Mama, is he my daddy?" Despite the uncanny resemblance, Prince still wasn't convinced.

Destiny nodded with tears in her eyes. "Yes, son, this is your daddy." She dived in and hugged them both, while Reece still held his son. "My god! I love you so much," Destiny whispered into Reece's ear. Seeing Reece with their son opened the floodgates to her feelings. She could no longer bottle up what she felt inside.

A part of Reece wanted to take Destiny and make passionate love to her right there on the spot—with Prince watching if need be. He still held a tremendous amount of feeling for her inside. Only thing he felt more was the stinging bite of betrayal embedded deep in his soul. It was that very ache of burning that kept him focused. Kept him from reciprocating the same sentiment Destiny issued him. Kept his eye on the prize.

Destiny pried herself away from Reece and Prince long

enough to offer him something to eat. Reece accepted, and they went into the kitchen to eat.

While Destiny set the table and took the roasted fish from the oven, Reece sized Destiny up. She had gotten a little thicker in all the right places. Her skin was just as smooth as ever. And she possessed a glow that would not be denied. When Destiny set the food on the table, Reece noticed her nipples harden, threatening to puncture her tank top. Destiny noticed Reece watching and blushed. She scurried back to the stove to retrieve the potatoes, shrimp, and salad. When she returned and sat at the table, Reece had stopped recklessly eyeballing her body and gazed intently into her eyes.

"So, what's on your mind Reece? What have you been doing with yourself these past few weeks?"

Reece sat little Prince on his lap and let his leg bounce reflexively. "Well, like I told you before, I'm catching up with things at the label. We gon' sign Niya. You know her, right?"

"Do I know her?" Destiny asked rhetorically. "R and B Niya? Of course! But isn't she signed to your parent label?"

Reece smiled. "Qwess's *former* parent label. We are independent again. I invested a little change to get things started off the right way."

Destiny sighed deeply, shaking her head. "Somehow I thought things would change," she said.

"What's that supposed to mean?"

"How you going to mix drug money with legal money? And how are you going to bring your drama in with Qwess and them? He has made a full transition and is doing so well for himself."

Reece shook his head. "See, you don't know the new me. I am no longer King Reece; I'm simply Reece, a man trying to put the pieces of his life back together after being betrayed."

Destiny caught the dig. "I'm just saying, you can't live a

double life and expect things to go your way," she stated. "Sooner or later you'll be caught."

"Now ain't that the pot calling the kettle black, Destiny, or should I say Katrina."

"Ouch."

"Yeah . . . ouch."

Silence descended upon them. Their attention fell upon the one thing they did right. Prince. They watched him as he watched them.

"I don't want to do this in front of him," Reece said. "This isn't what I had in mind when I thought about meeting my son."

Destiny dropped her head. "You're right. I apologize. Look, umm, you and Prince catch up on things. I have to run to the store real quick."

"Nah, chill out. It's all good. No worries. I understand what you were trying to tell me, and you're correct," Reece admitted. "I wouldn't do that to my brother, though. He's been through enough. I'm committed to doing things right."

Reece's cell phone rang, interrupting the mood. Reece recognized Qwess's number and answered it.

"Peace."

Qwess returned the greeting. Reece listened.

"What?" Reece exclaimed when Qwess told him the re- sult of the meeting. Reece listened some more, got details, and hung up.

He turned to Destiny. "See what I mean? They need me already. I gotta go," he said suddenly.

"What? What happened?"

"Nothing serious. Just business." Reece stood from the table and gathered his things. "Look, I'll call you, okay?"

"Reece, wait." Destiny grabbed his arm. "When will I see you again? We need to talk, like, seriously."

Reece nodded. "Yeah I know. I'll be back real soon."

"Okay." Destiny hugged Reece tight, as if she didn't want to let him go. "Reece?"

"Yeah?"

"I know you hate Destiny. Hell, I hate her, too. But my name is Katrina. Could you please try to give Katrina a chance?"

Reece thought for a moment, then said, "We'll see."

In reality, Reece was playing sheep. He had plans for Destiny or Katrina or whoever the hell she was. Big plans. If she could survive his plot, then maybe—just maybe he would forgive her.

Chapter 11

Amin, Qwess, Hulk, and Doe all sat in the conference room of ABP's studio Crescent Cuts. The studio was initially one office building located adjacent to Beauty Palace, Qwess's sister's hair salon. However, when Qwess purchased the property about five years ago, he eventually gutted and redid the whole property. Now, Beauty Palace was the most exquisite salon in town, and Crescent Cuts studios now boasted the actual recording studio, a game room containing pool tables, a seventy-inch TV screen equipped with a game console plastered on the wall, and two chess sets with gold and platinum pieces for one, and ivory and oak for the other. In addition to this, Crescent Studios also contained a huge conference room with cream-and-green marble floors, and an emerald and ivory conference table with matching chairs. The interior decorations of the studio cost more than the construction itself.

Qwess and company were waiting for Reece to arrive to begin their meeting to discuss a solution for the problem with Niya. Niya being with ABP was absolutely imperative for ABP to start back off on the right foot as an independent. Niya was guaranteed to go at least double-platinum. Qwess had produced the majority of her last album, so the music wouldn't take any dramatic changes. Niya's fans would still be pleased. Niya was already an accepted and established artist so ABP wouldn't have to engage in an extensive, costly promotional campaign like they would have to with their other acts. So far to date, Qwess had been ABP's top-selling artist, but he was officially retired. Both Flame and Saigon were expected to sell, but together they couldn't sell more records than Niya with the right formula. If Niya were on an independent, she could put out more edgy music, because she wouldn't be restricted to the ideals of the corporate entity that black music had become. All in all, ABP needed Niya desperately, but AMG refused to budge.

Doe was flipping through the pages of the premier hip-hop magazine while waiting on Reece. His heart was heavy because when he dropped Niya off at home, he promised her that he would do everything in his power to ensure her transition from label to label. Doe and Niya were experiencing their first major marital problems. She claimed he wasn't giving her any attention. He tried to explain to her the reason he had been so busy lately, but Niya pressed on. If he could swing this coup, then things would be lovely. ABP would truly be a family affair.

"Yo, is that Qwess on that cover?" Hulk asked Doe.

"Yeah."

"What does it say?"

"I don't know. I haven't gotten to it yet. Oh, here it is right here. 'The Dirty's Last Stand,'" Doe read aloud ceremoniously. Then he proceeded to read all three pages aloud.

He hadn't gotten to the third paragraph before Qwess started wincing. Apparently the reporter had decided to highlight the contradictions between Qwess's real life and his purported life on wax.

Doe was enjoying seeing Qwess squirm in his chair. Both he and Amin had warned Qwess about his indiscretions with his stable of beauties.

"Listen to this." Doe laughed. " 'When asked about his rumored romances with the actress Melinda Wolf and model Allysin, Qwess avoided the question like a seasoned boxer does a jab. However, he made sure to point out that he was *not* married and thus committed to no one.' "

"Qwess, she got you pegged, brother!" Amin laughed. Doe continued reading aloud.

"Ooh! Check this: 'For Qwess to be the self-proclaimed spokesman for the disenfranchised, he sure is not one of them. The Mercedes Maybach in this photo belongs to him. And we didn't begin to touch his car fleet in North Carolina.' Damn, you must've pissed her off," Doe said. Doe read on a little further.

"Well, it's not all bad. Listen to this: 'Qwess did prove true to his ethos about preventing black-on-black crime. While at a celebrity basketball tournament, Maserati, Qwess's rival, practically begged him to fight. However, Qwess graciously bowed out like a true gentleman.' "

"A true gentleman!? She making me sound like a bitch! Is this already on stands?"

"No. It's an advance copy. Alysia got it in the mail today. They want to know if we have any rebuttal," Amin answered.

"Hell, yeah. Tell Alysia to get them on the phone right now." Amin left to tell the assistant Qwess's demands.

"Well, it's not too bad. They made some valid points. It shouldn't hurt your sales on the album," Doe surmised once he completed the article.

"Um-hmm. Where is this brother at?" wondered Qwess, looking at his Jacob timepiece.

"Who knows?" Hulk quipped. "I'm still shocked he fucking with that bitch Destiny. I want to wring her fucking neck! Is that where he at?"

"I don't know." Qwess's mind was already elsewhere.

"Oh, shit! You got Quotable of the Month!" Doe exclaimed loudly.

"Word?" Qwess perked up at the mention of that. This was the ultimate confirmation for any rap artist.

"Well, actually not you, but it's your song 'Look in the Mirror.' It's Mysterio's part. Damn, this is hot." Doe began to read the verse:

> *"You think it's a game wait 'til those tempers blow,*
> *You got cats in here ain't never going home no mo',*
> *So be lucky they ain't bucking every chance they get*
> *While you runnin' round talking 'bout some count-time shit.*
> *And be lucky that you allowed to see yo' kids every day,*
>   *'cause kids in here would love to see your blood spray.*
> *So you say that we in prison cause of crimes of greed,*
> *Got you on your way to work just to turn some keys,*
> *Check your pedigree*
> *'Cause you look just like me,*
> *In the eyes of the law we ALL guilty.*
> *'Cause the law seem to see your odor as your crime*
> *Be lucky that your ass ain't doing no time*
> *And count your blessings instead of looking down yo' nose*
> *When you see a brother lusting off a new Black Gold*
> *We some grown men snatched in the midst of our prime*
> *How else we gonna deal wit' a high sex drive*
> *What you think everybody back here is a punk?*
> *Man killas don't come to prison just to turn into chumps.*

When Doe finished reading the verse, the room fell silent. The implications were clear. Everyone was thinking the same thing, but no one wanted to say it.

Finally, Hulk spoke up. "Yo, the way they digging Mysterio, we could break him first."

It was merely a thought, because Hulk and everyone in the

room knew exactly who Mysterio was, and they all knew he wanted nothing to do with the industry as an artist.

No one answered, still lost in deep thought. Doe continued to flip through the magazine. Amin returned with news. "Alysia is still trying to get through. She said she'd buzz us when she got through."

"Good. I'd like to tell them a thing or two," Qwess said.

"Oh, shittt!" Doe exclaimed suddenly. "Yo, Ock, check this out right here. Isn't this ole girl Lisa, the one you ran into in Cali?" He held the picture up for Qwess to view.

"Yeah. Let me see." Qwess reached to grab the book, but Doe held it from him.

"Nah, hold up. Damn, sis look good in this bikini."

Lisa was in the coveted Dime Time section, a section that put the most beautiful women in the industry on display. She was the featured model this month.

Doe continued to openly lust at the picture.

"Damn, is it blazing or what, brother?" Doe asked Qwess.

"I wouldn't know."

"What you mean, you don't know? You ain't smash it yet?" Qwess shook his head.

Doe smacked his head. "Aw, man! You been spending all this time with the broad, and you ain't hit. Hell, you even stayed out in Cali by yourself. Sent us back alone. What's up? You don't like chocolate, or sucking toes?"

"What you talking about?" Qwess was becoming agitated. He was a bona fide swordsman. Just the thought of someone questioning his status was an insult. Furthermore, he was still perturbed that he hadn't hit.

Doe clarified his question. "Well, it says right here that she likes her toes sucked, chocolate baths, and whatnot.

"Man, would you give me the book!" Qwess finally managed to wrestle the book from Doe's clutches. "You married anyway," he added.

"You might as well be. You can't hit nothing," Doe retorted.

Qwess observed the picture, scrutinizing it closely. All he could think about was smashing it. He couldn't recall the last time he was this smitten with a woman.

Qwess and Lisa Ivory had spent a considerable amount of time together compared to his other conquests. Thus far he had only gotten to second base: kissing, and meaningful fondling. He was eager to go further, but she was on some other shit.

"Damn, she is *fine*," Qwess admitted. "What would you do with that, brother?" he asked Hulk, showing him the picture.

"Nothing," he simply stated.

"What? Why?"

"Well, you know, some women are like fine art."

"Fine art? Fuck you talking about? I'm married and I would hit it," Doe interjected.

Hulk clarified, "Some women are like fine art: They're nice to look at, but you wouldn't want to smash it."

"Ooh," commented Amin. Just then their administrative assistant, Alysia, buzzed through. Qwess retrieved the phone out of the holder integrated into the table. Alysia put the call through.

Qwess immediately started telling Qima off. While he was talking, Reece sauntered through the door, greeted everyone, and took his seat at the table. He snatched the magazine up and began to flip through it until Qwess put down the phone.

"What's up, brah?" Reece spoke.

"A lot," answered Qwess. "I had to put this little chick in place about my article. She tried to make me look like a sucka."

"Word? What she say?" Reece asked.

"Nothing much. Talking 'bout she did it, so she could make sure she talk to me again."

"Who?" Doe asked. He wasn't paying attention to the conversation.

"Qima, the reporter from the magazine."

Doe chuckled. "Damn, she got good jokes."

"True, true. Let's get down to business now. We've been waiting long enough," Qwess ordered, looking at his watch, then shooting Reece a scathing glance.

Everyone took bathroom, water, and smoke—weed— breaks respectively then resettled at the opulent table to render a solution to their problem.

Qwess reiterated a complete rundown of the meeting to Reece. Reece sat thoughtfully for a moment then commented, "How bad do we need her to turn a profit immediately?"

"Bad." That was Amin.

"How could we turn a profit without her?"

"A miracle."

"Come on, Amin. I don't get down with the pie-in-the-sky bullshit. I deal with the actual factual. You a numbers man. Crunch numbers, nigga!" Reece chastised.

"How many times I told this brother about calling me a nigga?"

"Well, quit acting like one."

"What?!"

"Only niggas wait on pie in the sky."

"You a nigga!"

"I'm a god."

"You a nigga!"

"I'm a god—"

"Come on, brothers, chill out. We ain't get nowhere like this. Peace it out," Hulk ordered. He didn't talk much, but when he did he was obeyed.

"Word, word," Qwess cosigned. "Here's the real deal, a'ight. Flame and Saigon expected to go platinum, but AMG still own some percentages off their work. I *could* have another album out in six months—if necessary. If we can get Niya out of her contract, and signed with us, we'd clear out. Or . . ." Qwess looked directly at Reece.

"Or what?" Reece snapped.

"Or Mysterio could cut an album. Turn to page one forty-two. He got Quotable of the Month."

"Anyway," Reece dismissed. "So, you saying Niya is the equalizer?"

"Pretty much," admitted Qwess.

"What about the two bitches you was telling me about?"

Amin sighed heavily.

"Desire?" inserted Doe. "They not as established as Niya. We need Niya." Doe was still thinking about the promise he had made to his wife.

"And those fucks at AMG refuse to budge, huh?" asked Reece, voice laced with contempt.

"Yep."

"Okay, so who's in charge of her contract?"

"Directly? John Meyers, but everything is cleared through Linda Swansen," Doe answered.

"All right, and you've tried everything you're willing to try?"

"Yeah." That was a rhetorical question.

"And we really need her?"

"Yeah."

"A'ight. So you're giving me permission to try things my way?" Reece inferred.

Amin wasn't having it. "Nah, hold up. This ain't no street gang. This is a legitimate business organization—"

"That you can't handle, Mr. Business Manager," Reece interrupted. "I own a big share of this company. So, I gotta pull my weight, too. Let's see if you understand this: I must exercise due diligence to receive the best possible return on my investment." Reece was no one's fool.

Hulk had something to say. "I'm with Reece on this one. I mean if you've tried everything and we still don't have her, it can't hurt for Reece to try." Hulk wasn't the sharpest tool in the shed, but even he thought it feasible to let Reece try.

Amin's reluctance showed on his face, as did Qwess's. Amin's reluctance was speculative. Qwess's was factual. Qwess knew that Reece would stop at nothing to bring Niya over to the label. Truthfully, Qwess felt that that type of ambition was needed. Therefore, he said nothing, which was tantamount to agreeing.

"Well, it's settled, then. Given me some more details, and a few days and things should be taken care of," stated Reece, commandeering the conversation. No one said anything. Doe coughed up the details, and the meeting was adjourned shortly thereafter.

Before Reece left, Qwess cautioned him. "Be careful."

Reece bust out laughing and slammed the door.

Chapter 12

Two weeks after the fateful meeting with ABP, John Meyers was sitting at his desk finishing up some paperwork when ambition and determination came to pay him a visit in the form of three burly men. He was so immersed in his work he didn't notice the intruders until a meaty hand slammed into his desktop.

"We need to talk!" Samson demanded.

"Wha-wha, who are you? And how did you get past my security?" Meyers stammered.

"That's not important. This is!" Samson thrust a piece of paper on his desk. Meyers read it. It was a severance contract relieving Niya of all her responsibilities to AMG.

"Ah, no. I know what this is about. You tell Amin he can't scare us," Meyers insisted, shaking his head vigorously. "Mrs. Diaz is obligated to us for two more albums—at least—so don't come in here with scare tactics thinking that's going to change things."

Samson couldn't believe his ears. This scrawny pseudo-man was attempting to defy him.

"Muthafucka!" Samson struck like lightning, snatching

John Meyers up from behind the desk, dragging him to the middle of the office floor.

"I ain't asking you to do shit! I'm telling you. To refuse me is to refuse your life!"

Samson gave Chabo the nod, and Chabo came down hard across Meyers's back with his wooden baseball bat.

CRACK!

"Ahhh!" Meyers screamed.

Samson snatched him up off the ground into a full nelson and positioned him in front of Gil. Gil began raining blows into Meyers's midsection, then cuffed him with a stern left hook to the jaw. Blood spewed onto the ivory carpet. Samson released him, and he crumpled onto the floor wheezing and pouring blood onto the floor from his mouth.

Samson snatched him up by his neck and held him in the air. "You think you tough, motherfucker? Huh? I'm gonna teach you a lesson!"

Samson hurled Meyers into the air. He crashed into the wall, shattering a platinum plaque. No sooner than he hit the floor Samson was on him again, raining blows on him. He grabbed him by the back of the neck and dragged him to the desk.

"Now sign this fucking paper," Samson snarled.

"Argh god!" Meyers gargled through the blood pouring from his mouth. "What are you doing?!"

Samson smiled. "This . . . is Crew business." Samson booted him in the gut with his steel-toed boot. "Now listen . . ."

Destiny opened the door for Reece wearing a green lace teddy and kitten heels. The ensemble accentuated her healthy thighs so deliciously Reece couldn't keep his eyes off of them.

It had been a long time coming, but Reece's plans were finally coming to fruition. Prince was with Doe and Niya for the weekend, leaving Reece and Destiny alone. Reece had had to court Destiny all over again in order to regain *her* trust. Talk about paradoxes. In any event, Reece did what he had to do to get done what needed to be done. Now he was being thoroughly seduced. The best part about the seduction was that Reece held the actual climax in his possession.

Destiny led Reece through the house straight into her bedroom, where candles surrounded her bed.

"Damn, I feel like I'm being sacrificed or something," Reece joked.

"Ummm, maybe you are," Destiny purred.

Reece began kissing her deeply, luxuriating in the taste of Destiny's saliva mixed with the faintest hint of alcohol. Destiny returned Reece's kisses with equal intensity. Reece palmed Destiny's shapely ass, letting his fingers slide through the crack. He allowed his middle finger to explore shamelessly. Reece felt moisture on his fingertip so he dove his middle finger southward to the source of the wetness. When he found Destiny's eager hole, he began to finger fuck her softly, all the while kissing her passionately.

"I want you so bad," Destiny pleaded. "Please don't stop!"

Lisa Ivory walked into her palatial loft overlooking the Pacific and was greeted by a surprise. Pink roses engulfed the room, arrayed in beautiful bouquets placed strategically throughout the room. To her left, a trail of Hershey's kisses started and continued to lead all the way up on her stairs. Lisa was curious and a little afraid initially. Then she remembered the wink her security guard at the gate gave her when she drove through. He wasn't flirting. He was hinting.

Lisa ascended the steps slowly. She picked up one of the Hershey's and popped it in her mouth. Uh, how she loved chocolate!

When she reached the top of the stairs, she heard someone in her bathroom. She crept past her bed over to the closed door and put her ear to the door. She heard nothing, but she smelled a strong chocolate scent. Lisa slowly turned the knob.

When the door opened, she saw Qwess in a tub full of chocolate. His entire body was coated with fine milk chocolate.

"Surprise!" he greeted confidently.

"What are you doing?" Lisa demanded.

"Well, you said you like chocolate." Qwess spread his arms, presenting himself. "Here it is—in the flesh."

Lisa eyed him approvingly from head to torso. She bit her bottom lip, contemplating her next move.

"Stand up," she commanded.

Qwess did. Lisa took one look at his double-chocolate-coated penis and said, "Don't move. I'll be right back."

Samson gave John Meyers one last chance to help himself.

"Nigga, if you don't do right this time, we gon' kill yo' punk ass!" he promised.

John Meyers pulled himself up on his elbows to his desk. His right leg was broken at the knee courtesy of the baseball bat wielding of Chabo. Meyers's face was swollen on the right side. That was Gil's doing. His ankle was broken so badly, his left foot was almost facing the other way. He was lucky, because Samson had tried to break the entire foot off.

Despite this, Meyers still attempted to hold strong. That was, until Samson started to slowly slice his ear off. Samson wasn't a quarter of the way down before Meyers relented and agreed to call Linda Swansen and make the deal.

Reece and Destiny were lost in the throes of passion. They were making love missionary-style. An R. Kelly CD bumped profusely, setting the tone as Reece plunged his manhood deeper and deeper into Destiny's hot wet vagina. Just as Destiny was about to climax, Reece snatched his pipe out of her and immediately started eating her out. He took her clit into his mouth, sucking it ever so gently. Destiny cooed with pleasure. While Reece sucked on Destiny's clit, he steadily pulled his two fingers in and out of her. When Destiny was about to cum, Reece stopped long enough to look at her face.

Destiny was glowing like a midsummer day's sun. Reece flipped Destiny over on her stomach and planted a trail of kisses down her spine. He kissed both of her soft cheeks, then parted them with his long tongue. Reece ran his tongue between her cheeks just to the entryway of her asshole, paused briefly, then started licking it, too. He parted her cheeks wider before burying his tongue deep into her asshole.

Destiny couldn't take it anymore. She bucked violently, half escaping Reece and half surrendering herself to him. Reece gripped her tighter so she couldn't move. Destiny wailed out a primal scream as her juices gushed out like a water faucet. Insensitive to Destiny's feelings, Reece slammed her face into the bed so that her ass jutted into the air. He scooted up closer to her and entered her doggie style, commencing to pound her savagely.

"Oh, that feels so good!" Lisa panted. She had discarded her clothes and now lay in the tub of chocolate with Qwess sucking her toes.

Qwess dipped Lisa's left foot into the tub then pulled it back up toward his face. Chocolate dripped off her big toe into the tub. The chocolate contrasted with Lisa's light skin, making her foot resemble a vanilla cone with fudge topping. Qwess kissed her little toe affectionately, followed by the rest of them. Next, he started with the little toe again. This time he slid his tongue between the little toe and the one next to it, eyeing Lisa the entire time.

Lisa was struggling to keep her narrow eyes open. When Qwess stuck her big toe in his mouth, Lisa lost the battle. She allowed herself to luxuriate in ecstasy, nearly climaxing from the expert toe-sucking alone.

Lisa had no intention of sleeping with Qwess so early in

their courtship. She had heard of his reputation as a notorious playboy, and she refused to be a notch on his belt. However, a favor this good deserved one in return. So Lisa retrieved her foot from Qwess's mouth and began stroking his semi-erect penis. Once it was fully erect, Lisa dipped her hands in chocolate, dousing Qwess's penis. Then she methodically began licking it off, teasing the underside of Qwess's member with her tongue ring. Suddenly, she gulped Qwess's entire dick into her mouth, causing Qwess to suck in air. Lisa sucked and pulled while playing with Qwess's balls, attempting to take him there.

Qwess pulled Lisa up from his lower torso to kiss her deeply. He could read the passion in her eyes before he led her around one more time. This time instead of pulling her up, Qwess spun her around so her head was southward, and her beautiful snatch sat right in his face. Lisa continued to suck while Qwess sucked chocolate out of every inch of her lower area.

John Meyers replaced the phone into its cradle weakly. Samson placed the paper in front of him to sign.

"Sign it, you cocksucker," ordered Samson. Meyers did as instructed. Finally, he was broken. "Next time don't try to save someone who don't care about you. That bitch boss of yours didn't even offer to come assist you when she knew something wasn't right."

Samson looked to Chabo and Gil, who stood on either side of Meyers in their menacing killer-black uniforms. Abduction and extortion were their specialty, so they were right in their element.

"Ees that it?" Chabo asked.

"Yeah. Mission accomplished," Samson answered, wiping his mouth.

Chabo reached into his cargo pocket to retrieve the same tranquilizer potion that had been administered to John Meyers's security. He grabbed Meyers' arm and injected the solution. Meyers's body went limp immediately.

Simultaneously, Samson's cell phone rang. Samson looked at the clock on the phone screen, then read the number. He knew exactly who was calling.

"Come on, brothers. We got another stop to make."

The clock read 12:30, half past midnight.

Destiny lay asleep in Reece's arms with her head on his chest. The candles had burned completely down to the wicks, leaving a spooky light in the room. The mood fitted Reece's thoughts. As Reece looked down on Destiny, he almost regretted what he was about to do.

Almost.

He thought back on his years of incarceration and the tremendous amount of face he had lost in the sight of his comrades. He recalled nights when he lay alone in his cell and anxiety crept up on him and threatened to claim him. He relived those memories in real time. The memories reinforced his decision.

Reece's phone rang. He reached over the bed to retrieve it out of his pocket while scooping the other thing as well. Reece saw the five-minute warning etched on the screen. So he woke Destiny up.

"Hey, hey, wake up." Reece smacked Destiny lightly until she awoke.

"What? What's up, baby?" Destiny croaked.

"Remember when you told me, if you could, you would do my time for me?"

Destiny was confused. "W-what are you talking about?"

"You remember? You wrote me saying that."

"Yes. Yes, I remember. Let's leave the past in the past, baby." Destiny kissed Reece. Reece returned it, but said, "Okay, we will, but there is one thing first."

"What?"

"You gotta get your chance to do my time."

Destiny wiped her eyes and looked at the clock on the nightstand. "What are you talking about, baby?"

"You said that if you could, you would do my time for me. Right?"

"Reece, baby, let's leave the past in the past," Destiny whispered. She laid her head back on the silk pillowcase.

"We will, but first you have to do my time."

Reece gulped and closed his eyes. He whispered, "I love you."

Then he hit Destiny with the tranquilizer.

Samson pulled the Range Rover onto the curb right in front of Destiny's house.

"Wait here. I'll be back," he ordered as he jumped out, leaving the truck running.

By the time he reached the door, Reece was there with it wide open.

"Come on. Hurry up!" Reece ushered Samson in the room where Destiny lay sprawled on the bed in sweat pants. "Help me find her shoes."

"Fuck her shoes! Let's roll."

When Reece turned around, Samson had Destiny slung over his huge shoulder and was barreling out the door. Reece followed.

Once outside, Chabo jumped in the driver's seat while Reece and Samson jumped in back with Destiny. Gil left his post in the street to jump in the passenger side.

The truck eased off into the night as quickly as it came on a rendezvous with retribution.

Qwess rested peacefully in Lisa's California king–size bed, which dominated the entire second floor of her loft.

After the bathtub session of sucking, he and Lisa showered

together to wash the chocolate off before taking the show to the bed. Qwess ravaged Lisa's body so well that at times she felt as if she was being blessed by a sex god. The way he navigated her body left her mesmerized.

Now, she also rested peacefully beside him completing the spoon. Every now and then she would reach behind herself to play with Qwess's flaccid penis and giggle like a schoolgirl.

Both Qwess and Lisa were languishing in a post-sex after-glow when Qwess's phone began ringing incessantly. They ignored it at first, but it kept ringing and ringing.

"You might need to answer that to tell your other paramours that I have locks on you for the weekend," Lisa joked tenderly.

Qwess was feeling beside himself. Lisa Ivory had him wide open. He had never experienced anything like this in his life! She had him gone. He picked up the phone from the night-stand, recognizing the East Coast number, and told Lisa, "Here, why don't you tell her."

Lisa accepted the phone, moved her grizzled braid from her ear, and spoke very exaggeratingly chic-like, "Hell-o."

"You son of a bitch! You son of a bitch! You are going to so pay for this!!"

Lisa passed Qwess the phone. "I think it's for you."

Qwess put the received to his ear and was assaulted by the high-pitched screaming of Linda Swansen.

"Ho, ho, ho."

"Ho, my ass, you black bastard! You think you can get away with this? Do you? You just wait. You're gonna regret the day you ever heard of me."

"Wait!" Qwess screamed. "What's this all about?"

Linda crowed sadistically. "Oh, you don't know, do you? Sure you don't. Well, I'll tell you what, you fucker! You can have the little half-breed whore on your label. I'll see to it that she's blacklisted all over this industry. And the police will be paying you a visit. Ooh, I can't believe this shit! You're gonna pay, I tell ya. You just wait. I'm gonna have—"

Qwess clicked off the phone while Linda was still talking. He sighed heavily.

Lisa stroked his waves. "What's that all about?" she asked.

Qwess sighed again. "I gotta go back east."

Chapter 13

By the time Qwess touched down at Charleston International Airport, the news was all over the wire:

> *Music Executive Beaten within Inches of Death over Contract Dispute . . . More at noon.*

All televisions were displaying the same headline throughout the airport. When Qwess reached the curb, a limo awaited him. The chauffeur opened the door for him. Just as Qwess was about to get in back, he heard a distinctive horn blow. He looked up to see Doe in his Bentley Azure, with the top dropped. A little boy was strapped into the back seat. Qwess paid the chauffeur the requisite fee and a healthy tip for cancelling, then jetted to the Bentley.

"What's up, little man? What's your name?" Qwess asked the little boy while buckling himself into the back seat.

"Prince."

"Prince?" Qwess echoed incredulously.

"Yes, sir. My daddy was a king."

Qwess couldn't help but laugh. "Really?

"What kingdom?"

"I don't know." Little Prince shrugged innocently. "My momma told me that everybody called him King Reece before."

"Oh, I see." Qwess let the little one down easy. He ruffed Prince's dreadlocks before turning around to face Doe.

"Now tell me, what the hell happened?"

"I don't know. I had Prince all weekend." Qwess eyed Doe suspiciously. "What? I'm serious."

"Okay. So what's up with Reece?" Qwess asked. "Where was he?"

"Good question. I've been trying to get up with him since last night after Linda Swansen called Niya cursing her out."

"Her too?"

"Her too?"

Qwess relayed the phone call he received from Linda Swansen that prompted his swift return.

"So, she said she released Niya?" Doe clarified.

"Pretty much. I haven't spoken with Amin yet, so I don't know exactly what she talking about. Far as I know, we don't have Niya yet."

"Well, something's going on," Doe surmised.

"Let's see if Amin available yet." Doe entered the number into the car phone. The rings were audible. After just the second ring, Amin answered.

"*Salaam alayka,*" Qwess greeted.

"*Wa alayka salaam,*" Amin returned.

"Yo, what's going on?"

"Brother, you tell me. I just came home and found an envelope slid under my door. I opened it up and found a severance contract dismissing Niya from all obligations to AMG."

"Word?" Doe was ecstatic, but leery. "How'd that happen?"

"I haven't the slightest idea," Amin confessed.

"Seriously, brother," Qwess cautioned. "What do you know?"

"Brother, I don't know anything, but I'm thankful."

Qwess thought for a moment. "Well, something's not right so let's not get too excited . . . yet. Is there anything suspicious? Did you look over the release papers? Is everything in order?"

"Other than some red spots on the paper that looks like what I'm afraid to think it is, everything is fine."

Qwess and Doe shook their heads, sharing the same assumption: Reece.

Qwess said, "See if you can get up with Reece and hit us back."

Reece had been planning his revenge from the day he left prison. Every inch of his brain said kill her, but not too deep in his heart, he cared for her. Destiny herself had provided Reece a solution to his dilemma.

When Reece was incarcerated, Destiny wrote letter after letter without a response from him. In a last ditch effort, she sent Reece a heartfelt letter insisting that if it would make him forgive her, she would do his bid for him if she could. All she wanted was forgiveness.

When Reece was released, he wrecked his brain storming up ways of revenge. Surely, he couldn't let her transgressions go unanswered. The night of his party, while Bone administered street justice to the carjackers, Reece formulated his plot.

On the same piece of land the torture cabin occupied sat another building that was uninhabited. Reece canvassed the building himself and found it more than suitable for his plot. So, he along with Samson thoroughly cleaned the concrete chamber and turned it into a makeshift prison, complete with electric power, microwave, and a portable refrigerator. Reece then sent Samson to the store with a list of items resembling a prison canteen list. When Samson returned, they stocked the bunker and discussed the plot.

Rule number one: NOBODY knows nothing! Rule number two: NOBODY sees nothing! Rule number three: NO-

BODY hears nothing! This was to be a secret between the two of them. This would recement their loyalty to each other.

Reece would be the only person to attend to Destiny. If he was unable to tend to her, then only Samson would pick up the slack.

Destiny awoke to find herself on a hard cot. She rubbed her hand across her frazzled hair then observed her surroundings. Destiny's head was still spinning, so it took a moment to gather her wits about herself. When she did, she attempted to stand, but was advised by her excruciating headache to take it easy.

She sat back on the cot momentarily and began to observe her surroundings very cautiously. The mind of a highly trained agent still lived inside of her.

First things Destiny noticed were the oversize Dickie jumpsuit she wore and the huge pit bull chained by the entrance of the bunker. As soon as Destiny set her eyes on him, he set his eyes on her. They locked into an intense stare-off. When she moved an inch, the dog moved a mile.

Next, she spotted a metal shelf containing numerous cans of tall sardines and Pacific jack mackerel, instant rice, ramen noodles, bags of chips, candy bars, soda, and hygiene items. To the right of the shelf sat a table with a microwave, cooler, and bowls with utensils. In the corner was a miniature refrigerator. On the other side of her cot was a high wooden toilet, so tall that to use it, she'd have to literally climb up on. Next to the toilet was a tin bucket with bottles of water on either side of it. She concluded that was a makeshift sink. Aft of her cot, up about two feet, was a small window that a house cat would have trouble climbing through, but through that widow Destiny could hear a chain dragging the ground back and forth. Every now and then she could see the shadow of another dog outside the window.

Destiny was confused. The last thing she recalled was she and Reece making passionate love in her home. It was explosive . . . mind blowing . . . It was the perfect source of reconciliation. Or so she thought. Where was she now? Who had abducted her? And what about Prince? Did someone abduct him also?

Destiny began to panic. She looked around the room again, and the walls seemed to be closing in on her. Her eyes blinked involuntarily, and her mouth became bone dry. Currents of energy zipped through her stomach as panic settled into her core.

Suddenly she heard someone coming to the door. Keys jingled. Locks turned. Destiny swung her head toward the door just in time to see Reece walk in wearing a security uniform complete with baton, whistle, and flashlight. He patted the dog and tossed him a treat. Then . . .

"Brrrr!" Reece blew a whistle loudly. "On your feet, inmate. Shakedown!"

Destiny jumped from the cot fidgeting, shifting from foot to foot in her socks. She was now more confused than ever.

"H-hey, baby," she managed weakly. "I'm so glad you here. What's up?" Destiny asked carefully. She knew he was schizoid.

Reece ignored her. "You heard me, inmate. Shakedown!" Reece repeated.

"Baby, this isn't funny," Destiny whined. "I know we used to role play, but this is a bit much. I'm ready to go home now. You've made your point," she stated matter-of-factly. She reached out and tried to hug him, but Reece slapped her hands away.

"What's wrong with you, inmate? Don't touch me; that's assault on an officer!"

Destiny frowned. "Okay, Reece, baby, I'm scared now. This is a little too real for me."

"Inmate, this *is* real."

"Reece, you've made your point. I get it."

Reece burst into laughter. "No, honey. I have just begun to make my point. Now strip for a shakedown," he ordered again.

Destiny was fuming at this point.

"Reece, what the hell is wrong with you? What are you, fucking crazy!?" Destiny stood tall and proud. "Now I'm ready to go. Get me out of these funky clothes, this funky-ass . . . place! Away from that FUNKY-ASS DOG!"

Reece stood silent and defiant, unamused by Destiny's antics. Then suddenly he cackled loudly. "Baby girl, baby girl," he taunted. "You still don't get it, do you?" Checking his watch in mocking fashion, he explained to Destiny her dilemma.

"You won't be leaving here for the next . . . ohhh . . . four years and about six months."

Four years and six months . . . It finally hit Destiny what type of situation Reece was crazy and resourceful enough to pull off. Just the thought made Destiny lose her composure.

Was he doing what she thought he was trying to do?

"Reece . . . I'm not playing. Let me out of here right now!"

Reece jumped back into character. "Inmate, you will address me as Officer Kirkson from here on out." Reece was so true to the game that even playing an officer was rubbing him the wrong way. "Any insubordination will be met with disciplinary action."

Destiny realized that Reece was serious. He was really trying to hold her hostage. She felt like a fool for trusting him. She should've known that a man like Reece was unable to let bygones be bygones.

She began to sob. "What about my baby?" she asked, thoughts immediately transferring to the most important thing in her life.

"*Our* baby will be fine."

She leaked in her clothes a little, fear preventing her from holding her faculties together. "Reece, you can't be serious. What about last night? I thought you forgave me."

Reece looked at Destiny like she was out of her mind. "What would make you think that?"

"Because last night we made love. We made passionate, gut-wrenching love." She closed her eyes and reminisced.

"No! *You* made love. I fucked you like you fucked me."

"You bastard!" Destiny spat. How could he screw her brains out then throw her to the dogs? "I fucking trusted you. You trifling bastard!"

"I know," Reece sang. "Just like I trusted you."

"Get me out of this fuckin' place!" Destiny started to charge Reece, but the giant pit bull rose up, obscuring her path, making her freeze in her tracks. The dog growled viciously, baring its sharp teeth.

Reece grabbed the collar to pull it back. "Next time I won't hold him back," Reece simply stated.

Destin shrank back to her spot on the cot.

Reece walked over to her and broke character as he explained her predicament.

"It's like this, Destiny. I am not a man that believes in forgiveness. I believe in justice and equality. Now you wronged me in the worst way. You actually owe me your life, but there are only two things keeping you alive. One, I am a changed man; I'm done with the killing. I'm trying to go straight. Two, our son, Prince. I know that hurting you will hurt him, so I had to get creative with your revenge."

"You bastard!" Destiny cried. The fact that Reece was explaining himself so casually told her that the crazy was still in him. He had rocked her to sleep with his kind overtures, and now she was paying for her stupidity.

"I thought about the letter you wrote me not long ago. You swore that if you could do my time for me then you would. You begged for my forgiveness and said that if you could, you would. So here is my proposition to you . . . I did almost *five* years in prison because of your type of love. If you can do half of that in here and still love me, then maybe we can try again—for our son's sake."

Destiny couldn't believe her ears. Yet she knew Reece was serious. She made one last-ditch plea for mercy.

"Reece, don't do this. There has to be another way for us to handle this!" She attempted to blink away her reality. "If you don't want to be with me anymore, then fine. Just help me take care of our son. Okay?"

Recce shook his head and smiled. "See that? Haven't even spent a day in jail and already ready to leave me. Imagine how I feel."

Reece let his words linger in the air a moment before turning and walking to the door.

"I'll bring some books back to help you through your bid."

With that he closed the door on Destiny, leaving her alone with her pleas echoing off the walls.

When Reece strolled into CC studios an hour after leaving Destiny, he was walking on air. He had tied up two loose ends in twenty-four hours.

His first move had been designing the coup to snatch Niya away from AMG. Reece knew those arrogant fucks at AMG would never have released her without his intervention. Reece knew that in America people only understood two things: money and violence. They had offered them money and they scoffed at them. So, Reece resorted to what had never failed him in business: violence. He knew he had to keep his hands clean, so he had enlisted his ghost goons, the men who were undocumented. Reece loved it when a plan came together. He especially liked it after hearing how arrogant the execs at AMG had been with Qwess and the crew when they attempted to talk sensibly. Now let's see how they liked dealing with Crew business.

Secondly, he was able to finally begin closure on the past with Destiny. Reece had meant what he said about having something with her if she could survive her makeshift bid. He also was sincere when he told her if it wasn't for Prince, she would've been fish food long ago. However, seeing that his son needed his mother made him think twice. Reece's parents died when he was a teenager, forever leaving a gaping hole in his heart. He didn't want his own seed to experience the same, so he was very reluctant to do any real harm to Destiny. Reece had knowledge of self and realized the importance of having both parents around. Despite this, Reece felt his son's mother had some unpaid dues to reconcile that were bigger than little Prince. So, while Destiny paid those dues, Reece figured he would assume the responsibility of both parents—as had Destiny when he took his government-sponsored vacation.

Reece opened the door to the plush conference room of CC studios and was rushed by little Prince.

"Daddy, daddy!" Prince yelled, running to Reece with arms wide open. Reece had been spoiling Prince rotten since his release. He had already bought him a car, and the child was only five. Reece scooped his son into his arms before scanning the room.

Seated at the emerald-and-ivory-streaked table were Doe, Amin, Qwess, Hulk, and Alysia. The brains and brawn of Atlantic Beach Productions. They all wore indignant masks on their faces.

Alysia doubled as administrative assistant/public relations coordinator and had been receiving calls all day about the assault on John Meyers. The calls ranged from concern to accusations. She had contacted ABP's management staff one by one with questions. No one knew anything about anything. Reece was the only member she hadn't contacted. He had been unavailable for the past twenty-four hours, which was suspicious. It was now time to get some answers. Alysia didn't know much about Reece except that his capital was a huge reason ABP was able to go fully independent again. So in essence, he was one of her bosses as well as part of the reason for her huge bump in pay. She had heard stories of his street exploits as King Reece. After all, he was a street legend in the Carolinas. Now as she stood there peeping him with his knowing smirk, standing tall at the door, she knew this was about to be an interesting conference.

Reece strutted to the table confidently, his Durango boots click-clacking on the marble floor. He had changed clothes since leaving Destiny, and now wore a Rocawear jean suit with his platinum crown swinging to his navel.

"Peace, my brothers and sister. Why all the long faces?" Reece asked, as if he didn't know already.

"Go ahead and take a seat," suggested Qwess. Reece assented. Qwess continued, "Do you know anything about this?" He pushed power on the remote, and the flat-screen TV phased to life showing a prerecorded news segment about the vicious assault on John Meyers. All occupants of the room eagerly anticipated an answer from Reece.

Reece thought a moment and simply stated, "Yeah."

Moans and groans filled the room.

"Brother, what did you do? What did you do?" Qwess moaned with his hand to his face.

Reece scrunched his face up. "What you mean, what did I do? I handled business."

"See, Qwess, I told you you can't bring an animal out the woods an' expect him to be potty-trained," Amin jumped in.

Animal? Potty-trained? What the fuck!

"Hold up. I know y'all ain't bitchin' out on me? You gave me the task, and I handled it! The fuck is the problem?" Reece asked, taking offense.

"The problem is this ain't the streets. You can't go in assaulting people when you don't get your way," Amin reasoned.

"Shit, I can't tell this ain't the streets. That white bitch assaulted your manhood from what I'm told. They undercut you and left you helpless like a newborn baby and you still defending them," Reece scoffed.

Qwess, sensing things were about to get out of hand, interrupted the conversation. He gestured for Alysia to take Prince out of the room. When they left the room, conversation resumed with Qwess speaking.

"All right, brothers, calm down. We're on the same team. Now what we need to be concerned with is protecting ourselves: physically and legally. Now Amin has a point, Reece. We can't use violence all the time to get our way." Amin looked at Reece tauntingly. Qwess spoke on. "But what's done is done. We got to make sure we can't be linked to this."

"I'm saying, brother. Give me some credit. I handled that. Everything is love. All we have to do is fall back for a few, then make our move." Reece desperately wanted to impress Qwess. He still respected Qwess tremendously and had a lot of love for him. He wanted Qwess to see that he was trying to give his all to make sure their dreams were realized. By any means necessary.

"Okay, let me get this right. Say this blows over. Next time we have a problem with someone—what?—we beat them to death, too?" Amin couldn't let this fly. He had sacrificed too much to get taken down by some bullshit. Unfortunately, Reece had had enough.

"You know what?" Reece exploded. "What's your title?" he asked Amin.

Amin puffed his chest out. "Business manager, senior level."

"Um-hmm. For who?"

"What?" Amin scoffed.

"For who?"

"For ABP." He shook his head.

"Um-hmmm, you see this nigga. This nigga. And this nigga." Reece pointed to Doe, Qwess, and himself respectively. "We are ABP. You are an employee of ABP. You do what the fuck we tell you."

"Hold up," Qwess interrupted.

"Nah, ain't no holdup. This brother need to know where he stand. Like I said, you work for us. We call shots! You follow 'em. You really don't have anything to lose. We do. So, we gonna do everything necessary not to lose. I'm a winner. That's what winners do! Now you keep talking shit, and I will make you give me the respect I deserve. You better recognize who the fuck you talking to."

Finished with his speech, Reece leaned back in his seat to read the mood of everyone else.

Doe was still silent. Far as he was concerned, he was happy with the results. He had kept his promise to his wife. They were about to make more money than ever. And the industry had been sent a message that ABP was for real. Win-win situation.

Qwess was so consumed with thoughts, no definitive words came out. His first thought was that Reece was wrong for talking to Amin like that. Amin had picked up where Doe left off in areas of business and done a damn good job. Amin was responsible for a lot of ABP's success. He did an excellent job of product placement, communicating with television and radio stations, and other little tidbits that weren't his area of responsibility. On the other hand, Reece did have a point. As the third partner/owner of ABP, he was owed a certain modicum of respect. From day one Amin exhibited a grudge against Reece, either for his theological beliefs or his street rep and demeanor. Amin was really arrogant toward Reece and needed the "humbling" that Reece gave him. Qwess's final concern was the potential legal ramifications of Reece's acts. No one could afford to take a fall right now. As long as it was guaranteed not to come back on them, Qwess was cool with it. However, was anything guaranteed when dealing with the law?

Amin was seething! Who was this ruffian to put him in his place? While Reece was bidding, Amin had put his thing down for the industry, thus paving the way for Reece to be an employer. Amin felt all these things. Yet he said nothing. In fact, it was Hulk who spoke first.

"Listen, ain't no need for all the drama. It's simple. We needed Niya. We got her. Maybe some things could have been done different, but they weren't. So, we just be happy and deal with whatever, whenever," he said in his gruff twang. Lately, he had become the voice of reason.

Qwess sighed audibly. "Hulk is right. What's done is done. It's water under the bridge. Amin, draw the contract up for Niya so it'll be official. I'll call my dad to put him on standby on the legal end." Qwess massaged his temples. He hated to break up his parents' vacation. "So it won't be any drama, we'll hold off making an announcement that Niya is signed to ABP until Flame's album release party in Atlanta. By then some of the heat should die down."

When Qwess spoke, it was law. Everyone agreed to his suggestion.

Amin still had unresolved issues, but they could wait until a later point. For now, he was cool.

For now.

Chapter 14

"Come on, more passion! More, more!!" Blow screamed. Blow was the premier director for music videos and was currently directing Flame in his follow-up video for his new album. His lead single "Cack Life" was already climbing the charts to number one, so Doe decided they'd follow up with another one. You know. Hit them in the head back-to-back. Doe, along with his wife, was present to supervise things.

The video was being shot in Myrtle Beach. So a lot of it was shot in The Playhouse, ABP's mini-mansion situated oceanfront inside of a gated community. Doe laughed to himself when he thought about how things had come a long way. Back when they were younger and he was starting out his corporate job as an accountant, he used to figure out ways for Qwess and Reece to hide money from the government. Fast-forward a few years. Now, he was coming up with different ways to claim money for the government to see. Like shooting the video in the mini-mansion allowed them to receive tax breaks at the end of the year since it was used in the line of "work." Indeed things had changed.

"Okay, take ten!" Blow screamed, muttering to himself.

Blow's contempt sprang from the fact that the featured model, Dana, refused to act engaged in the scene. The video shoot had moved to the beach, so now the models and extras wore their swimwear—including Flame, who wore black trunks and nothing else. His diamond-encrusted platinum ABP chain draped proudly around his neck, do rag plastered over his waves, Flame embodied the contemporary hip-hop artist. Earlier in the day he had dunked Dana in the saltwater, messing up her hair as she attempted to sunbathe. This, among other things, was what caused Dana's reluctance during the shoot. Flame had been trying to get with Dana ever since she arrived the day before. He took her out to a fancy restaurant, insisted that she stay at the house with Doe, Niya, and the others while the remainder of the video girls were put up in hotels. He even tried to spend the night in the guest quarters with her, but that was where Dana drew the line. She was not interested. Besides, she had already set her sights on a lofty goal.

The shoot resumed after Blow spoke to Doe for a hot minute. Doe had helped come up with the video treatment himself, so he was adamant about making sure things went how they were supposed to go.

Doe observed closely behind his designer shades. When Flame mouthed the words, "I'm lusting and I can't change," Dana was supposed to come around to the front of Flame, shoot him a sultry look, and walk off seductively. That's what she was *supposed* to do, according to the treatment. What she *did* looked like a bad rendition of birds flirting, her walk more chicken than peacock, her look more bat than parrot. Doe was forced to call for a break.

"Blow! Cut, Cut," Doe snapped. "Shorty, come here a second."

When Dana reached him, Doe rebuked her diplomatically. "Shorty, wassup—"

"Dana."

"O-kay. Dana, wassup? You not feeling my man or some-thing?"

"Um-umm. Not really."

"Ooh. Word? Why? Wassup?"

Dana rolled her neck just a little. "Because he think I'm some groupie or sumthin'. Like I'm supposed to be all over him or sumthin'."

Doe chuckled a little. "But, damn, shorty—Dana—you are. At least for the video." Doe removed his sunglasses so as not to feel impersonal. "Now, baby girl, you are costing me a gang of grip with all this stopping. Now I know you got it in you. Your profile said you want to be an actress, right?"

"Yeah." She returned his gaze aggressively.

"Well then, you gotta act!" Doe allowed himself to smile to break the brunt of his command. When he looked at Dana again, there was an unmistakable hint of lust in her eyes.

Doe leveled his eyes and spoke barely above a whisper, "Now you see that look you giving me right now?"

"Um-hmmm." It was more of a grunt than a word.

"That's the same one you gotta give him."

"Well, he's not you."

Was she choosing?

"Well, uh, give it to the camera." Damn, this caught Doe off-guard.

"Well, what about the walk?" She blew her words at Doe.

"Now, I know you got a strut to go with those curves." Ah, what the hell. If it gets the job done.

"Oh, you wanna see it?" Still flirting.

"Uh, yeah." Doe looked around, embarrassed. "Show me when you walk back over there. I'll let you know when it's not right."

"Oh, it's right."

"Well, show me then," Doe challenged.

"You ain't saying nothing."

And he wasn't. For when Dana sashayed back over to the shoot, she pulled out all the stops. She pulled her turquoise bikini out of her cheeks, knocked excess dirt off, and paraded her tight ass back over to Blow with such aplomb, any working girl would be put to shame. She tossed her silky Hawaiian hair over her shoulder to let the sun kiss her smooth, light bronze skin—and to make sure Doe was watching.

He was. In fact, Doe was a little too enthralled with Dana's strut, evidenced by the bulge that now occupied his linen shorts.

Just mere feet away, tucked under a canopy, sat Niya. She had observed the whole exchange from behind her tortoise-shell Chanel frames. To her, it seemed innocent enough. At first. Then she saw what appeared to be shameless flirting. When her husband turned to walk back toward her, she knew they were flirting. Her husband's dick was harder than the Statue of Liberty.

"Please do something about that. It's disrespectful," Niya requested once Doe reached her.

"What?"

"This." She grabbed Doe's pipe and held it.

"Yo, come on, babe, chill." Doe laughed, jumping hysterically.

"All right then. Get right," Niya snapped. She couldn't believe this brother was playing her like that! She had convinced him to come to the beach to spend some quality time. Much needed quality time. He hadn't been home much, just as predicted. Now that he was, she tried to keep him interested. Niya was now twenty-eight years old, but she knew she still looked very good in her peach thong bikini. Hell, even the video honeys were cutting envious eyes at her. Not to mention Blow himself.

"Aw, come on, bae. You know these chicks can't hold a candle to my baby," Doe submitted. However, he couldn't shake the wanting look in Dana's eyes.

★ ★ ★

Destiny had been in her makeshift prison for the better part of two weeks. During that time, she had become nauseated, then completely sick. In the beginning, she had refused to eat anything or drink water. She had become content with the thought of exiting into eternal peace. She had become tired of life with the man called Reece. Unfortunately, he had a twisted concept of love. Sort of a yin and yang. See, he would take her to incredible highs (trips around the world) to incredible lows (threats on her life). He would make her feel like a flower in full bloom (when she climaxed repeatedly); then she would be made to feel like the bride of Hades (being a prisoner).

Unfortunately for Destiny, she and Reece were inextricably entwined. Her five-year-old son, Prince, made that a fact.

Her son. Her dear son. According to Reece, Prince was the *only* thing that kept her breathing. He didn't know how right he was: If it wasn't for Prince, Destiny would have given up long ago, letting herself wilt away in her prison. The endless diet of candy bars followed by diarrhea and shitting on a makeshift *wooden* toilet that kept her droppings in a barrel just underneath the rim were becoming unbearable. *This can't be life*, she thought. She would rather die than live like this.

To his credit, Reece had personally come to check on her every day. After removing the shit bucket to get it cleaned out, he would come back to keep her company. They mostly talked about the books he would bring her to read. Books like *The Blackwoman's Guide to Understanding the Blackman* by Shahrazad Ali and *The Art of War*. Reece would always put an interesting spin on things, always stressing having knowledge of self, knowing your role in the black family, microcosms and macrocosms, basically things that he studied when he was away. It was refreshing for him to hear a female's perspective. Conversing about these books made them grow closer. It was really like she was in prison and Reece was visiting.

After they talked, Reece would pull the sink bucket close to Destiny's bed and wash her tenderly. At first, Destiny recoiled when he told her what he was about to do, but as he explained to her, it was either she let him or she linger in stank-a-dank-dank. The decision was a no-brainer, and ever since the first time, Reece washed her daily.

The bathing was starting to become a ritual Destiny enjoyed. It was then she was allowed to see the tender side of Reece, the part she had fallen in love with so many years ago. As Reece washed her he would open up and discuss things with her, exorcising his demons through their conversations. He would share with her things going on in his new life and how he struggled with being three people: who he had been, who he was now, and who he was striving to become. At times the battle felt as if it would tear him apart, but he always managed to get through the tough times.

Reece reiterated to her why he was doing what he was doing. It seemed to Destiny that Reece was doing this to her to gain face among his comrades more than to actually punish her. She had seen Reece at his worst, and this was not it. She knew that Reece could be an animal when prodded. What he was doing to her was just the rigmarole. Tough but not difficult. Maybe deep down inside Reece realized he had gotten off easy with five years. That if it wasn't for her cracking up on the stand and refusing to testify he could've really gotten hit hard, maybe even faced the death penalty for killing a federal agent. Five years was a drop in the bucket compared to what he could have gotten.

A part of Destiny felt sorry for Reece. During those moments of vulnerability when he broke down and bared his soul to her, Destiny wanted to hold him to console him. Even in her predicament, she still wanted to protect him. The irony. If this wasn't love, then why did she feel that way? Love is insanity.

Keys jingled. Locks turned, taking Destiny off guard. She had been expecting Reece hours ago. He always visited her around the same time each day. When the door opened, Destiny was shocked. It wasn't Reece at all. Instead, it was a very tall, very broad, bald-headed man. He petted the now-docile pit bull and Destiny noticed something eerily familiar about him, but she couldn't place him.

The giant walked over to her and passed her some papers. "King Reece said read this," he commanded.

When he spoke, his voice hit Destiny like a blow from a heavyweight boxer.

Samson!

The last time she had seen Samson was on the tarmac. Reece had blown one of her colleagues' head off so that he could escape.

It was at the airport hangar more than five years ago when Reece was apprehended. Reece and Samson had caught wind of the federal investigation and were fleeing to Mexico for a much-needed hiatus. Reece's supplier was furnishing a private jet for them to depart in. Realizing it was now or never, Destiny had alerted her handler, "Uncle Lou," aka Lieutenant Harris, and issued him the details. The feds put agents in place at the hangar to impede their departure until backup arrived. Reece, Destiny, and Samson arrived at the hangar early, and when the agents in place attempted to thwart their departure, Reece reacted, killing one instantly to save Samson's life. During Reece's trial, the FBI interviewed Destiny intensely. They thought she had colluded with Reece and Samson in their enterprise. According to the FBI, Samson was on the lam in Mexico terrorizing shit, becoming more powerful than ever. He was number three on the FBI's Most Wanted list.

Now he was here.

Of course, he looked different. Had put on some pounds of musculature. Face looked altered. But when you're as big as Samson, there wasn't much one could do to change his appearance. One thing Destiny did notice was that he walked with a lot more authority now. It was like his nuts wore a ton.

"Uh, hi, Samson," Destiny managed. At one point, the giant had been like a little brother to her. He had accompanied her and Reece everywhere, so naturally they became close.

Samson cut her off. "Look, save the nice attitude, you deceitful bitch. I don't like you, and I never will. If my man didn't want you alive to suffer, you'd be dead already. Prob'ly would've snapped yo' neck ma'self," he stated matter-of-factly.

Destiny nodded and gulped a ball of fear. "I understand, Samson. I don't blame you. If I were you, I would hate me, too."

"You could never hate me as much as I hate you. The king loved you! He gave you the world. He even sacrificed his own life to save your lying ass," Samson reminded her. "If he would've just killed you, then he wouldn't have done a day in prison."

"I was just doing my job, Samson. Don't you get it? Now sometimes in our line of work we have to do things that we don't like to do, but when we swear our allegiance to something we have to carry it out."

"Is that so?"

"Yes! Just like when you swore your allegiance to the Crescent Crew—whatever your bosses ask you to do, you had to carry it out."

Samson snarled, "First of all, I don't have a fucking boss. And don't ever compare your job to what we have. You work for the government; we built our *own* government."

"Worked for the government," Destiny clarified.

Samson smirked. "I forgot, they fired your ass. Anyway, King Reece said to tell you he won't be able to make it today."

Samson looked like he was about to leave but thought better of it. There was something on his mind. "Why, Destiny?"

"Excuse me?"

"Why?"

"Why what?"

"Why not just kill yourself and save us all the sin? We treated you like family! He really loved you, and Reece never loved nobody. And you betrayed that trust."

The giant freak walked closer to Destiny where she sat meekly on the bed. Samson bent down to look her square in the face. With veins bulging out his neck, he said, "I swear I don't doubt the god, Reece, but if it's one mistake he made, it's keeping you around. Ahhhh!" He screamed, unable to contain himself in the bunker. "But it's cool. By the time you finish five years in here, you'll be crazier than a junebug."

Samson stood to his full height and bumped his head on the ceiling. He recovered and looked upon Destiny with pure hatred. His eyes blazed.

"Samson, I'm sorry," Destiny said weakly. "I was only doing my job, but I'm not with them anymore."

Samson scoffed. "Whatever. Look, like I said, Reece said study that packet. Don't know why he wasting time trying to teach you that anyway," mumbled Samson. As he turned to walk out, he stopped to pat the big dog on the head.

"Hey, boy. Hey, boy," Samson taunted while playing with the dog. Then he suddenly shouted, "Watch her!" The dog jumped to attention immediately, in the direction of Destiny, clipped ears perked, tail standing straight up, low growl emitting from his throat.

"Atta boy," Samson commended. He eyed Destiny one last time, then eyed the paperwork she held and grunted before walking out.

Keys jingled. Locks popped.

Destiny looked at the title of her packet.

"The (5) P's of Perdition."

The video shoot was wrapping for the day when Doe went over to consult with Blow about the next step. Doe had barely gotten in two sentences before someone tapped him on the shoulder. He turned around to find Dana.

"Can I speak with you a second?" she requested. She was still wearing her turquoise bikini. Her silky hair was damp and matted to her forehead.

"Uh, yeah, just a second."

Doe wrapped up the conversation with Blow and returned his attention to Dana.

"A'ight, what's up?"

"Ah, nothing much. I just wanted to thank you for giving me motivated inspiration to finish." Dana laughed. "For a minute I got worried."

"Ah, come on, it wasn't that bad, was it?"

"Shoot. You just don't know." Dana laughed again. "This shit could get to you. Come on, let me see more ass, show something for the camera," she joked, imitating the director.

Doe laughed with her. "True, true. But hey, you're living out your dreams, aren't you?"

"Kind of sort of." She gave Doe a longing look.

"Kind of sort of? Well, what's missing?" he asked. Dana fixed Doe with a penetrating stare.

"I'm really missing a good man. You know any?"

There she goes with this flirting.

"Well, uh—"

"Any good man that's not *happily* taken?" She put extra emphasis on "happily."

"I'm ready to go, Daddy." Niya appeared from out of nowhere, interrupting the exchange. She clutched Doe's arm in a vise grip. "You done?"

Doe was taken aback, and for a minute thought he had gotten caught up. One glance at Niya showed him different.

He had escaped—this time.

"Yeah, Sunshine. I'm ready."

"Good. Come on." Niya led the way toward the parking lot where Doe's Ducati was parked.

"Guess I'll see you later," Doe told Dana half-heartedly. "You coming to the release party, right?"

"Wouldn't miss it," she promised.

"A'ight. Peace."

Doe and Niya arrived in the parking lot. Niya slipped on

her shorts while Doe took the bike off the kickstand. Niya was seething. Her day had started out well. She and her husband had brought the sun up with fabulous lovemaking, followed by breakfast in their birthday suits. Niya left the house feeling all warm and fuzzy. She just knew her marriage was getting back on track. They had been married three years, and Doe was already on the verge of being an absentee husband. Niya had considered getting herself a jump-off, but decided to give her husband more love instead. She thought things were getting back to normal. . . .

Until she saw her husband's dick getting hard twice for the same chick in the same day. Yeah, she'd definitely have to keep her eye on her husband.

Chapter 15

Qwess was thousands of feet above the clouds in a private jet, but that wasn't the reason he was in heaven. Lisa Ivory, Slasher Extraordinaire, was inducting him into the mile-high club for the second time in three days.

They were on their way back from Jamaica in a chartered jet from a trip that Lisa had designed and starred in—all on her dime. She had called Qwess at his home four days earlier telling him she had a surprise. While she was on the phone with Qwess, his buzzer at the front gate buzzed. Before Qwess answered it, Lisa told him who it was: a car that she had sent. She instructed Qwess to just get in. No clothes. No bags. No nothing. Just bring himself. After a few phone calls to his other partners, Qwess was whisked away in the limo. The limo went to the airport, but detoured to the hangar where the private jets docked. Qwess boarded the Gulfstream V and settled into its plush confines. In no time he was asleep. He awoke in Kingston, Jamaica, where a car was waiting to take him to the port. At the port, he boarded a ferry to a private island. When the boat docked and put Qwess off, he stood looking at a red-roofed villa—the only building in sight. Surrounding the villa were the usual perquisites of vacationing: pool, tennis court, basketball court, etc. Qwess walked up the sand to the villa and was greeted by a very happy Lisa wearing nothing but a smile and her trademark braids. Needless to say, they sexed each other away for the remainder of the day into the night.

The next day, Lisa fed him in bed. After that, she led him to a room inside the villa that had been converted to a massage room. Aromatherapy candles burned throughout the room. Lisa instructed Qwess to lie down on his stomach so she could massage him. Lisa poured hot oil on Qwess's back and began to knead it in. Before long, Qwess felt two pairs of hands on his back. Startled, he turned over quickly to find a beautiful, buxom woman with flawless chocolate skin sitting on the edge of the table. She was as naked as Qwess and Lisa. Initially, Qwess was shocked. Not to find a naked masseuse. After all, he was an international player. He was shocked that Lisa didn't mind, or better yet that she had arranged it. Then it hit him. He suddenly realized what was happening. His suspicions were confirmed when Lisa smiled at him and started kissing the girl. Seeing the encounter aroused Qwess immediately. His dick stood straight up like a flagpole.

It wasn't ignored long. Lisa bent over and put the whole thing in her mouth—very slowly. By the time she caught a rhythm, the other woman started eating her out.

It was true. Lisa played Ironman; she played both sides of the field—men and women.

The woman ate Lisa out like she owned that pussy. Like she knew it well. Like she had been there before. She made Lisa moan and shake almost harder than Qwess. She stopped munching Lisa long enough for Lisa to straddle Qwess. When Lisa began riding Qwess like a prize jockey, the woman came around to sit on Qwess's face. Before Qwess could resist, Lisa stopped her. Instead of the woman straddling Qwess face, Lisa did, while her companion straddled Qwess. Lisa and the woman kissed each other while Qwess pleased them both. When the other woman was about to reach peak satisfaction, Lisa sensed it and prevented it from occurring. It appeared she was on the verge of spazzing out! She violently pushed the woman off of Qwess, but regained her composure shortly thereafter. Lisa decided no one would climax from Qwess's skills but her. So to keep the action going, she made the mystery woman lie on the massage table spread-eagle and began tasting her juices while Qwess watched. Before long, Qwess had had enough watching, so he entered Lisa from behind while she stood, bending over, lapping up her companion. Much of the rest of the day was spent in some freaky form or fashion.

The next day when Qwess awoke, Lisa was on one side, the other woman was on the other. Qwess had experienced his first ménage à trois and it was *wonderful!* He had screwed the finest women the world over, but never had he experienced a ménage. Now that he had, nothing else would be sufficient.

Later in the morning, the woman left, leaving Qwess and Lisa alone. They ate. Talked. Fucked. Ate some more. Now they were on their way back home in a private jet that was plushed out and cost about $40,000 a day. Lisa footed the bill for the whole excursion. And as if that wasn't enough, she was presently trying to suck the soul out of him.

Qwess moaned louder and louder as Lisa's movements intensified. Then suddenly she stopped.

"What's wrong?!" Qwess gasped.

"Nothing," Lisa stated flatly. She got off her knees and sat in Qwess's lap. "I want to talk some more."

Qwess regained his composure and obliged her. "What's up, Ma?"

Lisa smoothed her hair before laying her head on Qwess's chest.

"You know I was just thinking. I really like spending time with you."

"Uh-huh. And?"

"And I was thinking about moving closer together."

Qwess cleared his throat. "Excuse me?"

"I mean, just think if we could spend every day like we did at my villa this weekend—minus the help, of course." Lisa chuckled then thought about something. "By the way, how do you feel about what happened this weekend?"

"What you mean? It was straight. Food was nice. Weather good. Weed was blazing. What more could I want?"

"You are a mess." Lisa tapped Qwess playfully. "You know what I'm talking about. The massage."

"Oh. The massage was excellent. Left me very relieved."

"Uhh! Qwess, I'm serious." Lisa flapped her arms in irritation.

"A'ight. A'ight. For real. I'm cool with it."

"Really?" She perked up.

"Of course. Why wouldn't I be?"

"Well, you know . . ."

"I know what?" prodded Qwess.

"A lot of people look at me differently when they find out I'm greedy."

"Greedy?"

"Yeah, see, I'm not gay, bisexual, or nothing. I'm greedy. I want it all. Women and men."

Qwess chuckled. "Girl, you crazy."

"Nah, really." Lisa straightened up to drive her point home. Looking Qwess straight in the eye, she proceeded to make her case. "As you know, I'm an overachiever. I have to master everything I do. Like, I can't just sing. I have to act, model, produce, the whole shebang. I have to be a Slasher," she explained. A Slasher was an artist who mastered more than one skill. "Well, that same drive applies to everything I do, including my sex life. I mean, I love men and the way they make me feel, especially when they know what they're doing—shout-out to you . . ."

Qwess blushed.

"But I also love women. They're beautiful creatures. Their curves, skin, smell, everything."

You're preaching to the converted, thought Qwess. What he said was, "I feel you."

"You do?" Lisa was surprised. For so long she hadn't dated because she was afraid of being judged.

"Of course."

"Good. So you don't think any less of me?" She had to be reassured.

"No. Why would I?"

"O-kay." Lisa was convinced. She replaced her head on Qwess's chest. Then she had an afterthought.

"Do you want to know who that was?"

"If you want to tell me," Qwess responded nonchalantly.

Lisa pinched him. "You don't sound too enthused, or curious. Anyway, her name is Ruquiyah. We've been getting . . . intimate . . . since I was twelve. She's also my best friend in the whole world. We've shared everything together. She is the only person that didn't change up on me when I became famous. She always tells me to watch out for men like you. You wouldn't believe how I had to convince her to go along with this."

Qwess was curious. "What did you tell her?"

"I told her I was in love."

Did she say love?

Qwess let her comment linger in the air. For the remainder of the ride, he relaxed and enjoyed the company of a beautiful, successful woman.

When their plane landed at the private hangar in Charleston, South Carolina, their paradise weekend was abruptly interrupted as they had company. A black Tahoe idled on the tarmac just outside the door.

"Who is that?" Lisa wondered aloud.

"I don't know," Qwess admitted. "But we're about to find out. They're coming this way."

The stairs to the plane opened up, and two tall white men in dark suits boarded the plane. One of them made himself comfortable and took the open seat across from Qwess, while the other man stood closer to the open door of the plane.

"How's it going, superstar? My name is Agent Michaels; I'm with the FBI."

Qwess tensed up a bit. "What can I help you with, sir?"

The agent gestured around the cabin of the plane. "You came a long way from a prison cell, Qwess. You living good. And you've come a long way from the Crescent Crew . . . or have you?"

"Baby, excuse me for a second, please," Qwess said to Lisa.

"Wait, Qwess, are you okay? Are you in some type of trouble? Because I can get my lawyer on the line right away."

Qwess gave her a crocodile smile. "Nah, baby, I appreciate you, but I'm good. Just wait for me out there in the car."

Lisa exited the plane and climbed into the Bentley that awaited them on the tarmac. When she was out of the area, Qwess turned his attention to the agent.

"Now what were you saying, sir?"

Agent Michaels leaned in closer, to just inches away from Qwess. "Qwess, I like you a lot. I can respect a man that came from nothing, a man that walked away from the game and never looked back. If you tell me that's who you really are, then I'll walk away and you'll never see me again. But if I find out you're still doing Crew business, I will put you back in the same cage you left when you were twenty-one."

Qwess shook his head. "What you say your name is again? Agent what?"

"Michaels."

"Well, Agent Michaels, can you please tell me why you came on my jet and interrupted my vacation? You better have a good reason for this, because I'm about thirty seconds away from having your badge," Qwess promised.

"You know what this is about."

"Enlighten me."

"Don't play stupid."

"Fifteen seconds are gone."

"Do I have to say it?"

"Ten seconds left."

"The beating of John Meyers. You ordered it."

Qwess allowed himself to relax a little. He thought for sure that Reece was back to his old ways and had committed a cardinal sin. This he could deal with.

"I don't know what you talking about," Qwess said.

"Soo . . . it's just a coincidence that AMG released one of their biggest artists to you after their executive was savagely beaten?"

Qwess shrugged. "I don't know how AMG conducts their business. I'm a businessman; I see an opportunity and I take it. My new artist is a great opportunity for my business."

Agent Michaels huffed and leaned back in the plush leather seat. "You know, Qwess, I really thought this could have gone differently. This isn't 2004 anymore. King Reece doesn't have any more lives to give for your freedom. If I find out you ordered the beating, your ass is going down!"

At the door, a brief commotion ensued. A few seconds later, a huge shadow loomed behind Agent Michaels. It was Hulk.

"Everything all right here, Qwess?" Hulk asked, itching for some action. His disdain for law enforcement was apparent.

Qwess stared at Agent Michaels with a poker face. "Everything is fine, big guy. Agent Michaels here was just leaving. Can you show him out, please?"

"Qwess, let me leave you my card—just in case you learn anything that can help us." Agent Michaels slid his card onto the wooden table.

"Agent Michaels?"

"Yes?"

"Get the fuck off my plane."

★ ★ ★

Destiny and Reece were in her "cell" discussing the packet he had sent her while Reece showed her how to make a "setup." Reece had been visiting Destiny regularly for the past couple weeks. Sometimes he would just come in and sit on the edge of her cot and watch her while she slept. Other times they would have engaging conversations.

Over the weeks, Destiny had seen Reece's heart soften. Initially, he was hell-bent on revenge, forcing her to go through everything he experienced while incarcerated. It seemed the more she whined, the more he enjoyed it.

Then she stopped whining.

See, Destiny knew Reece's Achilles heel. The only thing Reece hated more than a traitor was a coward. He absolutely loathed a person who begged for mercy. In his sight, the world never showed him mercy, and he had had to learn the hard way. He had to adapt and overcome or perish by the wayside. He figured if he had to take his pain like a man, then everyone else had to take theirs, too. Destiny knew this. She came to the conclusion that Reece was going to be whatever he wanted to with her, regardless. Begging would only incite him to other things. Her main priority was to survive and get to her son. So she played the passive-aggressive role each time Reece came around. She could see that it was working. She was slowly wearing down his resolve.

Reece poured the soup into a bowl and began mixing it. "So, what did you learn from the papers?"

Destiny sat cross-legged on the bed, then answered, "Well, I see some valid points, but why philosophy?"

Reece put down the bowl, then turned to give her his full attention.

"See, you got to think of all of them in order. They're all predicated on one another. Call 'em off in order—" He used his fingers as totaling points. "Philosophy, propaganda, politics,

police, and penal. Put together you have the five P's of perdition. This concept has been used to destroy societies, while
making the rich protected."

"You still haven't answered my question, Reece."

Reece chuckled a little. "Everything starts from philosophy. You gotta understand what philosophy is. In the dictio-
nary there are about ten definitions. Well, you can sum all ten
of them up by saying that philosophy is the system of values
incorporated based on long pondering of theories, histories,
and subsequent hypotheses."

"Subsequent what?" Destiny was educated, but she was
finding it difficult to keep up.

Reece continued, "Okay now. Knowing that, you'll know
that all societies' value systems start with philosophy. Once the
framers of a society determine what's moral—based on their
adopted philosophy—then they start with the propaganda.
The propaganda is to inform the masses of what's acceptable
or true based on the pondering of the forefathers. Once they
use the media to get their points across, they enact *policies*.
Hence the politics. The mind state being, 'look, this is what's
up. You know this is what's up because we told you what's up
with our propaganda machine.'" Reece was hyped now. He
loved a good build.

"Now that you know this is what's up, we are gonna enact
policies because of what's up—whether good policies or bad
policies—we're enacting them to deal with what's up. Ya follow me?"

Destiny nodded. She was finally beginning to understand.

"Okay. Now, it's like this: This is what's up. You know this
is what's up because we told you this is what's up. Now as a result of what's up, we made these policies. You ready for this?"
Reece asked.

"Yeah."

"A'ight. Now we are going to enforce these policies with . . ."

"Police!" Destiny blurted the answer like a child in school.

"Riiiight! And the police are going to *penalize* you, by beating, incarceration, et cetera, until you get in line with the original philosophy."

Destiny nodded vigorously. She finally understood.

"By applying these methods over time, the masses are stripped of free thought or any revolutionary drive because they've seen what happens to people who 'get out of line' with the original philosophy. As a result, the masses of the people are like cattle. Only reacting, never acting."

The bowl inside the microwave sizzled and popped, interrupting Reece's class. He retrieved the bowl, stirred the salmon, added butter and a little water, and then replaced it in the microwave on two minutes. Next, he added pepper, onions, and butter to the soup. With that done, he continued the class.

"As I was saying, the masses are blind, deaf, and dumb. Eighty-fivers. Then you have ten percent who know but conceal the truth. Then you have people like me, the—"

"Five Percenters, or Poor Righteous Teachers who are supposed to civilize the uncivilized," Destiny finished his statement for him.

Reece couldn't help but smile. She remembered. After all this time she remembered the basis of his way of life.

"Yeah. The Five Percenters," Reece confirmed, unconsciously rubbing the crescent-moon-star-seven tattoo on his right forearm.

Reece stared at Destiny in silence, no doubt recalling all the good memories they shared. Recalling all the things they had in common. Like the fact that they had no family. Destiny, like Reece, lost her parents at an early age. Their similarities were what drew Reece to her. The thing that made their bond so strong was that for once in their life, they had found someone they could love: each other.

But was it all a lie?

That was the thing Reece couldn't get past. During their time spent in the bunker, his heart had softened, but when he thought about tomorrow it hardened again.

"You remembered?" Reece told her.

"Of course I remembered. How could I forget?"

Life could be a terrible thing. Love made Destiny remember. Hate wouldn't allow Reece to forget.

Lisa had dressed and now sat in Qwess's lap feeding him and herself from the gourmet platter the in-flight chef had prepared. Between bites Lisa and Qwess discussed past relationships. He informed her of Hope, his ex-fiancée who now worked as the director of public relations for Renaissance Records, the Yankees of the music industry. She had been his first love and his first heartbreak. Then he also told her about Shauntay, the woman he was with during his grinding days coming up in the industry. She was murdered on the night of his birthday party celebration when he accepted his first deal with AMG Records. After she was killed, it was discovered she was carrying his baby. It seemed like ages ago.

What he didn't tell Lisa was why she was killed. Her killers actually mistook her for King Reece. He definitely didn't share with her that Shauntay's death was the impetus for the Crescent Crew wars, the bloody retaliation carried out by the Crescent Crew on the Blood Team and the old heads who hired them. No, he didn't tell her that. Qwess learned that women in the industry claimed to love street dudes until they actually got with one. He only explained that it was mistaken identity.

However, this revelation brought up a point Lisa had been dying to inquire about.

"Um, Qwess, I'm curious about something," Lisa said.

"What's up?" Qwess was now reclined in the plush seat, stroking the lacquered wood, thinking about how bad he wanted a jet. Lisa was stroking his waves.

"Now you know I'm not nosy," she prefaced. "But is it true what they say about you having something to do with your old boss getting paralyzed?"

"Who?"

"You know who. John Meyers. They say you had him hit because he wouldn't agree to your demands to re-sign you."

"What? That's crazy! Who is they?" Qwess demanded.

"People in the industry."

"Well, people don't know what the fuck they talking 'bout. I was with you. Remember?" Qwess was agitated that the story was getting crossed up. He was making some major moves that required he keep a clean image.

"I know, poo-pee. Calm down," Lisa soothed.

Qwess relaxed a little. He had to nip that in the bud immediately. Word traveled fast in entertainment.

"See, that's what's wrong with niggas now. Always starting rumors. Then when a nigga box 'em in the mouth, they looking stupid." Qwess looked every bit the part of scorned artist. He was putting on a good show for Lisa.

"Come on, poo-pee. Don't let the haters vex you. This is our time." Lisa planted kisses all over his face.

Lisa was clearly open. Qwess had really put his thing down on the young girl. She didn't want him to leave her sight. "I wish I had two of myself. I'd keep one with you at all times," she whispered in his ear.

"What?" *This broad is loco*, thought Qwess.

"Ya feel me," Lisa continued. "I just like being with you. You really understand me like no one else does, and you allow me to be me. When are we going to spend some time together again?"

"I don't know. I gotta shoot to Atlanta to make sure everything is right for Flame's release party. Plus we got a major announcement to make that's going to shock the industry."

"Really? What is it?" Lisa jumped like a little kid.

"Nah, I can't let the cat out the bag, but you will know." Lisa was disappointed. Here she had shared the most intimate details of her life, and he was keeping a funky little business move from her. She didn't like it, and she told him as much.

Qwess understood, so he swore her to secrecy, then told her, "Niya is now with ABP."

Lisa's jaw dropped, and she sat in silence. Maybe the rumors were true. When she told Qwess what the industry was saying, she meant just that. The *industry* was saying that. However, Linda Swansen had paid her a personal visit to warn her about the dangers of getting too wrapped up with Qwess. Linda's message was simple: *If Niya signs to ABP, Qwess is poison. Stay away.*

Now, Lisa knew Niya was signed to ABP, which must mean Qwess was poison, according to Linda.

Qwess was a very potent poison that changed the tables. Most poisons killed you, but Lisa felt that she would die without this poison. She was in love.

Oh, what to do?

Destiny and Reece were finishing up the last portion of their "setup" meal. Reece had added Veg-All to the salmon and soup, which set the meal off proper.

Destiny was still in thought about the lesson Reece had given her about the five P's of perdition. She definitely understood it, but she was unsure why Reece had bothered to explain it to her, especially since he was going to make her live in this bunker for the next four years—if he was going to let her live at all. Reece was likely to spazz out at any time and extinguish her life.

"Reece, why are you sharing this with me?" Destiny finally asked.

"What? This knowledge?"

"Yeah."

"Well, I see it like this," Reece began, straightening himself up on the cot to look at Destiny. "You're the mother of my seed. Which means you have to be able to endow him with proper education. Knowledge of self. The first principle of proper education is knowing the basis of the education of the masses. What is known as 'the box,' because it closes people's minds."

Destiny got the point. "But why are you teaching me this if you're going to keep me here for four years? I mean, you have possession of Prince now. You can teach him yourself. By the way, where is he?"

"Vyshay has him."

"Who?"

"Vanilla," clarified Reece. "And I am teaching him. I just want you to know so you won't be a stranger to it."

"Who is Vanilla?"

"She's one of my partners. She held me down when I was away."

They sat in silence for a few seconds before Reece asked Destiny, "What's wrong with you? The whole time I've been talking you've been preoccupied."

What's wrong? I'm locked in a fucking concrete bunker! "Nothing," said Destiny.

Reece eyed her suspiciously.

"Nothing you care about anyway," she clarified.

"Try me," Reece offered.

Destiny measured her words. "I'm late."

"You're late. Late for what?" Reece mocked, checking his Jacob and Company timepiece. "You ain't going nowhere."

"I'm late late."

Reece jumped from the cot, clearly vexed. "Dammit, Destiny, don't do this shit! Don't pull the pregnancy stunt on me. You fucking playing me like I'm stupid! I try to show you a little compassion, and you take my kindness for weakness! Fuuuuck!"

The pit bull started barking and going crazy upon seeing his master upset.

"Wait, Reece!" Destiny cried out, pulling his arm back. "Baby, I'm serious. I haven't had my period for weeks now," Destiny claimed. "I wanted to tell you, but I knew you'd act like this. I didn't want you to think I was soft."

Reece slowed his roll from the door. He turned to look at Destiny. She looked sincere, but hell, she looked sincere the whole couple of years she was setting his ass up. She had Reece thinking she was a daddy's girl going to school. Truth was, she was just as parentless as he, and she was a federal agent. If it wasn't for the vigorous inquiry he had conducted, he wouldn't have been convinced she wasn't a cop now.

Destiny continued with her pleas. "Reece, listen. At this point it doesn't matter. I've already resigned my fate to you. You're gonna do what you wanna do. As long as Prince is taken care of I couldn't care less. But please believe it: I haven't seen my period in weeks. Just thought you should know."

Reece was silent. All he could think about was how she was trooping so strong. He was almost proud of her. Then she had to pull a pregnancy stunt.

"Sooo . . . if you are pregnant, are you saying the child is mine?" Reece asked.

"Fuck you, motherfucker!"

Reece shrugged his shoulders. "I'm saying, I just came home; I don't know who you was fucking while I was away."

Destiny crossed her arms. "Fucking while you was away, huh? After the ordeal that you put me through do you honestly think that I will be out here fucking someone else? It took me a year to just get over the devastation of what happened with you! And please tell me, who do I follow up with after dating you?"

Reece stared at Destiny and nodded. "Pregnant, huh?

A'ight. We gon' see. I got this release party in a couple of days. After that, I'll get back with you. And Katrina?"

Destiny perked up. "Yeah?"

"You better not be fuckin' playing with me. Ya hear?" Reece walked out the door.

Keys jingled. Locks turned. Destiny was alone with her thoughts.

If she was pregnant, would Reece let her go?

She could only hope.

Chapter 16

Club Crunk was Atlanta's new premiere nightspot located in the Buckhead section of town. It got its name because the proprietor was none other than Atlanta's godfather of crunk music. He had invested a healthy portion of money to make Club Crunk just as popular as his music. He had succeeded, too. On any given night, one could spot a number of entertainment's glitterati perusing the club. Add the fact that ballers the world over visited Club Crunk regularly, and you would have to concede that Club Crunk was the "it" spot for the southeast. And it more than accommodated its audience. Sitting on more than 20,000 square feet, Club Crunk was tri-level. The bottom floor boasted a full-size pool for the infamous Wet-n-Wild Wednesdays when female patrons were known to strip down to their birthday suits and skeet-skeet up the place. The middle floor was the biggest, containing three full bars, two dance floors, pool tables galore, and numerous "privacy" booths. The third floor was where the ballers played. The entire third floor was reserved for VIPs.

Not one of those hide-me-I'm scared-to-be-touched VIP

sections either. This VIP section was so big it could've been a separate club itself. Fitted with state-of-the-art technology, this room was made to be adored. Plasma screens made up one wall, a full bar made up another. A dance floor sat center of the room so people could really let their hair down. Tucked into a neat corner was a black room. Called that because the lights were low, and inhibitions were lower, the black room was where jump-offs happened. No one said, heard, or spoke of anything in the black room.

Admission to the third floor started at a thousand dollars.

When Atlantic Beach Productions hosted the release party for one of their premiere artists, Flame, everyone who was anyone came to frolic. Word was on the wire that Qwess had strongarmed his way out of a contract with AMG, so in certain circles he was beginning to be revered with respect. He had done to the Matrix—the mainstream that controlled artists like puppets—what so many others desired to do, but never did. He had literally taken his destiny into his own hands. He was a bona fide shot-caller in the industry, so people wanted to be associated with him in any way.

The admission extended around the corner, far from under the courtesy canopy, which stretched a nice way from the entrance door. People from all walks of life eagerly anticipated entrance into Club Crunk. Pimps strutted in loud three-piece suits. Ladies who looked like they should've belonged to the pimps stood proudly in sheer miniskirts and six-inch stilettos. Ballers repped in everything from ostrich boots to Timbs.

A convoy of white Benz limos pulled up beside the long line right in front of the club. The three chariots idled a moment before the passengers emerged, one car at a time.

In the first limo was Doe. He placed his marble-print leather shoe on the pavement and let it linger a second for everyone to see. The marble shoe was an idea he was pitching, so he decided to test it this night. All eyes were on him, indeed, when he fully emerged in an all-gold leisure suit, with his wife, R & B sensation Niya, on his arm. She wore a brown satin dress that complemented Doe's suit, and matching heels. Her neck, wrist, fingers, and ears were all flooded with the finest ice. Her hair pulled into a bun, mink stole around her shoulder, she looked more like a model than a singer. Amin followed her in a simple gray suit. Six-foot-five Mustapha was assigned this detail. He ushered them inside.

Flame bust out of the second limo wearing a Carolina-blue silk-linen blend suit, with matching gators. His diamond-encrusted ABP chain swung defiantly at his neck. Ladies attempted to rush him, only to be held back by club security. Flame's best friend, 8-Ball, tailed him, wearing identical colors but a different ensemble. He was hooded out. As Flame walked toward the door a young woman yelled out, "I love you, Flame!" She tossed her panties at him.

Flame caught them, smelled them, and then flashed his new platinum grill. "I love you, too!" Six-foot-six Abdullah escorted him inside.

In the third limo sat Qwess. He waited a few minutes for the crowd to calm down before he poured out in an off-white linen suit, with green shirt. The coat stretched to just above his knees. His green-and-white gators announced his arrival proudly. Once he stood to straighten himself, the R & B duo Desire stepped out of the limo to join him. Melinda (the red one) wore a green slip dress, limited jewels, and a ton of makeup. She was clearly a bottle beauty. She grabbed Qwess's left arm. Her sister Clarinda was naturally pretty, but her beauty was further put on display by the cream dress with the plunging neckline she sported. Her hair was pulled up into a neat coil. She clutched Qwess's right arm. Qwess tilted his cream-colored brim over his left eye, and the paparazzi unleashed a volley of flashes. The diamonds Qwess flaunted on his wrist were so pure, they flashed back like they were taking pictures. Qwess strolled to the entrance with the limo door still open. When most of the focus was averted from the car,

Reece slid out in a dark-green silk suit. His bald head and be-jeweled grill competed for shine. Hulk picked up the rear in a no-nonsense black-on-black suit, replete with earpiece and scanner to stay in contact with the rest of his security team.

Inside, Club Crunk was already packed with people who were afforded the luxury of not having to stand in line. Ac-tresses, models, porn queens and kings, players from the At-lanta Hawks and Falcons, legendary hustlers, everybody was up in the joint. ABP had reserved an entire corner of the club. When they arrived at their tables, Cristal, along with an assort-ment of appetizers, awaited them. Numerous local radio and television programs were broadcasting live, as well as a rep for BET. The attention was focused more on the organized assault on AMG's offices than on Flame's actual album. Flame was popular, but he didn't warrant that much attention. Also, one of ABP's PR reps had leaked to the press that a major an-nouncement was to take place at the party. Therefore, every station wanted to be first to break the news.

Once the entourage was settled, everyone relaxed and kicked the bobo until it was time for Flame to perform. He was doing a couple of songs off his new album to generate buzz. There were also plans to give out CDs with bonus mate-rial, along with a *Making of . . .* DVD.

Desire sat underneath Qwess, each sister under a respective arm. One would think that Qwess had boned them both be-cause of his reputation as a philanderer. Truth was, he hadn't sampled the goods of either sister. He didn't believe in mixing business and pleasure that close to home. Plus, he didn't want the chicks to think he owed them more than he did. Leave it to a broad to think that just because you laying pipe, they de-serve some of your pie, when in actuality the woman received more satisfaction than the man. That's how Qwess saw things anyway.

"Yo, Flame, remember what I told you when we first

met?" Qwess asked Flame, who was sitting beside Clarinda. "Tell 'em."

Flame scooted closer. "What, dawg? You told me a lot of stuff."

"Well, what did I promise you?" Qwess clarified.

"Oh. You told me that if I do the right thing, you'd make me a star."

"Riiiight. Did I?"

"Hell yeah, dawg. I shine like the sun, baby. Haha," Flame joked.

"See, I tell you. Just be patient. It'll come. Things don't happen overnight," promised Qwess to both sisters. They were beginning to get discouraged because they hadn't seen any light yet, other than attending industry events as spectators.

Flame spotted the girl from earlier who had lent him her panties. "Yo, pardon me for a minute." Flame excused himself.

"Yo, where you going?!" Qwess gasped.

"I gotta go pay somebody back what they lent me," Flame answered, holding up the satin panties.

Qwess shook his head as Flame and 8-Ball tore through the crowd. "Don't get lost! Business first!" he yelled, but his voice was drowned out by the deafening bass of the crunk music.

Niya and Doe were busy enjoying the appetizers and getting busy with the free drinks while observing the scene. Reece was beside him talking animatedly on a cell phone, while Hulk posted up beside their table. After drinking too much, Doe told Reece, "Yo, cuz, watch my wife while I go use the bathroom. I'd hate to have to fuck one of these brothers up about mine."

Niya blushed. She loved to hear her husband talk like that, especially in light of the problems they had been having lately.

Doe maneuvered his way to the bathrooms located by the elevators that led to VIP. He had quite a time getting through because of the people scattered about inside, sniffing cocaine in ciphers, and smoking sherm blunts. He could just imagine how many people were already on X pills. Doe handled his business and was accosted at the sink by a woman who recognized him. (Yes, the middle-floor bathrooms were coed.) She demanded Doe autograph her perky breasts. Doe obliged her with no hesitation and peeled out. On his way back to the table, he inwardly checked himself on how easily he had agreed to sign the woman's breast, right above her nipple. Months ago that would've been a definite no-go.

Lost in his thoughts, Doe never even saw Dana until she grabbed his arm.

"Hey, stranger. I've been looking all over for you," Dana greeted.

Doe started looking over her. "Oh yeah?" Doe was unnerved, as he was obviously attracted to Dana.

"Um-hmmm. You look nice," Dana complimented. She had to reach up and whisper in Doe's ear because of the music.

"You too," yelled Doe.

Dana was wearing a turquoise spaghetti-strap dress of light material, which cupped her ample bosom nicely and accented her smooth Hawaiian skin. Her hair was pulled over to one side with a colorful flower holding it in place.

"Thank you. So, am I going to get a chance to dance with you? After all, this is a party."

"I don't know about that. My wife is with me," admitted Doe.

"Damn, she got the cla-clink on yo' ass!" Dana demonstrated with her wrists outstretched. "You must've been a bad boy before?"

Doe allowed himself a brief laugh, "Nah, nothing like that."

"Well, you know," Dana began, her voice taking on a sultry sincere tone, "I'm a very persistent person. Intoxicating, too. One dance could lead to a lot more. It's a good thing the ole ball and chain is with you. I see something I want, and I will get it."

Doe had to indulge her. "What makes you think I want you? I *am* a married man."

"Oh, you want me." Dana was confident, which Doe was finding irresistible.

"What makes you so sure?"

Dana looked around to ensure not too many eyes were on them before she pulled closer to Doe.

"Because your dick is hard." She cupped him in her hand and held him there, looking deeply into his eyes. "Don't deny yourself what you really want. Later."

Just like that, she was gone, leaving Doe with hard thoughts and a harder dick.

When Doe arrived at the table he was surprised to see Reece conversing with Samson and Bone. Ever since the incident at AMG, Samson had been laying low. Now here he was in the flesh, in a club full of industry folk. Sure, he wore a Kangol pulled down over his eyes, but Samson wasn't the type of person you looked over—even if his Kangol wasn't cream-colored, which it was. Doe surmised that Samson came to view the fruits of his labor firsthand. Doe had no qualms with him being there. If not for Samson, Niya would've still been a slave for AMG.

"*Salaam alayka*, Big Sams," greeted Doe.

"Peace, Blackman." Samson enveloped him in a tight embrace. "What's the deal?"

"Chilling."

"I see the lady looking good," Samson commented, giving Niya the once-over.

"True, true."

They talked a little with minutes slipping away. Soon it was time for Flame to perform, and he was nowhere in sight. No doubt he was wilding away with the broad from earlier.

Just as Qwess was about to send Abdullah to search for him, Flame popped up wearing just his trousers, boots, and a wife-beater T-shirt. In his hand he held his top shirt, which was soaking away. Flame's braids were soaked as well.

Qwess shot Flame that knowing glance. Flame gestured for Qwess to chill. Qwess didn't get a chance to rebuke him because the emcee called Flame to the stage.

Flame took the stage while the instrumental to his new single gripped the powerful system. The crowd swayed and started murmuring the words to the song before Flame even spit one word. Patrons from VIP even came down to witness the mini-concert.

Flame ripped through his new single, some old classics, and freestyled a bit, while his chubby sidekick 8-Ball played hype man. As quick as it started, the performance was over. Flame called Qwess to the stage, and he commandeered the mic.

"Yo, give it up for my man," Qwess exhorted. "Fayette-nam's finest!" The audience applauded. "A'ight. Now, there is another piece of business we want to share with you. As you know, ABP prides itself on bringing up the best *quality* music in the game. Emphasis on quality. Now in keeping with that tradition, we added someone else to the family. Someone I know you love." Qwess paused for effect.

"Please, Atlanta, help us welcome to the family the newest addition to the ABP roster—"

Cameras poised, tapes rolled, silence ensued.

"Niya!"

Niya sashayed on stage, all tanned legs and diamonds, with panache, amid healthy applause. Right behind her was Doe, holding his wife down every step of the way. Niya walked up to Qwess, planted a kiss on his cheek, then grabbed the mic. The crows lowered a bit.

"I'd like to thank you for your support. You mean the world to me," Niya gushed. "I'm looking forward to blessing you, as you have blessed me with the hottest music to come out in a long time! Know what I'm saying. I'm thrilled to bring my music home. I'm sure you all will reap the benefits." Niya's voice dripped of a B-more accent, as did her style. Ladies in the urban jungles of America thoroughly identified with her music.

Qwess regained the mic, spoke briefly, then called all members of ABP's recording staff on stage. Once assembled, Qwess raised his arms grandly and announced, "We present to you the future of hip-hop!"

Some applauded. Some didn't. Qwess was set-tripping in a *big* way. Nonetheless, they all left the stage to resume partying.

When Qwess exited the stage, he felt a tug at his arm. He turned and looked into the eyes of Qima, the reporter from the magazine.

"Hey there," she offered. "Yo. Okay, I see. You still salty about the joke, huh?"

"Nah, I'm just messing wit' ya. What's the bizness?" asked Qwess.

"Nothing with me. Everything wit' you."

"What you mean?"

"You're quite the talk of the industry."

"You think?"

Qima scoffed. "Uh, yeah."

"Anyway," Qwess said dismissively, "I'm sure you didn't come over to tell me I'm popular."

"Actually, I came to buy you a drink." Qwess was surprised, but the act humbled him. "Nah, let me buy you one. Come on."

Qwess and Qima journeyed to the table. As they arrived at the table, Doe and Hulk were leaving.

"Where you going?" Qwess asked them.

"Following these fools to VIP." Doe pointed to Reece and Samson, already ahead by a few steps. "Damn, shorty, you look different. Kinda cute. Good looking out on that article," Doe shot at Qima. He was aroused, so all his senses were heightened.

Doe, Hulk, Samson, and Reece entered the third floor amid stares. The two giants with them made it appear that two bigshots needed their bodyguards to party. That wasn't the case at all. It was just family chilling, catching up on old times. Still, people got out of their way. Some people recognized Reece from his *Don Diva* magazine article, which caused them to whisper and point slyly. The crew snagged a table in the cut to parlay. Yet they couldn't help but trip off the wannabes inside VIP like the nut who walked around with a drippy jerry curl à la 1985. Or the other brother wearing a chunky wacky chain. It was clearly a cheap grade of silver, but he flaunted it like he wore a mil around his neck. And he had the nerve to put diamonds in it. The crew couldn't help but laugh, especially Reece. Gossip was something the god didn't usually do. He felt that was for hoes. However, being new to the streets again, he couldn't help but comment on how the quality of brothers had dropped significantly.

They were still lost in conversation when Dana popped up out of nowhere. She was determined this time, evidenced by the way she grabbed Doe's hand.

"Can I speak with you a moment?"

"Sure, speak," Doe told her, refusing to meet her gaze.

"More of a private setting would be nice." She pulled Doe's hand. He didn't resist. Next thing he knew they were in the black room.

Doe didn't club too much, except for business, so he was green as to what went on nowadays, especially in VIP. Even if he did, he wouldn't have been prepared for what met him in the black room. The black room encouraged people to "black" out. Hence its name. People paid the thousand-dollar cover to the third floor just for the black room. That being the case, it shouldn't have surprised Doe that people were jumping off in the black room. Not that he could see anything. His nose worked well, though, and all he smelled was pussy.

Dana commandeered a corner and put Doe's back to the wall. She whispered in his ear, "It's time to stop fighting it. Let me give you what you want."

She cooed oh so softly in his ear. Doe couldn't see her eyes, but he could smell her sweet breath. He could feel the warmth emanating from her body. Dana rubbed her fingers across Doe's upper lip, letting him smell her juices. She had been playing with herself since the moment they stepped into the black room.

"Taste it," Dana encouraged. "Taste my pussy. Your pussy . . . if you want it." Dana slid her fingers into Doe's mouth, then slid closer to him, her breast flattened against his chest. She put both arms around his narrow waist and spoke into his face.

"I'ma show you how you're supposed to feel all the time," she promised.

Doe shuddered with desire in her arms. Dana could actually feel him shake, and she knew she had him. And she could also feel the centerpiece of his arousal, harder than brick, at the pit of her stomach.

Dana sank down to her knees. All the while she held him close, falling down his shirt front, past his faux marble belt, coming to rest on the part of him that refused to be denied. She allowed her face to linger there a moment, absorbing the heat from Doe's member. She rubbed her face on it from cheek to cheek. Dana felt it pulsing, threatening to bust through the flimsy trousers. She felt how big he was, which made her want him in her mouth more. Right now. She found his zipper, slipped it down smoothly, and released the monster from its prison. Doe's love muscle fell out into Dana's waiting hands. She held it like a prize, savoring the moment. She opened her mouth and placed the head on her tongue, letting it sit unperturbed. Using her tongue ring like a trained expert, she titillated the underside of his dick until neither one of them could stand it. Feeling Doe was on the verge of release, she deep-throated him in one smooth motion. Doe groaned loudly in surrender. The sound of others getting busy around them heightened the experience. Dana continued to deep-throat Doe, all the while using her arms to pull him closer. Doe was in another world! His wife never gave him professionals so well. He was about to release his juiciest into Dana's mouth when suddenly she stopped.

Doe cried out, "What the fuck!"

Dana ascended from her knees, put her fingers over Doe's lips, and whispered to him, "I only swallow what's mine."

Doe had to struggle to regain his composure, but he did. "Yo, Dana, chill, ma. You know I got a wife," Doe reminded her.

Dana was on point, though. "I know, and I don't wanna break that up, but I do want you. So what's up?"

"What you mean?"

"I mean this: We can take it however you want to. I'll respect your boundaries with your wife as long as you're there for me when I need you."

Doe knew things were fishy. A broad this bad wanting to be his mistress. First thought: She was a gold-digging groupie. Second thought: He didn't give a fuck. With head skills like that, he could imagine what the fuck game was like. He had money to burn; wasn't shit for him to sponsor a broad. He would only allow her shovel to go so far into his money pit.

"Yo, you serious?" Doe asked.

"As a heart attack."

Doe contemplated a moment then pulled Dana closer to him. "I'm down, but know this: If it's mine, it's mine exclusively," he whispered into her ear.

Dana sounded offended. "Of course. I'm not the type of girl to sleep around. Now let's go before you're missed."

With that, they maneuvered out of the black room. As they neared the door, Doe could've sworn he heard Flame in there with them, talking dirty to some chick. Doe moved a little more cautiously toward the door, paused a moment, then slipped out alone.

Back at Doe's table, Samson and Reece were conversing about Destiny.

"So, you sure you took her the test?" Reece asked Samson.

"Yeah, god."

"Was it positive?"

"I don't know. I just dropped the shit off and dipped," Samson answered, "Yo, god, what's up with that broad? You gon' handle that bitch, right? 'Cause it seem like you getting soft on her all over again. I know my dawg ain't going down like that?" Samson made light of the question but he was dead serious.

"Hell, nah. That bitch put a chink in the Crescent Crew armor. That shit can't ride. Pregnant or not." Reece said the menacing words to his comrade, but he felt different. Despite himself he was starting to feel for Destiny all over again. Maybe it was her willingness to learn, or her courage. Reece knew many men who cringed in his presence. Men, if put in the situation Reece had put Destiny in, would've probably killed themselves by now. But not Destiny. She held strong.

"That's what I'm talking 'bout," Samson countered. "I wanna kill that bitch myself. You just don't know."

Reece cringed inwardly with the thought of Samson breaking his girl's neck. His girl? What the fuck? Reece had to catch himself.

"In due time, Poppo. In due time," promised Reece.

Out of nowhere Mustapha rolled up with Niya in tow.

"Where's my husband?" demanded Niya.

Reece and Samson looked to each other, remembering who Doe had stolen away with.

"Um, I don't know. The nigga was just right here, li'l cuz," Reece attempted to say.

Niya narrowed her eyes. She knew something was up, but before she could investigate further Reece informed her, "Oh, there the nigga go right there."

Doe arrived at the table and spoke to his wife.

"Hey, patnah. Where you been?" Niya attempted to kiss her husband but Doe turned to give her his cheek.

"Um-um. I've been calling Earl," sidestepped Doe. "This shit is messing up my stomach."

Niya accepted his excuse but was reluctant. She smelled the faintest hint of perfume around his collar when she went to kiss him. She overlooked it, though.

"Good, because Qwess said he's about ready to go. Y'all ready?"

"Yeah, no doubt. Where's Flame?" Doe asked.

"Who knows?" Hulk answered.

"Baby, give me your two-way." Niya passed Doe her pager, and he began typing. "Man, I told y'all to keep an eye on him; y'all know how he get at these parties," Doe chastised while typing Flame a message.

Everyone gathered their things and prepared to leave. Hulk, Samson, Reece, and Mustapha went first while Doe and Niya lagged behind them, hugged up like lovebirds. Before entering the elevator doors Doe spotted Dana at the bar. She blew him a kiss. He returned a wink. The elevators doors closed, reopened, and put them out on the second floor, where they linked up with Qwess and company. Qwess informed them that the cars were waiting.

They moved through the crowd bidding farewell to those who mattered. Flame caught up with Qwess at the door and told him he wanted to kick it a while longer. Qwess wasn't too enthused since he knew how Flame could get taken off track with those broads. They had an in-store CD signing at one o'clock the next day. From previous experience, Qwess knew Flame was liable to party until daybreak. Flame told Qwess that he would check him at the W Hotel no later than three a.m. Flame practically promised Qwess, so Qwess relented and left for the night.

Outside, the limos were parked curbside idling. Doe and Niya were already in their limo with Mustapha. The chauffeur closed their door and pulled from the curb. Qwess went to inform Flame's driver to stay put for a while. Qwess could've easily gotten someone to do it for him, but he was a micromanager.

Micromanaging was his downfall this night.

As Qwess walked to the car, shots rang out into the night. The first volley of rounds shattered the passenger-side window of the limo. It exploded, bursting onto Qwess. He crouched on the ground next to the limo looking for cover, reaching for a pistol that wasn't there. There was a temporary lull in the gunfire. Qwess peeked his head up to see where the danger came from. More shots shook the Atlanta night. Qwess tucked himself behind the limo again.

"Stay down!" Hulk yelled. He fired suppressive shots into the air then ran to retrieve Qwess. Focused on his boss, Hulk never saw the second gunman. Reece did.

Reece laid down a volley of shots from his .45, causing the second gunman to take cover behind a parked car.

"Come on!" Reece yelled, directing them back inside. Hulk ran toward the club with Qwess sheltered under one arm, his Desert Eagle in the other hand.

Reece took his eye off the car the gunman had ducked under for a second, and it cost him. As he was making a way for Hulk and Qwess, the gunman crept from behind another car and opened up, hitting Qwess high in the thigh.

"Ahhh!" Qwess yelled in agony, clutching his leg as he tumbled to the ground.

Reece ran to meet Qwess as he hit the ground and was bombarded with shots, causing him to fall short. Just as he was about to crawl over, he spotted the first gunman walking toward him, the embodiment of cool. The gunman wore a derby pulled low over his face, a scarf mummifying the lower portion. Reece knew it was over. He saw his life flash before his eyes: the moment his parents died in a car wreck, meeting his cocaine connect who made him rich, trips to the Bahamas with Destiny, making love to Destiny in his mansion, his son, Prince.

Reece saw it all flash before him in an instant.

He met the gunman with a warrior's glare, welcoming death. Reece had never been a coward in life, and he wouldn't be one in death, either. He smiled at the gunman as he advanced on him. Reece had waited all his life for his death. He was embracing the moment.

The gunman raised his weapon. Reece saw the dot reflecting from his forehead. Seconds later, he heard an applause of uninterrupted gunfire and saw the gunman's body flail to the side, breakdancing like a choreographer.

Samson ran up on the gunman and delivered the coup de grâce to his head, then turned to help his brother with Qwess until Reece pointed, screaming, "It's another one!"

Samson went into war mode, crouching low with his Tec-9 in his hand, surveying the whole street from behind parked cars. Hulk dragged Qwess back inside the club, then returned to help with the search.

Out of nowhere popped the gunman running down the street full speed. Samson tore off behind him, stopping every few feet to lick shots. He saw his shots whizzing by the gunman, just missing him by inches.

Suddenly, the street was ablaze with lights flashing everywhere.

"Freeze, drop the weapon! Now!" an officer screamed at Samson and Hulk. Samson paused but didn't drop the Tec-9. The Crescent Crew's motto was to hold court in the street. The courts didn't give men like them justice.

"Drop the weapon!"

Samson's eyes went from the police to his gun.

Then he saw the pig's barrel down on his brother, Hulk, who was following his lead. He could sense Hulk's thoughts telepathically, *You shoot. I shoot.* After all, they were twins. No amount of plastic surgery could alter the blood that pumped through their veins.

Samson took inventory of the situation. Hulk was legal. He was not. They were holding some change now, so he could make bond before they found out who he really was. As long as he didn't bang out with the big dogs. Time was of the essence.

So Samson made a decision.

He threw down his Tec-9.

Police clouded him from every angle, taking him into custody.

Chapter 17

Qwess awoke to a room full of balloons, get-well cards, and Lisa Ivory. Upon seeing him awake, Lisa began showering him with kisses.

"Good afternoon, handsome. How are you feeling?"

Qwess rubbed his head groggily. "Not too good. What's up? What's going on?"

"Well, what do you want to know? Where do you want me to start?" Lisa inquired. "You know you were shot, right?"

"No shit!" Qwess countered. "What are they saying, though? 'Cause I can't feel my leg. My shit is numb. My whole fuckin' left leg!" Qwess began to panic. "I'm scared to look down. Is it there?" He fanned his hands. Qwess was getting more excited by the second. "Is it there?"

"Calm down, baby. Calm down." Lisa rubbed him comfortingly. "Everything's going to be all right. They had to operate on your leg so it's still feeling the effects of the medicine. It's still there. Hold on a second."

Lisa went out the door. When it opened, Qwess could hear a lot of commotion in the hallway. Then the door closed, leaving him all alone in the room.

He took the time to check out his surroundings. There was a vast array of flowers displayed throughout his room. Immediately, he spotted a bouquet of black roses. Qwess had been in the streets long enough to know what that bouquet symbolized. In fact, he had sent a few in his time himself. It was sent to announce to the world that a hit had been made. Normally, it was done when the hit was a success. In this case, Qwess assumed someone wanted to send the message that the violence wasn't random. This was a planned assault.

Qwess noticed the television was still broadcasting the news of the incident, trumpeting his misfortune like a sport. Incensed, he changed the channel, only to be met with the same press game on different stations. When he couldn't take it anymore, he flipped off the tube. Just as he was about to lie back down, Lisa busted back in the room along with his mother, father, Doe, Niya, and Hulk, who posted up by the door.

"*As-salaam alayka*, son!" gushed Qwess's mom, running to the bed to hug her son.

"*Wa alayka salaam*," Qwess returned weakly.

"How are you? We returned as soon as we heard. We've been here all day waiting for you to wake up. What happened? I told you those streets don't mean you no good," Aminah scolded.

"Aminah, give the boy a break," Khalid swore, as only a husband to a wife could.

Niya came over to extend her regards, as did Doe. There was a lot to be said, so Khalid dismissed all the women. When the door closed, only Hulk, Doe, Qwess, and Khalid remained. Khalid pulled up a chair next to the bed and began the meeting.

"Who do you think did it?" asked Khalid with cold sincerity.

Qwess was pressed as far as answers were concerned. "I don't know. I have an idea."

"The white chick?"

Qwess nodded.

"Um-hmm. I thought so, too," Khalid agreed. "Well, that's not the biggest concern. Do you know about what else happened the other night?"

Qwess shook his head slowly. Khalid called Doe over to relay what had transpired two nights ago after Qwess was dragged inside. Qwess listened with a heavy heart as Doe told him Reece, Samson, and Hulk were all locked up on weapons violations that night. Hulk had just made bond that morning and headed straight over to the hospital to stand guard at Qwess's room against any more attempted attacks.

"So, what's up with Reece? Why isn't he out yet?" Qwess asked.

"Well, the feds trying to drag him through the mud a bit because of his felony conviction. You know he not supposed to be carrying any weapons. Plus, they trying to get his ass behind that Crescent Crew stuff anyway." Khalid chuckled a bit before continuing. "Ole Prosecutor Long still want him. He the same fool that was after me all those years. Don't matter, though. They'll have to give him bond, eventually."

"Hulk, tell 'em what happened to you," said Doe.

"Aw, man. Those bastards just knew they hit the jackpot. They kept harassing me thinking I was my brother. They showed me pictures of dead police in Mexico, talking 'bout they finally got me. They moved him up to number two on the FBI's most wanted list."

"Damn, we gotta get him out before they make the connection," Qwess said. "Surgery can only hide so much." Even injured, Qwess was loyal.

"I don't know how. It's going to be a little harder than we thought. For some reason they won't give him a bond," Khalid stated flatly.

Samson was led into an interrogation room in chains at the Fulton County Detention Center. An officer was on either side of him holding his massive arms, guiding him. He took a seat in a room that contained a long metal table with chairs bolted to the ground on opposite ends. One wall was dominated by a long mirror, which Samson assumed was a two-way mirror. Samson steepled his hands together as close as the tight cuffs would allow, then leaned back and waited. He knew it was always best to let others speak, then decide which angle to go, based on what was said.

The officers chained Samson's leg irons to the floor, then left him. Moments later, two plainclothes detectives entered the room, a black one who was tall, dark, and almost as muscular as Samson and a small white cop with gray hair. The white cop spoke while the black one played the cut, looking menacingly at Samson, while flexing his muscles in his tight shirt.

"Now, Mr. Divine, let's get one thing straight right now. We don't believe your mother named you God Cipher Divine, or that Divine is even your last name for that matter. Furthermore, the only time a grown man trifles around without ID is when he is on the lam." The white detective pulled his sleeves up. "Now, what are you hiding from?"

Samson said nothing.

"Oh, you will tell us, or we'll find out eventually," the black detective swore, balling up his fist in threat.

Samson shot him a glance and scoffed. *Wish he would try that strongarm shit,* he thought.

Someone buzzed the room. The white detective excused himself, then returned minutes later with a package in hand. He wore a smirk like he possessed the Holy Grail.

"You still playing Helter Skelter, huh?" the detective taunted Samson, who remained mute. "I bet you wanna talk after this."

The detective poured the contents of the envelope on the table in front of Samson, while fixing his partner with a jackpot stare.

Samson looked at the photos as they fell and knew exactly what they were. Surveillance pictures from AMG's office cameras. On them, he, Gil, and Chabo shined bright as day. Like they posed for the pictures, their faces were unmistakable. Numerous still shots showed them tranquilizing the guards, ducttaping them, then putting them in storage closets. More shots showed them entering various offices looking for info. And the last frames taken in John Meyers's offices depicted them beating him mercilessly. A separate photo accompanied every blow delivered.

Someone had fucked up—*big* time.

Gil and Chabo were supposed to cut the power a good thirty minutes before they entered. The generator power was supposed to leave enough energy for work to be done, but not enough power to run their sophisticated security system. So they thought. Unfortunately, they thought wrong.

"Still nothing to say, tough guy? Oh, we're sure you got something to say now. Hmm?"

Samson smirked. "I want to talk to my lawyer."

Qwess was still receiving the run-down from Hulk at the hospital while his dad, Khalid, listened in silence.

"Then, to top things off, those two Mexicans keep calling, harassing, talking 'bout they had some business to take care of." Hulk was adding to the story. "Like I didn't almost get throwed. Ya feel me?"

Qwess didn't like the sound of things thus far. A night of celebration had turned into disaster. It seemed to Qwess that every time he was about to fly, something happened to attempt to bring him down.

"Where's Flame?" Qwess sat up higher in the bed to appear strong, but his ashen complexion betrayed any vigor.

"He out in the hallway. He been in here a few times, but you were asleep," answered Hulk. "You wanna see him?"

"Nah, I'll see him later. Is that all?"

"Pretty much," said Doe.

Khalid had been nursing his words until everyone said

their peace. When they were finished, he spoke, "Listen up, and listen well. Like I told Salim a long time ago, you can't play both sides of the fence. I know you thinking revenge, revenge, but that's not what's up right now. Even if we did know who did this madness, retaliation wouldn't be a good idea right now." Khalid looked at all of them before continuing. "At some point you have to decide to leave the streets in the streets. Ya understand?"

Qwess wasn't buying it. "Nah, Pop. They violated me! I didn't bring street shit—stuff—to them. They brought it to me."

Khalid shot him an accusatory glance.

"Well, I didn't do it directly," Qwess corrected. "But still, I might not ever walk again, and you telling me to let it ride? You didn't raise me like that, Pop! You didn't raise no coward!"

Khalid shot him an accusatory glance. "I'm sure once you calm down a bit, and think, you'll see it's best to hold tight—for now."

For the first time, Qwess caught the "for now" his father was using. They made eye contact, and Qwess got the message. His father wasn't saying not to do anything at all. He was just saying not now. Qwess caught the point. That's how old-school gangsters handled business. They may wait a couple years before they got their man, but in the end, they *got* their man. And they never, ever let their left hand know what their right hand was doing. The big guns were called in now, so he had to play by the big gun rules.

"A'ight. We'll let things play out," Qwess agreed, playing along. "We'll see what the cops can come up with. After all, I'm a legitimate businessman that's been assaulted. That warrants investigation," he added, feeling important.

Doe was relieved there would be no more bloodshed. In a way he felt responsible. If he hadn't persisted about relieving his wife of her burdens, this would've never happened. Still, if given a second chance, he would've done the same thing. Doe was finally realizing that everything in life had a price. There could be no progress without struggle. His only regret was seeing his main man laid up in the hospital and his cousin in jail.

However, these were regrets he could live with.

"Hey, brother, I wouldn't get too excited about them finding who did this. They still haven't found the killers of Pac and Biggie," joked Doe. Everyone laughed, and the mood was lightened.

There was a knock at the door. Hulk allowed the doctor entrance. He was holding a chart in his hand, his mood somewhat jovial. He addressed Qwess.

"Mr. Wahid, I have some good news and some bad news."

Qwess cringed.

"The good news is your surgery was a success. We were able to remove the bullet before it did major damage. However, it did some damage to your hip. Luckily, your periosteum prevented major damage. So, you should be able to walk with no problem once the cast is removed. Now, you may have a slight limp for a while, but other than that you should be okay in a few weeks. We'll transfer your therapy sessions to North Carolina for you, and like I said, you should be okay."

Qwess was relieved. No major damage, but there was something else.

"What's the bad news?" Khalid inquired.

"The bad news is . . ." The doctor removed his wire-frame glasses. "You have to eat this food for two more days. You can't leave until all your tests are completed."

A sigh of relief entered the room.

"Not so fast," the doctor advised. "There was an additional problem."

"What kind of problem?" Qwess demanded.

"Umm, can we get a little privacy please?" the doctor asked. "This is a private matter."

Qwess excused everyone until he was alone with the doctor.

"Talk to me, doc. What's going on?"

The doctor spoke softly. "There was a problem with your blood work. We had to send it over for more testing."

"More testing? What kind of testing?!" Qwess exploded.

The doctor measured his words carefully. "Well, we can't get a positive reading on your HIV test."

"That's good, ain't it?"

"No. Not positive in that way," clarified the doctor. "We mean it's inconclusive so we have to send it over for more accurate testing."

Qwess was on edge. He had hit a few broads raw-dog in his lifetime. More like a few hundred if getting brain counted. Excluding blow jobs, he could count ten right off that he had smashed this year alone. However, most of them were high-profile actresses and models. Surely, they didn't have anything. Did they?

"In light of everything, I'm sure this is the last thing you needed to hear. Maybe it's nothing," Doc reasoned. "But again, we have to be sure. Of course, all of this is confidential, so your lady friend doesn't know."

Qwess excused the doctor, leaving him alone with his thoughts. There was an eerie silence in the room as Qwess began to tally up the number of lovers he had been with unprotected. Who was he kidding? He couldn't begin to think of an accurate count. He had sowed his seed from Fayettenam to the Philippines and everywhere in between.

Guess when it rains it pours.

Chapter 18

Reece bopped out of Fulton County Detention Center a new man with his lawyer, Malik Shabazz, at his side.

It was a bright Monday morning. Reece had spent five days in jail. During that time the investigators had tried every tactic possible to break him. Out-of-towners had turned their city into a war zone, and someone had to pay. Especially rich, black out-of-towners. One may not know it by the bright lights of Atlanta, but racism was still very prevalent in Georgia. Driving ten miles outside of Atlanta, a black man was still liable to get hung.

Reece knew that Federal Prosecutor Long was still after him. Fortunately, this was not his jurisdiction, though he knew Long still wielded great weight.

In the end, his influence wasn't enough. They had to set Reece a bond. His charges: Possession of a Firearm by a Convicted Felon, Discharging of a Firearm in Public. Bond? Fifty Gs cash. No surety.

The magistrate grudgingly issued him a bond. He didn't want to, but with Malik Shabazz on the case, it was a done deal.

Malik Shabazz had been Reece's trial lawyer when he went to court years ago. It was Shabazz's spectacular performance that allowed Reece to get so light a sentence offered for a plea. Reece wouldn't have had to take it, had Long not rounded up Doe and Qwess on bogus charges. Nonetheless, Reece took it.

Since the trial, Malik Shabazz had amassed a formidable list of clients, wealth, and prestige. His name rang bells like those of Johnnie Cochran and F. Lee Bailey. When Malik Shabazz rolled into Fulton County heads turned. A star was in the house. The amount of time it took for the paperwork to be processed was how much longer Reece would remain in jail—not a second more.

Now, Reece and Shabazz proudly strolled to the parking lot to retrieve Shabazz's Jaguar, Shabazz in a blue pinstripe suit, Reece in his wrinkled green suit from the party.

No sooner than they settled into the plush confines of the Jag did Reece put the press on him about Samson.

"Listen, brother, you can't go back up yet until you get my man out," Reece pleaded when they left the parking lot. "Seriously, brah. Time is of the essence. Ya feel me? Whatever the cost, I got you."

"Relax, Brother Reece. They can't link that body to him. Look, it's a clean shoot. Your man, the security fella, is licensed to carry, as well as kill if necessary. Authorities found a gun on the dead guy, open-and-shut case," Shabazz explained. Then he added, "They're just giving him the runaround. If his lawyer representing him now can't come correct, then I'll step in, and believe me, brother, they do *not* want me to handle that." Shabazz slapped the leather steering wheel for emphasis.

Reece let it sink in. He did not know that Samson was being investigated and possibly charged with what happened in North Carolina. Therefore everything sounded good to him.

"This is a nice li'l car here," Reece commented, changing the subject.

"Thanks. It's an XKB. I'm glad you like it. You bought it."

"What?!"

"Ah, come on, brother, let's face it. Over the years you have made me a wealthy man. Not for nothing." Shabazz chuckled hungrily.

"A'ight. A'ight. I get it."

"Good. Do you want me to swing by the hospital to see your friend? He's being released today."

Reece looked at Shabazz skeptically, "How you know that?"

Shabazz tsked. "It's all over the radio. The main talk is about that singer, what's her name? She's a hot item in the press these days. I wouldn't mind that myself if—"

Reece glared at him.

"Anyway, everyone is over there. News, radio, paparazzi. Your boy has made good for himself."

Reece could imagine the scene: vultures everywhere taking advantage of his man to leech info about that broad. Nah, he didn't want any part of that.

Furthermore, he had more pressing issues on his mind. In his brush with death, he had had an epiphany, so he decided to follow up on it.

"Nah, I don't want to go over there. Let's hit the highway. I'll give him a call in a few hours."

Reece leaned back into the plush leather guts of the Jag. He had a lot on his mind. Right now, he needed to rest. He closed his eyes and zoned out.

Hospital staff and well-wishers waited at the door to see Qwess off. A lot of celebrities came through these hospital doors, but few caused as much raucous attention as Qwess. People from all over sent their regards in the form of flowers or cards. Phone inquiries numbered into the thousands. Media people stayed camped outside. Through it all, Qwess remained a gentleman. For that the hospital staff adored him. Even his girlfriend (everyone assumed), Lisa Ivory, Slasher Extraordinaire, was a sweetheart. Though she never left his side the entire time he was there, she never got in the way of the staff doing their jobs. She didn't throw any diva antics, either. For that, she had respect in their eyes.

It was checkout time for Qwess, and as Hulk pushed him toward the door in the wheelchair, he had a lot to be thankful for. He looked to his right at Lisa, who had rolled with him like a trooper throughout his whole ordeal. Qwess couldn't help but think how he had exposed her. Fortunately, his test came back HIV negative, but oh, the possibilities. Qwess shuddered to think of the thought! He was speeding on thirty-five with no kids to boot. Previously, that was how he preferred it. He had seen too many brothers crash and burn hitching to a woman, only to be dividing his possessions later. He always vowed that wouldn't be him. He wasn't changing his mind, but he couldn't help but wonder how long one could live dodging HIV.

When Hulk rolled Qwess through the revolving doors outside, he immediately spotted a hunter-green Rolls-Royce Phantom right in front of the door.

The car was sick, but Qwess wouldn't have noticed it twice had it not been for the red ribbon tied prominently across the hood. Being that they were in Atlanta, it could've been anyone's, but Hulk rolled Qwess right up to it. The moment Qwess was about to question Hulk, flashbulbs pulsed sporadically.

Lisa yelled, "Happy belated birthday!"

"What is this?" demanded Qwess.

"Your birthday present. You think I forgot you turned thirty-three two days ago? Nope, sure didn't."

"But this is a Rolls!" Qwess objected. He was thinking more like a $300,000 Rolls.

"And?" Lisa challenged.

"And, and. . . ."

"And nothing. You won't be able to drive yourself for a while, so I figured you and big man here can ride in style." Lisa took charge. "Don't even try to object, because I know this is what you like. You told me already so here it is. Happy birthday. Watch your foot."

Lisa helped Hulk place Qwess in the back seat while reporters looked on in envy and awe. Hulk popped the massive trunk, threw the wheelchair in, and then helped Lisa get in back with Qwess. Apparently, a throng of reporters had blocked the suicide door to ask questions. Hulk flexed bad one time, and the crowd parted like the red sea. Hulk tucked Lisa in, got in himself (with the ribbon still on the hood), and peeled out to I-85.

Doe was feeling re-energized as he luxuriated in new snatch. Dana turned around on him while he was up inside her and proceeded to ride him like a prize jockey while offering a splendid view at her beautiful ass. The shot was so good. Doe tried to think about boxing, baseball, vomit—anything—to keep from busting. Nothing helped. Just like the last time, he exploded again uncontrollably.

Doe had been with a lot of women before getting married, and none since. Before or since marriage, he had never, ever, had pussy so blazing! Dana's shit was tight, shallow, warm, wet, and she knew how to use her muscles. Really knew how to use her muscles! She had told Doe that she could pick a flat quarter off the ground, and flip it twice, using just her coochie muscles. After the way she rode Doe, he believed it.

See, Dana had this thing she did. She would sit all the way down on the dick, then rise up slowly, applying different amounts of pressure as she ascended. When she got to the head, she would wrap her lips around it and squeeze like she was milking a cow. All the while she would wrap Doe into those green eyes of hers. Talk about sex! To top things off, Dana was a real freak. She was down for anything—and she locked his toes. In fairness, Doe hit her off. He definitely didn't condone eating out, but after the things Dana did, it was the least he could do. She came again and again, too.

How did it get to this?

Upon returning to North Crack, Doe had to hook up with shorty. The black room episode had him open. He had to sample the goods, so he told his wife he was going to pick up Qwess from Atlanta, but instead he made a detour to Columbia, South Click. He had left Dana instructions at the Marriott desk on what to do when she arrived. She followed them perfectly. Doe drove a bucket and wore a low hat so as not to draw attention. The clerk still almost recognized him. He thought he had left a trail until she called him Ice-T. That was one time Doe didn't mind being mistaken for the Cali rapper. Other than that everything had gone off without a hitch. He had the plastic on extra-tight, and he practiced *fitrah*, or shaving of the public hairs. So wasn't any Kobe Bryant situation popping off. As long as Qwess hollered at him before he made it home.

Ah, shit! Qwess!!

Doe grabbed the phone from the bedside and dialed Qwess's cell.

"Come on, brother. Pick up," Doe begged. On the fourth ring Qwess answered.

"*As-salaam alayka.*"

"*Was alayka Salaam. Hablame en español,*" Doe suggested.

"Why? What's up?"

"Listen, don't call my crib until you see me."

"Clown, what you do?"

"Nothing."

"Nothing?"

"Nothing. Just don't call my house."

"Okay."

Qwess ended the call.

"Who was that?" Lisa wondered.

"Doe."

"Oh. Why didn't he want you to call his house?" she asked, to Qwess's surprise. He knew she was eavesdropping. He didn't know she spoke Spanish fluently. "Why you looking like that? Didn't know I spoke that, huh? Don't worry. There's a lot you don't know about me, but I will give you the chance to find out."

Lisa cozied up to Qwess, putting her head on his strong chest. His casted left leg was stretched out over the spacious ivory-colored back seat, while Lisa matched his position oppositely. Up front, Hulk navigated the behemoth like he had been born driving. Everyone was beyond comfortable traveling on I-20.

Then the phones rang again, one after the other. First Hulk's. Then Qwess's.

They answered them simultaneously.

On Qwess's phone was his father. Qwess yelled, "What?!" He couldn't believe the news. He and his father exchanged a few words before hanging up.

Qwess went to tell Hulk, but Hulk was still on his line talking. After a moment, Hulk hung up as well. His expression had changed drastically. Qwess knew that he knew also.

"Samson?" Qwess queried.

Hulk nodded.

"That was my father. He just told me. He also said that Reece posted bond a few hours ago. Matter of fact, he should beat us back to town."

"Uh-huh." Hulk nodded. His mood was somber because his brother was in danger. Samson was being extradited back to North Carolina to stand charges for the vicious assault on John Meyers. Samson had told Hulk about the photographs of the scene and informed him that the only charge that had stuck in Georgia was the gun charge. Therefore, Hulk had acquired a body in the line of duty. No doubt, it would greet him on the entertainment news shows upon his return home.

He was cool with it. He would take the blame for a hundred bodies if it meant keeping his other half free. From jump, Hulk was screaming that it was he who marked the would-be assassin. They didn't want to believe him, but had no other choice. Apparently, it was a clean shoot. A bodyguard protecting his client. Of course, po-po felt something else was amiss, but without evidence, they had to release him.

Now, his brother faced another dilemma, and there was nothing Hulk could do about it until they set a bond—if they set a bond. Not to mention the very real possibility of them finding out who he really was.

Damn, shit was getting thick.

The minute Reece was dropped off at home, he jumped in his Lac and headed to Fayettenam. He had to holler at Bone. Bone had been with Samson that night in Atlanta, but when the smoke cleared, he was nowhere to be found. Reece knew Bone wasn't soft. He had recruited him himself. However, things weren't right. Crescent Crew was taught to never leave a comrade in battle. Never. Bone wasn't just a member, he was a captain. Hell, he ran Fayettenam and the surrounding cities. Plus, he would be a heavy contender for boss of the Crew if something were to happen to Reece or Samson. And that's what was tugging at Reece.

Reece pulled up on Murchison Road Car Wash and spotted Bone right away. Stunting in his tangerine-colored '71 Impala, Bone drew all the attention. Of course, the top was dropped to show the white guts, and women surrounded the car. Bone was a millionaire a few times over. He had a big house out in the country, a small fleet of luxury cars, and numerous spots in different cities. Yet he could always be found on his block among the proletariat. The hood was his home, and no amount of paper was going to change that.

Reece crept up beside him in his Lac.

"Peace," Reece saluted.

Bone was a little shocked to see Reece so soon, but he took things in stride. "*Salaam.*"

"What's the bizness?" asked Reece. Bone had one of his young'uns riding shotgun, so Reece made sure to save his face. "I need to holler at you a minute."

"No doubt." Bone instructed his young'un to take a hike, then suggested Reece get in with him. Reece left the Lac where it was at, joined Bone in the street to talk. Reece wanted to know a few things about Bone and his allegiance. The best way was to talk to him.

Reece really wanted to leave the game alone. He was a wise man, so he knew if he played both sides of the fence, he would eventually fall. Yet he couldn't shake the pure adrenaline rush of killing. The arousal of being known. The luxury of knocking off the baddest chicks on the strength of who he was. Take for example the way the females who were around Bone's car when he pulled up now gravitated toward him. Sizing him up. Trying to glimpse their reflection on the diamonds in his teeth. Unfortunately for them, he wasn't interested in them.

Reece owed it to his Crew to make sure they were put in the best position possible before he deserted them. In theory, anyway. Truth was, he would never really leave. Crescent Crew to the death was his motto.

When Bone suggested Reece join him in the car, Reece initially hesitated. He despised drop-tops. They were so vulnerable. But when he saw they could get no real privacy any other way, with great reluctance, Reece joined Bone in the 'vert. Bone drove off in the direction of Fayetteville State.

"Yo, so what's the deal? What happened to you the other night?" Reece demanded. He was never one to mince words.

"Shit, my nigga, everything happened so fast. One minute we chilling in the Range puffing, next minute this nigga pulling a John Wayne! By the time I got around the corner, the Rollers had mobbed up. So I dipped. I figured wasn't no use in every-body going to jail. Ya feel me?"

Reece hesitated before answering. He was busy matching the events of that night with Bone's narration. It matched so far. "I feel ya," Reece finally said.

"So, what's up with Samson?" wondered Bone. "They gave him a bond yet?"

"Not yet. They just giving him a hard time now. He'll be home soon, though," Reece assumed.

"Word. That's what's up!"

Bone pulled over in front of a house two blocks down from the college. "Be right back," he told Reece as he jumped out, never bothering to open the door.

Reece watch Bone bowleg up to the house and still won-dered if something wasn't right. For all intents and purposes, Reece was out of the Crescent Crew—street side. So he tried to let it be. Unfortunately, he kept getting sucked back in. It was like things couldn't run right unless he injected his will into situations. Not that the captains were incompetent, but they seemed to lack the big picture. The Crescent Crew wasn't de-signed to be a run-of-the-mill street gang. It was designed to be an organization willing to do anything necessary to achieve greatness. The way Reece saw it, anybody could sell drugs or shoot somebody. It took something special to be a part of the Crew. Everyone always marveled at the Italian mob, but truth be told, they didn't do anything that couldn't be done by any other group, especially blacks. The same thing that made them such a force was the same things that other groups supposedly stood on: loyalty, respect, ruthless ambition, and knowledge of self. KOS was key because they understood who they were. More important than that, they understood that others knew who they were and hence weren't going to give them shit! If they wanted something, they had to go out and get it. The only thing given in life is life itself. Everything else is taken. That was Reece and Qwess's mind state when they founded the Crescent Crew. The early members understood this. Now, the ranks were flooded with a bunch of misfits, with the exception of a few notable standouts like Bone. The Crescent Crew was Reece's baby, and he refused to see it go the way of the mob.

Bone peeled out of the house just as quickly as he had gone in. When he jumped back in the car he had some news for Reece.

"Yo, dawg, them Mexican cats getting to be a nuisance," relayed Bone.

"Why, what's up?" This was news to Reece.

"Nuttin really. Them mu'fuckas just keep calling my spot with dat bullshit."

"What bullshit?'

"Looking for Samson. Talking 'bout they had something important to do, and us going to Atlanta fucked things up."

"What?! And?"

Bone nodded vigorously as he pulled away from the curb. "I know. I know. That's what I been telling 'em."

Reece was seething. "Let me talk to them fuckin' wet-backs," he swore. "Everything we do is important. Fuck they think they are?"

Bone liked to see Reece upset about the Mexicans. Maybe Reece could talk some sense into Samson about them.

"Man, the whole crew has been warning the brother about that, but he insist that that they his new business partners," Bone said. He turned onto Pamalee Drive heading toward the mall.

"Business partners?" Reece frowned. "Ain't no business partners outside of the Crew. Now I let that shit ride because I believe in a man making his own bread, but the Crew come first. The Crescent Crew always come first!"

Reece paused to let his words sink in. Bone loved it. This did not sound like a man on the verge of losing his edge.

"What kind of business is it anyway?" Reece asked.

"Don't know. From what I'm told it's a 'bag or tag' operation in Mexico."

"Bag or tag?" Reece wasn't stupid. "Bag or tag" was a kidnap scheme where someone would kidnap someone dear to someone else for money or favor. Reece had pulled a bag or tag on one of the jurors when he went to trial. Bag or tag was profitable, but it was very risky. Too many uncontrollable variables, too many emotions. Too much attention.

"Yep," Bone said.

"Why would he risk that? He ain't hurting for money?"

"I believe—now I don't know for sure—Samson got a baby by one of their sisters in Mexico. The family was kind of poor so Samson threw the brother a bone. Gave him a way to make some money. Bag or tag is what's up in Mexico, so that's what they did," Bone explained.

To Reece this was bittersweet. He loved Samson for trying to give someone a chance just as Qwess had done for him and his brother Hulk so many years ago. Reece was all about helping the "little guy." By the same token, though, he did not need the drama. Sure, Samson was being housed with some Mexicans who looked out, but they were straight. Samson didn't owe anybody shit! Reece had made sure of it.

Then Samson's dick had to go putting him in debt. Reece understood perfectly the dilemma. Samson was put in. Mexicans were extremely family-oriented. By Samson knocking the Mexicana up, he had forever solidified a place in the family. The Mexicana had brothers (who were more than likely overprotective). What better way to woo them than by putting some cash in their pockets, making them men. Reece definitely understood the dilemma, but that was beside the fact. Wasn't no other outsider going to belittle the Crescent Crew.

"So, basically you saying they still doing this?" Reece asked.

"Yeah, I guess so. What else would they be talking about?"

"Well, it don't matter. Samson got other issues now."

Just then Bone's c-phone rang. When he answered it, Reece could tell it was a woman by the way Bone spoke. Then, suddenly, his tone changed. He was practically screaming while at the light on Skibo Road.

"Yo, who the fuck you talking to?" Reece prompted. Bone covered the phone and answered.

"The Mexican."

"Give me the phone." Reece grabbed Bone's phone.

"Hello?"

"Ello, ooh es dis?"

"This Reece. Who dis?"

"Ah, *mi amigo*. Ju jes de person I want talk to," Gil said in broken English.

"Yeah? What about?"

"It seems we 'ave a pro'lem, Vato. Ju see ween Monstruoso go weet ju, heem leave us weet a bag, ju know?"

"How is that our problem?" Reece asked. He was ready to put it down on these cats. Samson was Crew, and Crew first.

Gil chuckled lightly. "Aye, *mi amigo*. Ju no 'ave a pro'lem."

"Hell, you say?" Reece checked him.

"Ay. I do say. Monstruoso, heem and we partners. We 'ave much *negocios* in Mexico. Heem owe us."

"Hold up. Hold up." Reece had had enough. "First of all, Samson is in jail, so whatever plans y'all had, you can cancel. Second of all, Samson is our business partner, our brother. So, I don't give a fuck how much business y'all got in Mexico. Business here comes first!" Reece exploded into the phone. Passengers from other cars looked at him in the convertible with wild eyes. Reece looked in the side mirror and saw that he was foaming. He wiped his mouth and continued.

"Samson should be home soon, but when he do we got *business* to take care of, too. So, I suggest you fuckers head south of the border," Reece suggested.

Gil's tone was repentant. "Ju know, Vato, I sorry ju feel dat way. A man weet so many skeletons in is closet should 'ave more *respeto*. No worry. Ju weel soon, vato loco. Ju 'ave me respect soon," Gil promised.

"Yeah, well, fuck you very much! Hello? Hello? Bastards hung up," Reece told Bone. Then he remembered the other thing he had to handle. "Yo, take me back to my car. I gotta go handle something while I'm on this end," he said suddenly.

"A'ight. What's up with the Mexicans?" Bone was curious.

"Don't worry about it. You shouldn't hear from them again no time soon."

"Good."

Bone busted a U-turn in traffic to go back whence they came. Things were looking up. The boss was back in rare form, the infiltrators were out. Things couldn't get better.

But they could get worse.

Chapter 19

Doe and Niya were visiting Qwess in his home on the Wahid compound. Qwess was in his movie room surrounded by his nephews. They were watching *Goodfellas* on the movie screen. Qwess's leg was propped up on a futon, a bucket of popcorn sat in his lap. When he saw Doe and Niya, he happily ushered them in.

"Heey. *Salaam alaykum!*" Qwess sang. "Come on in. Have a seat. Keyshawn, go get more drinks." One of the twins got up to retrieve the drinks. "What's happening, good people?"

"Just chillin'," Doe offered. "Niya wanted to come see how you were doing. She hasn't seen you since we came back from Atlanta."

That was Doe's signal to Qwess: *Make sure you remember we came back from Atlanta together.*

"Oh, yeah, sis. I was kind of salty that you didn't come see me off from the hospital."

Niya blushed. "Well, somebody insisted on going by themselves. What was I to do?"

"I feel you," Qwess offered. He could sense that he was in the beginning stages of a jousting match.

"By the way, who all came back with you all?"

Here it comes.

Qwess was careful. "Me, Hulk, Lisa, and Doe."

"Um-mm."

"Why?"

"Just curious. Where is Lisa at, anyway? I heard about your gift," Niya said, changing the subject.

"She had to fly back to L.A. She wanted me to go with her, but I told her we got business to handle."

"Uh-oh. Sounds serious. Don't tell me Mr. Philanderer is turning over a new leaf," Niya joked.

"Nah, sis. It ain't even like that. She good people, though."

"A'ight, Qwess. Don't hurt my girl. She really dig you."

"Your girl?" both Doe and Qwess questioned.

"You don't even know her," Doe set the record straight.

"We kicked it at the party a little bit."

"What party?" Doe asked.

"You know the one last year. Anyway she's a friend in my head." Niya finally left it at that.

"Whatever."

Qwess decided to change the subject.

"Li'l sis. You know this here don't stop nothing." He pointed at his leg. "As soon as I can get off this dope, we gon' get it cracking in the studio. Gon' smash the game, too!" he assured her.

Each time Qwess mentioned his leg, Niya winced. Deep down inside she felt that she was responsible. Additionally, it could have easily been her husband that had been hit. No one had told Niya what transpired to get her off AMG, but she knew something real gangsta had gone down. When Linda Swansen had called and cursed her out with threats, Niya knew things were serious. People didn't get that upset when regular business deals went wrong, so that tipped her off. Her suspicions were confirmed yesterday when she learned someone was in custody for the beating of John Meyers. When

Samson's mug shot flashed on the screen, Niya easily put two and two together.

"Qwess, I know we are gonna smash the game," Niya agreed. She paused a second, taking Qwess's hand into hers. "I really appreciate everything you've done for me, too. I really do. And I'm sorry about your leg." This was all Niya said, but she was also thinking about how he was covering for her husband. However, she would let that ride for now.

"It's nothing. I'm sure you would do the same for me." Qwess readjusted himself in his seat. He was uncomfortable with the way Niya peered at him. Like she was looking for something in his eyes.

"Have you heard from Reece?" Qwess asked, looking at Doe. Anything to change the subject.

"Yeah. He's with his son. Ever since he came back, they've been inseparable."

"I still can't believe that girl just gave up her son like that." Niya shook her head.

"Hey, seeing is believing," quipped Doe. Qwess said nothing. He knew something still was not right about that.

"Anyway, me, him, and Amin supposed to get up later to discuss some things," Doe volunteered.

"Does he know about Samson being extradited back to face charges on that AMG stuff?"

"Yeah. He vexed and worried, too. He told me something about cursing out those Mexican cats."

"Word?" Qwess was surprised. "What for?"

"Don't know." Doe shrugged. "All he said was he put him in his place."

They talked a little more about catching up on things. Then Qwess asked Niya to excuse them.

Niya left the room in a huff. When Qwess and Doe were alone, except for the twins, Qwess pulled Doe closer so he could whisper. Qwess had picked this up from his father.

Somehow it made things seem urgent, which suited things perfectly.

"Talk to me, bro. Who is she?" Qwess asked in a scolding tone.

A load was lifted from Doe's shoulder. Surely, he could tell Qwess how he felt. He of all people would understand the inevitable draw of a beautiful dame. Doe didn't know what had gotten into him, but he had to have Dana.

"Aw, man, you remember ole girl from the video?"

"Which video?"

"Flame's joint 'Lusting.'"

"The Hawaiian broad?" Qwess smiled.

"So, you feel me." It was more of an affirmation than a question. "Brah, I just had to have her. Remember the night of the party? Brah, the broad sucked my shit like a pro . . ."

'Cause she probably is a pro, Qwess was thinking.

"I didn't hit that night, but that was the beginning. She tutored me right in the black room. Shit was so erotic!" Doe gushed.

Qwess listened but didn't like it one bit. This was not Doe's game. Doe was the balance, the stability. Plus it had been a while since he played out in the rain. He was liable to drown.

"Dude, dude, dude, listen." Qwess shook his head repeatedly. "This is not what's up," Qwess stated firmly.

Doe looked at Qwess, shocked. He thought Qwess would be happy for him. After all, wasn't it Qwess who always joked about him being stuck with the same trap forever?

"You smarter than this. You a married man, brother."

"But wasn't it you who said marriage is a prison?"

"Yeah, man, but that was from my point of view. That was because I'm too selfish to commit to one woman. You're stronger than me. Smarter than me . . . Brother, you gotta end this," Qwess decided.

"But she makes me feel so good!" gushed Doe.

"That's all the more reason you gotta end it," persisted Qwess. "Brah, you are married. To a beautiful woman who worships the ground you walk on. Now is not the time to start fucking that up."

Doe finally relented. "I know all that, but—"

"But nothing! Look at all the shit we went through to get her straight." Qwess focused on his leg. "That was because she family. Niya good peoples, and I won't lie for you again. So tighten up," Qwess snapped.

Damn, that was harsh. Doe couldn't understand why Qwess was flipping on him. After all the times he had had his back? Doe didn't realize that Qwess admired his resolve. Respected his chastity. Especially in a sex-driven industry like modern hip-hop. Doe didn't understand that not thinking rationally could crumble everything that they had accomplished. The very thing that some had risked their lives to see brought to fruition.

After such a strong lashing from his best friend in the whole world, Doe was ready to leave.

He stood to leave. "A'ight. I got you, brother," Doe said, giving Qwess dap.

"Do you really?" Qwess wondered.

"No doubt."

"A'ight then. Go handle your business. Go make your wife feel special." Qwess patted him on the back.

Doe left to join his wife. He had understood everything Qwess said, but right now his passions were his lord. Try as he might, he just could not extract Dana from his mind. Her smell. Her softness. The way she moaned in desire.

Shook in ecstasy. All this made for an intoxicating package that was truly unforgettable. Yet he knew he had to let go. He loved his wife. And though Dana made him feel like a teenager again, he wasn't. He was a grown-ass man who understood that what happened in the dark eventually came to the light.

Eventually.

★ ★ ★

"Pow! POW! Pow!" The gun erupted. "Look, Daddy, I shot you."

Reece snatched the gun away from Prince.

"Stop, son. You're not shooting nobody. What's wrong with you?"

Little Prince was visibly disturbed. He went to pouting immediately. "But I heard you shoot people. I want to be just like my daddy."

"What? Who told you that?"

"She did." Prince pointed at Vanilla, who was sunbathing by the pool.

"Prince, go inside and play," Reece ordered. "Now! And give me that." He snatched the toy gun from his hand.

Reece stormed over to Vanilla and snatched off her sun visor. "What the hell is wrong with you telling my son I shoot people!?"

"You do," Vanilla stated flatly. "I just thought the kid should know who his daddy is."

"You don't tell my five-year-old son that I shoot people!" Reece was livid.

"Don't you want him to be just like you?"

"Hell, naw! I want him to be better than me."

"You didn't turn out so bad," Vanilla reasoned.

Reece looked at her like she was crazy.

"I didn't turn out so bad? I'm a dope-dealing murderer! Fuck you talking 'bout?!"

"It didn't seem so bad before. You wore it like a badge of honor. Besides, you haven't done so badly for yourself." Vanilla gestured at the spacious mansion.

Reece shook his head defiantly. "Don't get it twisted. I was dealt my cards, and I played them. But this life isn't cool for everyone, especially not my son. Nah, I want him to be better than me. I bloodied my hands so he won't have to."

Vanilla had never seen this side of him before. King Reece

was never repentant. In fact, she didn't believe him this time, either.

"Whatever, nigga," she told him.

"What?" Reece stalked her lounge chair. "What you say?"

"Nothing." Vanilla attempted to cop pleas, but it was too late. Reece scooped her in one motion and threw her into the pool. She hit the cool water with a big splash.

"Don't talk slick to me," Reece commented as he went to join his son inside his mansion.

Reece found Prince in front of the PlayStation as usual. Reece flipped the screen off.

"Let's talk, son."

Prince sat on his father's lap. "What's up, Dad?"

Reece grinned at how grown his son seemed. Wouldn't be long before he was causing problems.

"I was serious about not shooting no one. That's not cool. You're going to be a lawyer or something. Not a gangsta. A'ight?"

"But, Daddy, you're a gangsta," innocent Prince acknowledged.

Reece couldn't fool this one. "True," he admitted.

"So, why can't I be like you?" Prince wanted to know.

"Because you can be better than me. I'm gonna make sure of it. Besides, gangstas need lawyers. You can take all their money legally. And that's really gangsta!" Reece coached his son.

"Okay, Daddy. If you say so. Daddy, when is Momma coming back?"

"Tomorrow."

It was true. Reece had been giving his life a lot of thought. The shooting in Atlanta, Samson in jail, the crew under siege . . . It made Reece ponder things like life and happiness. He concluded that he was happiest when he was with Katrina. He had found himself looking forward to their time together. When he visited her in her bunker, as medieval as it was, it felt like a vacation to him. The conversations they engaged in were like salve for his soul. She had shown her growth, and even challenged him on some things.

When his life flashed before him in Atlanta, the happiest moments in those quick snapshots were with Katrina. He could no longer deny it, he was at his best when he was with her.

It was then he realized he really cared for her. More than any woman since his mother.

He also realized the only way his son would have a chance in this world was with his mother in his life. Reece had damaged enough lives in his lifetime to warrant saving one, especially his own flesh and blood. During his twisted plan of retribution, Katrina had proven herself tougher than most men he knew. For that she deserved a chance to live. Only with him, of course. Any jumping ship would result in an immediate death sentence.

As far as how he looked in the eyes of his comrades, fuck 'em! He was the boss. He couldn't pardon who he wanted? What was the use of being boss if you couldn't make executive decisions?

Reece had indeed made up his mind. The only way to live the present and prepare for the future was to leave the past in the past. So, if Katrina could forgive his transgressions, he could forgive hers.

First thing in the morning, Reece planned to find out.

Destiny writhed in pain as she rolled over on the bed. Her stomach felt as if someone were inside trying to slice their way out with a razor. Her body felt weak because she'd had a horrible bout of diarrhea. As if the pain wasn't enough, her resolve was weakening. It was one thing for her to be strong in the presence of Reece, but in truth, she was growing tired of her predicament. She missed her son like crazy, and she was beginning to doubt Reece's sanity. What type of man would subject a woman to these types of conditions? What kind of man would risk the life of the mother of his child for a vendetta? Had he no heart?

During their talks when Reece visited, Destiny remembered why she had loved Reece so much at one point. However, it was moments like this she remembered why she hated him as well. Reece was an enigma, a complicated man who lived life to the beat of his own drum. With the psychology that he was attempting to inject into her mind with the literature he brought her, she was able to delve deeper into his mind. She concluded that there was a thin line between genius and insanity. But was this roller coaster worth it? Should she give up the fight and succumb to Reece's crooked vendetta or should she continue to hold strong for their child?

A terrible pain ripped through her stomach again. Destiny clutched her belly and prayed to God for help. She knew that she did not have much fight left in her.

Chapter 20

Reece walked into the master bedroom in his mansion and found Vanilla relaxing inside his Jacuzzi. She was smoking a blunt and sipping Cristal champagne from a flute while she watched the movie *Paid in Full* on the huge television hanging on the wall.

"Hey, babe, watching this has me thinking about you. You should do a movie on your life," Vanilla suggested.

"You think so?" Reece gave a half-hearted smile. His heart was heavy, his mind was scrambled, but his conscience was about to be clear.

"Yes, definitely!" Vanilla assured her. "The life you've lived, and the way you built the crew, it's worthy of a movie."

Reece sat beside the tub and took his shoes off, then he dipped his hand in the water. "I might think about that one day."

Vanilla stroked his arm. "What's wrong, my love? Something's on your mind."

"That obvious, huh?"

"Yeah, it is." Vanilla beckoned him toward the water. "Come tell me about it. Let me wash you while you tell me about it, then I can give you your surprise."

"Surprise?"

"Yep, you know it."

Reece stripped and joined Vanilla in the water. He sat between her legs, leaned his head back on her chest, and exhaled a sigh high into the air. He grabbed the blunt, and he puffed away in silence, mulling over his predicament.

Vanilla had been loyal to him for years. She had done more than prove herself to him prior to his incarceration, and she had proven her worth in more ways than one. True, she used to be a stripper. True, she wasn't what one would consider good stock when it came to becoming a wife, but Reece himself was off the beaten path. He wasn't a traditional man, so a traditional woman would never be right for him anyway.

"So are you gonna talk or what?" Vanilla asked as she rubbed suds on his bald head.

"Just thinking about everything." Reece whispered.

"Like?"

"Yo, you ever had a family?" Reece asked suddenly. "Like, a real family—mother, father, the whole nine?"

"Where is this coming from?"

Reece shrugged, "Just thinking about life, ya know?"

"I see," Vanilla said. She sighed and took the blunt from Reece. She inhaled deeply and watched the smoke rings waft into the air.

"Well, my father broke my heart before any man could," Vanilla whispered. "He made me promises and broke them repeatedly. I mean, when he was good, he was great, but when he was bad, he was horrible. He drank—a lot—and he was an occasional drug user," Vanilla shared.

"One night, I must have been around eight at the time, he came into my room and just stood over my bed staring at me. At eight, I already had a little ass and titties for my age, but I was still clearly a little girl. So anyway, while I was fake asleep, he slid under the covers and began touching me. I'm thinking, this is my daddy so the touches can't be wrong, right? Well, the more he touched me, the more it became clear that the touches were inappropriate—"

"Yo, you don't have to tell me any more."

"No, Reece, I want to tell you," Vanilla insisted. "I've shared so much with you, I want you to know who I really am. You know Vyshay; I want you to know how I became Vanilla."

Reece shook his head and smoked the blunt, still deep in thought. It was true that he didn't really know her. All those visits, and they never talked about her. It was always him, and what his dreams and aspirations were. They had discussed his past, his violent climb to the top. Reece discussed murders with her in vivid detail, things he had never told anyone. They had laughed on visits discussing murder as if they were talking about the latest television show. Vanilla never appeared to judge him; she never even blanched when he told her how he had cut a man's throat in front of his three-year-old child. Vanilla was just as twisted as he was. She was more like one of his niggas than his woman. She just happened to have a wicked vagina.

"Damn, that's fucked up, Vee," Reece whispered. "But let's not talk about that anymore. If you want me to, I will hunt that bastard down and cut his dick off," Reece volunteered.

Vanilla's gaze fell off into the television. "No need; I already did it."

"Word?"

"Yeah. I ran away from home when I was fourteen. Started stripping to provide for myself. One night, this sick bastard came in the club and paid for a lap dance with me. Then, he offered me two hundred dollars to go back to a hotel and trick with him. Said he was addicted to my good pussy. Well, I went back to the room, took his money, and then I took his dick. Yep, I put something in his drink and knocked him out. He thought I was going to give him some head. He closed his eyes, and I sawed that motherfucker off with my blade and watched him bleed to death. It was the best orgasm I ever had.

"I left New Jersey after that and moved to North Carolina. I started dancing here immediately and met you a year later."

Now it all made sense to Reece. Vanilla was attracted to him because she knew that he would protect her. When he first met her, she was actually trying to *break herself* to him. (She had offered to give him the money she made that night to go with him.) Reece's name was bubbling in the streets, and she wanted in. She was loyal to him because he was everything her father wasn't.

Vanilla passed Reece a fresh blunt and washed him while he puffed in silence. On the screen, Rico killed Mitch, and Reece scoffed—just as he always did at this part of the movie. To him, disloyalty was an unforgivable sin, which is why his heart was heavy.

A knock at the door interrupted Reece's thoughts. He craned his head back to Vanilla. "Yo, who is that?"

Vanilla smiled. "It's your surprise."

The door glided open and in walked an exquisite form of feminine perfection. She was tall with lean muscles in her legs flexing as she walked. She wore nothing but a long, sheer lime-green wrap that contrasted with her dark skin. As she walked to the tub to meet them, she exposed her bald vagina.

"Whoa, what's this?" Reece said with a chuckle.

"It's your surprise. We haven't gotten down since you've been home, so I wanted to give you a gift."

Reece didn't understand what was going on with himself. He didn't recognize what he was feeling. Here he was faced with two of the most beautiful women in his world—one of them strange pussy at that—the fruits of his labor, yet he couldn't bring himself to arousal.

All he could think about was Destiny.

She had plagued his thoughts, haunted him. He could no longer deny that he wanted to be with her. He had come to visit Vanilla to tell her what he planned to do about it. Then she hit him with this.

The exotic woman stood in front of the Jacuzzi and disrobed. She took a moment to pose for her audience. She knew she was bad and she wanted them to pay homage to her beauty. Reece picked himself out of his funk to admire the visual orgasm standing before them. He *was* still a man. His eyes roamed the curves of her body, from the smooth chocolate skin covering her six-pack to her muscular quads. Her high cheekbones and hazel eyes spoke of her exotic pedigree.

"I flew her in from Brazil just for you," Vanilla whispered, confirming his suspicions. "She doesn't even speak English. I paid for her for you . . . us."

The beauty climbed into the Jacuzzi and joined Reece and Vanilla. She waded through the misty water like an apparition drifting into Reece's arms. Her skin was supple . . . soft . . . and she smelled like heaven on earth. She wrapped her arms around Reece's neck and kissed him passionately on the mouth. Reece's manhood rose out of the water and touched her slit.

"I had her tested, my king. She's clean. You can fuck her raw . . ." Vanilla whispered in his ear from behind. They were in tune with each other. Everything he thought, she verbalized for him.

Vanilla floated around Reece and sank under the water. Seconds later, Reece felt her warm lips wrapped around his hardness. As the Brazilian beauty kissed Reece and massaged his shoulders, Vanilla sucked him with her familiar mouth. Reece caressed the soft cheeks of her perfect ass and slid a finger inside her tightness. She felt as if she had never been defiled.

Vanilla came up for air and gauged Reece's reaction. She knew Reece, she could tell he wasn't the same. She felt as if she was doing something wrong, as if he was numb to her pleasures, so she shifted the new beauty into his lap. Vanilla guided the Brazilian onto Reece's dick slowly. The woman hissed in ecstasy and laid her head back. Her long tresses fell into the water as she rode him slowly. Vanilla sank underwater and found their connection. She took Reece's heavy balls into her mouth and suckled him while the beauty rode him. To her surprise, she felt Reece's dick thump her cheek.

He had gone soft.

Vanilla came up for air and stared at Reece. "What's wrong, Reece? Do you not like her? Is she too dark?"

Reece leaned his head back and sighed. "She's fine. She is gorgeous, Vee. You did good."

Vanilla was confused. Reece never had erectile problems. He could go for hours, and the only thing he loved more than fucking one woman was fucking two—at the same damn time.

"So what's wrong?" Vanilla grabbed Reece's limp dick. "This isn't you."

"Nah, it's not that."

"So what is it?"

Reece shook his head. "I don't even know."

Reece was telling the truth. He didn't know what was wrong. He had never experienced true love, the ebbs and flows, the incredible highs and lows that love brings. In his life, everything was black and white (and green). Love was intangible and could not be quantified. It just . . . was.

"Maybe it's the water," Vanilla suggested. "Let's go to bed."

The trio ventured to the bed. Vanilla guided Reece to lie on his back. Both women caressed him simultaneously. Vanilla took one side while the Brazilian took the other. The Brazilian took Reece's semi-flaccid penis inside her hands and massaged him to a firm erection. She placed her mouth on him and sucked him slowly. Her rhythm was slow and methodical. Professional. Reece's body responded to her skills and, despite his tortured mind, he began to enjoy the escapade.

The Brazilian mounted him with a smile. She positioned her wet slit on the shaft of his dick and moved slowly up and down the length of his shaft, never allowing himself to glide inside, teasing him. She lifted slightly and took his head inside her tightness. Reece moaned and groaned. The feeling was exquisite, but he couldn't get in the mood. Physically his body was there, but for the first time in his life physicality wasn't enough.

He closed his eyes to savor the moment, and a vision of Destiny popped inside his head. He grunted. The women thought he was groaning out of pleasure, but it was pain that birthed his grunt.

The Brazilian took his grunt as her cue. She went into her bag and pulled out all her tricks. She squeezed him with her vaginal muscles, she licked her full lips, and kneaded her firm, supple breasts, but Reece never saw any of her moves. His eyes were closed and he was in his head. Inside his mind, he was inside of Destiny.

He had broken the threshold.

All of this time, he wasn't sure if he could be with Destiny because he couldn't see himself being intimate with her. Their relationship had been based on love, and their sex was a byproduct of that love. Because of her betrayal, his heart had shut down to sex with her. Now, because of the near death experience, he had been liberated.

Reece stopped the women from pleasing him. He removed himself from the room and walked onto the balcony to process his thoughts. Now that his decision to be with Destiny was final, there was only one thing left for him to do.

Reece's empire only held room for one queen. Sure, he would allow himself paramours, but none of them could know the things that Vanilla knew. Over the years, Reece had confided in Vanilla because he couldn't foresee a day when she wouldn't be a part of his life in some capacity. This was before he realized she loved him. It was obvious and undeniable now. Vanilla loved Reece, but Reece loved Destiny.

This was a problem.

"Hey, baby, are you okay?" Vanilla had joined Reece on the balcony. She had wrapped a satin robe around her naked body.

Reece looked over his shoulder. "Yeah, I'm good. Where is ole girl?"

"She's getting dressed to leave now. I figured you wanted us to be alone."

Reece chuckled. "Yeah."

"You ready to talk to me?"

Reece glanced at her. "Not really, but I guess I need to."

"What is it, Reece?"

"Destiny." He said the word as if it would make everything clear, but it only confused Vanilla more. She had no idea about Reece's diabolical plan.

"What about her? Please tell me you finally killed her. I know you have your son, but I never asked what became of her. I assumed you killed her when you took your son."

"Well, I definitely tracked her down, but ahhh, I didn't kill her."

"You want me to do it?"

Reece closed his eyes and swallowed the lump in his throat. If he loved Vanilla at all, it was because of her unyielding loyalty.

"Nah, I took care of her. Sorta."

"Sorta? What does that mean?"

Reece was silent for a while. He couldn't bring himself to look at Vanilla as he bared his truth. "I couldn't do it," he admitted.

Vanilla scoffed. "You couldn't do it?"

Reece turned to face Vanilla. "The truth is . . . I still love her."

Vanilla's strong façade cracked. "Are you kidding me? You love her?"

Reece dropped his head. "Yeah, I do, and I plan to be with her after tomorrow."

"You're fucking crazy! Ain't no way!"

Vanilla stormed inside the room, leaving Reece in silence on the balcony. She returned minutes later wearing tight jeans,

Timberland construction boots, and a dark sweater. In her hands, she clutched a pearl-handled pistol.

"Where is she?" Vanilla demanded. "Tell me where this bitch is so I can do what you don't have the nuts to do. This bitch betrayed you, played you for a fool, and took your empire from you." Vanilla shook her head vigorously. "There is no way I'm going to let the man I love look like a fool out here any longer. *I'm* going to protect this thing *I* helped you keep together."

Vanilla paced back and forth on the balcony. "Now either you tell me where she is, or you can go with me and watch me do it. Either way, she has to go!"

While Vanilla ranted, Reece continued to hang his head. He was replaying all of their time together, all of the times Vanilla had displayed her loyalty to him. She had been more loyal than most men. And now he was going to repay her loyalty.

"Vanilla, calm down," Reece croaked. "Give me the gun."

"No, Reece, because you were just talking some weak shit just now, and over my dead body will you let this bitch live."

Reece shook away the lone tear in his eye and raised his head. "Yeah, you right. I was tripping," he said. "The bitch does have to go. Fuck was I thinking, yo? That's why I'm glad I have you to keep me on point. That's why I love you, Vee."

The L word had caught Vanilla off guard. "What did you say, Reece? You love me?"

Reece nodded. "Yeah, I do. Now let's go take care of our Destiny."

Vanilla beamed a beautiful smile. "I love you, too, Reece!' She wrapped her arms around his neck.

"Whoa, whoa, careful with that burner," Reece said, chuckling. He reached for the gun, and Vanilla loosened her grip on the weapon and gave it to him. "Come on, let me get dressed so we can handle this business. I know just where she is."

Vanilla turned to walk inside with Reece right behind her.

She was used to him walking behind her because he was always enamored with her wonderful shape. She loved to put a little extra twist in her hips when she knew he was watching. This time was no different. Vanilla twisted her hips as if she was trying to throw her hipbone out of place.

Reece wasn't paying attention to her hips. He was too busy aiming her pistol at the back of her head. Before Vanilla could take five good steps, Reece pulled the trigger.

POP!

Vanilla collapsed to the ground and rolled over on her side. Her body heaved and convulsed as her eyes flitted from Reece's face to the gun in his hand. She tried to say something, but her words came out as wheezes.

Reece bit his bottom lip and shook his head. A lone tear slid down his brown cheek. "Damn, Vee . . . I'm sorry, girl." Reece fired four more shots to her face, ending her suffering. There was one more round in the gun. For a split second, Reece thought about putting the gun to his own head. He felt like shit, and he thought about alleviating his pain the same way he had alleviated so many others in pursuit of Crew business.

But this was different. This wasn't for Crew business. This was for his Destiny.

Heavy is the head that wears the crown.

Chapter 21

Destiny awoke when she heard sounds. She had no time-piece. But based on her calculations from the sun's rising and setting, it had been days since she'd seen Reece, or anybody for that matter. Last time she'd seen anyone was when Samson came by, tossed her a pregnancy test, and said, "Reece said take this!" He slammed the door back and Destiny had not seen anyone since. That was a few days ago. Her food supply was short since she shared scraps of her food with the dog, and her patience was even shorter. She had gone along with this little charade, but enough was enough. She missed her son, her clothes, and she missed life.

Damn Reece.

When Destiny heard someone fumbling around outside, she just knew it was Reece, and she was going to let him have it. However, Reece never came in. Whatever it was he was doing, it had him perturbed. Destiny heard him fumble around the back of the bunker, but he quickly moved to the other side when the pit bull on that side threatened him. Destiny giggled at Reece's arrogance. What made him think he could come pet the dog after he hadn't fed him in days? Destiny's amusement ceased when she heard someone talking. Reece wasn't alone. She craned her ear to the window to listen. Destiny heard Reece go to the car. Then she heard him close the trunk.

She had been out of the field for a while, but her instincts were still intact. She inwardly praised herself.

Destiny heard two sets of footsteps at the door and stood readying herself. She was going to let Reece have it, no matter who he was with!

A pause at the door then . . . *BOOM! BOOM! BOOM!*

Three deep explosions blew the door off the hinges! The explosion blew Destiny back against the wall where she slid down. She was barely conscious, but when the smoke cleared partially, she saw two men standing in the doorway. In front of them lay the once-killer pit bull. The dog was dead, with shrapnel and gunshot wounds to his head and abdomen. One of the figures had a shotgun in his possession.

Destiny began to panic. This was not Reece. The only question was who was it?

Doe laid in amazement at the cosmic fellatio he was receiving. The rhythm was right, as was the pressure. In fact, everything was right, which was making the encounter even harder to bear.

Doe had snuck out earlier in the morning with the excuse that he had to see Reece about something. If Qwess wasn't down to lie for him, surely Reece would have his back. Besides, he only wanted one last romp with Dana before he ended things. He knew he couldn't turn a hoe into a housewife. He had married his wife for a reason. She was a keeper. She was special, she was loyal, she was smart. Yes, he had played outside his pasture, but now he was ready to return home to till his own land.

But first he wanted to roll in the strange grass one more time.

When Doe called Dana, she was available as always. She seemed like she lived for Doe's call. Doe laid his game down, and an hour later he was being pulled into a hotel room on the twentieth floor of the Hilton.

Dana wasted no time removing Doe's clothes and giving him what he came for, only how she could do it. When she sensed Doe about to peak, she stopped. This was Dana's specialty. Prolonged, delayed ejaculation made for a more intense orgasm.

She led Doe over to the balcony, to resume their intercourse outside. She wanted Doe to give her back shots while she overlooked the city. Doe obliged her happily. This was what made her memorable. Made her worth coming back for. Made her worth risking a marriage for.

Dana stopped Doe short of climax yet again and led him back inside. She wanted him in the shower. They went into the shower. Doe slayed Dana up against the wall. She then washed him, and they exited after tremendous luxuriating. Dana was drying Doe off when the buzzer rang. Thinking it was room service, he put on a robe to answer the door. He started to answer it naked he was feeling so good, but he thought better of it. He *was* a big-time music exec.

Doe swaggered to the door with big nuts and flung it open . . .

And Niya punched him dead in the face.

Gil and Chabo had gotten wind via television that they were wanted men. Samson's picture was being flashed on the tube every half hour with the word "Charged" tattooed at the bottom of the photo. Gil and Chabo didn't speak much English, but they understood what that word meant. When their pictures flashed right after Samson's with the word "Wanted" plastered across it, they understood really well what that meant.

It was time to get the hell out of Dodge.

They had no qualms about going back to Mexico. However, because their stateside partner was in jail, they had no way of getting to their real money. Samson had left them in a bind—broke and wanted, which was a deadly combination. However, the ingenious brothers devised a plan to put some money in their hands to flee the country with, and it involved King Reece.

Gil and Chabo had first discovered the bunker when Samson brought them along to drop off something for Reece. Samson's instructions were explicit to the brothers: This place didn't exist. He explained to them that Reece would spazz out if anyone came near who was inside. Gil and Chabo thought it was weird that the great King Reece would confine someone he loved to conditions so medieval. They dismissed their confusion as cultural misunderstanding at first. However, curiosity overwhelmed them, so they prodded a little further and found out that the person inside was actually the mother of King Reece's child.

That's when things made sense to them.

They figured that King Reece hid Destiny away from the world because he wanted to protect her from his enemies or the prying eyes of law enforcement. They labeled him a genius for the move, because no one would think to look for her out in the woods. Nobody but them. They figured that this was King Reece's hideout, and if this place was good enough to stash his woman, then surely his money would be on the grounds as well. If anyone knew where some of King Reece's fortune was hidden, it was Destiny. If they could convince Destiny to reveal the whereabouts of King Reece's fortune, they could be halfway to Mexico before anyone knew what happened.

The brothers staked the bunker out for a day, then decided to make their move. After a little observation, they ascertained the grounds were empty except for the dogs. Ready for war, they approached.

Gil grabbed the shotgun, Chabo the machete. On their way to the bunker door, Chabo sliced one of the dogs so smoothly, the animal didn't have a chance to yelp.

At the door, Gil charted out the hinges as he had done a thousand times in the past, aimed the shotgun accordingly, and pulled the trigger. *Voilà!* The door rocked from its hinges.

When the dust settled they stepped inside to find a lone woman cowering in the corner. The place reeked of feces, and a slain dog lay at their feet. They deftly stepped across the dog in the direction of the damsel in distress. Gil palmed her face, looking at her carefully. She was cute despite the ragged jumper she wore.

Destiny attempted to speak, "W-Where's Reece?" she sputtered, clearly befuddled.

Gil looked to his brother and smiled.

"He's not here, but I have a message from him." Gil paused a moment. "He said to take us to where his money is."

Destiny was confused. "What?"

"We can do this nice or the hard way," Chabo said as he approached Destiny where she cowered in the corner.

"Wait, so you don't work for Reece?" Destiny asked.

The brothers looked at each other and shared a laugh. "Not anymore!" they chimed in unison.

"We came for the money, *puta*! Where is Reece's money? Tell us and we will go."

Destiny frowned. "I have no idea what you're talking about."

Gil struck first. He lashed out with an open-palmed slap to Destiny's jaw. The blow echoed inside the tiny chamber, and Destiny slid across the bunker floor into the corner, sobbing pitifully.

"What are you doing?" Destiny cried. "No . . . no . . . please don't do this. I don't know anything about any money."

"You lie!"

The brothers advanced on opposite sides of her. Gil grabbed her left arm and Chabo tried to clutch her right, but Destiny maneuvered out of his clutches and kicked him in his legs. Chabo stumbled, but when he recovered he smacked Destiny in the face with his heavy hand. Blood poured from her nose as she tumbled back onto the bed.

"*Toma!*" Chabo yelled triumphantly.

Gil turned Destiny over and sat on her chest on the cot. He rained blows on her mercilessly. She attempted to shield her face with her hands, but a good blow slipped through her guard and knocked her in the head.

"Where is the money?" Chabo asked.

While Gil sat on her chest, Chabo ransacked the bunker looking for signs of a safe or a secret compartment. Meanwhile Destiny lay on the cot drifting in and out of consciousness, shaking her head slowly.

Suddenly Destiny gathered a burst of energy and rolled Gil off her chest. He tumbled to the ground, and Destiny managed to rake her fingers across his eye.

"Ahhh!" Gil yelled, clutching his eye. "*Chinga puta!* I'm going to kill you!"

Chabo rushed to his brother's aid and caught one of Destiny's legs. He dragged her over to the cot and kicked her in her midsection. Destiny rolled into the fetal position to protect herself from the blows. Gil and Chabo commenced to beating Destiny together, kicking her savagely.

Chabo wrapped his hands around Destiny's neck and hoisted her high into the air. "Last time, where is the money?"

Blood poured from Destiny's mouth, and a huge knot lumped up on the side of her forehead. She was dizzy but coherent. "I don't know where any money is," she insisted, then added, "And even if I did I wouldn't tell you—*puta!*" Destiny spit a huge gob of blood right into Chabo's eyes.

Chabo dropped Destiny to the floor and wiped the blood from his eye. As soon as she hit the floor, Gil was on her. He raised the butt of the shotgun high in the air and smashed it into her face. A sickening thud echoed throughout the bunker, and Destiny collapsed. Gil racked a round into the head of the shotgun and pointed it at Destiny's head.

"Wait, *hermano,* if you kill her then we cannot get the money. Let's tie her up and torture her. She'll tell us where the money is."

Gil turned Destiny's limp body over on her stomach while Chabo looked for something to tie her up with. Destiny stirred a bit, and Gil clocked her with the butt of the shotgun again.

"Careful, don't kill her," Chabo warned. He found a strip of clothing and began to tie her up.

Suddenly, they heard a car roaring down the trail.

"You dirty muthafucka!" Niya stole on Doe again, knocking him to the floor. She jumped on top of him and dug her nails into his face.

"I trusted you, you lying piece of shit!"

Hearing the ruckus, Dana ran from the bathroom naked. Her eyes locked on Niya, and she almost shit on herself. She tried to run back whence she came, but Niya caught her, wrapped her pretty hair around her hand, and commenced to wailing on her head while she dragged her toward the door.

"You trifling *whore*! You looked me in my face and now you fucking my husband?! I'ma kill both you no-good cheaters."

Niya dragged Dana out into the hallway naked, kicking and stomping the breath out of her. Niya was taking it back to B-More on that ass. "I ain't no punk bitch! I ain't no punk bitch!" Niya swore with each kick. Dana rolled around on the floor, maneuvering from the blows.

Doe recovered from his spot on the floor and tried to pull Niya back, but Niya would have no part of it. She stopped long enough to look at Doe and ask, "Oh, you trying to protect yo' hoe?!" After that, she was swinging again, this time on Doe.

Hotel security came rushing, followed by a man in a cheap suit. Cheap Suit rushed past security and yoked Niya up.

"Niya, please, you swore you wouldn't do this! Calm down," Cheap Suit begged.

Niya was still tripping, but being restrained, she finally stopped swinging.

Through blood on his face, Doe saw the man in the cheap suit calming his wife down. He didn't like it one bit.

"Who the fuck is this?" Doe demanded to know.

Reece whipped his Cadillac down the trail in a rush. He couldn't waste another minute. He had slept on his decision and felt even better about bringing Destiny home. He had had breakfast with Prince and dropped him off at his uncle Qwess's house. He left Prince with a couple hundred dollars in case he needed something while they were out, promised him a surprise, and jumped in his chariot to claim his queen.

Reece had finally realized the secret to a happy life. No matter how rich you were, how ruthless you were in the sight of your enemies, how respected, feared, or whatever, without someone to share it with, life was meaningless.

Reece had screwed women the world over, but never had he encountered chemistry like he shared with Destiny. Before she removed her façade or after. Reece didn't believe in soul mates, but what he and Destiny shared was undeniable. He couldn't hide it any longer. It was time for him to be happy.

What Reece saw when he rounded the bend to the bunker made his heart drop. Like a trained assassin, he took in everything with one good look. The late-model Chevy. The slain dog. The bunker door blown from the hinges.

Reece knew all along that this scene was not the work of the authorities. This was done by people on the other side of the law. Only question was who?

Reece palmed his .45 in his right hand and reached in the glove box for its twin. He exited the Cadillac cautiously to learn who had infiltrated the king's court.

Reece crouched low, scanning the grounds as he approached the bunker. He planted his back to the wall of the bunker and began sliding down the outside of the bunker checking for his intruders. Going down the east wall, he saw no one. However, he did see footprints. Two sets. Reece peeked around the corner before turning it. Coast clear, he slithered around with his two heaters spread out and leading the way. He resembled a crucifix on the wall.

Seeing nothing on the outside of the bunker, he carefully came around to the entrance. Reece peeked inside and lost it!

He saw the dog first, sprawled out on the concrete floor with a huge hole in his bloody head. A horrible stench singed Reece's nose. His eyes followed the scent, and there he saw the love of his life sprawled on the cot twisted up like a contortionist.

Reece raced inside, forsaking all danger, to Destiny's aid. He threw one of his pistols on the cot and grabbed her hand to check her pulse.

It happened so fast. A burst of pain hit Reece as a bullet slammed into his back. Simultaneously thunder boomed inside the bunker as Gil fired another shot and missed.

Chabo and Gil emerged from each corner of the bunker with their guns blazing. The shots turned Reece around, and he instinctively squeezed off a few rounds at them. The first shot imploded Chabo's chest. The rest missed their mark, as the cannons made their presence felt inside the cramped space.

Gil saw his brother go down and rushed toward Reece with his .38 blazing. Reece met him step for step, bullet for bullet. Five of each. The two collided into each other with Reece falling underneath the bigger Gil. Both men continued to pull their triggers. Unfortunately for Gil, his trusty .38 would be his downfall this day, for while he pulled his trigger, the hammer snapped and snapped with no report.

Reece's .45's answered each time he called on it. Seven more shots lifted Gil clean off of Reece's body. Reece turned over on his side and sent a fatal round to Gil's face.

As soon as he saw his bullet hit its mark, Reece collapsed on his back. Darkness threatened to envelop him, but Reece remembered Destiny and fought through the fog. He was losing energy rapidly. He didn't know how many shots he had taken and he didn't care. He had to check on Destiny.

Reece crawled toward the cot. He crawled until his knees collapsed. When he couldn't crawl anymore, he dragged himself toward Destiny on his arms. He reached her eventually but couldn't muster the energy to mount the cot. *Damn, why didn't he bring her a bed?*

Unable to mount the cot, Reece draped his bloody arm over the bed and paused to gather his strength. No matter how hard Reece tried and tried, he couldn't gather the strength to mount the cot. He was losing blood, and numbness and pain began settling in. His head swooned, and his face plopped on the floor with a thud.

Reece lay dying in his own blood, the love of his life inches from him yet so hard to touch. Unable to move, Reece allowed his eyes to wander across the floor. Maybe to take a last picture with him to the afterlife. Maybe because that was the only thing his sight would grasp. Nonetheless, they wandered.

His eyes caught the used ramen cups. The old jack-mac cans. The partially eaten cookies.

The EPT pregnancy test.

Reece squinted and saw the plus sign in the window. He heaved one last deep breath.

Then darkness enveloped him.

Doe and Niya were locked in a heated argument. The room had cleared out. All who remained were the chief of security, Doe, Niya, and Cheap Suit. Dana had been allowed to put on some clothes before being escorted off the premises. After much pleading (and a stack of hundreds) Doe had managed to stay in the hotel long enough to talk to his wife.

Doe held a bloody rag to his face while he demanded answers.

"I'ma ask you one more time, Niya, and I'ma fuck you up if you don't answer. I'ma fuck you up anyway about my face," Doe promised. "But I wanna know who this cheap-suit-wearing mu'fucka is?"

Niya looked at Doe like he missed the butt end of a cruel joke. "You still don't get it, do you?"

"Get what?!" Doe roared. He was getting more pissed off by the minute.

"Get this!" Niya reached into her Coach bag and started throwing pictures on the bed. "And this. And this. And . . . this!" She flung picture after picture on the bed.

Doe's mouth gaped open in surprise. On the pictures Dana was riding Doe. The pictures were taken from their Marriott episode. Obviously from an adjacent hotel window.

"I had you followed, you dirty bastard," Niya explained.

Then it hit Doe. Cheap Suit was a private investigator. He had been trailing Doe. That was how his wife found out about him being there.

Doe blanked out and charged Cheap Suit.

A couple minutes later, a gang of hotel security guards were pulling Doe off of Cheap Suit.

A hazy plus sign was what Reece saw as he drifted in and out of consciousness. The little bit of his mind that still functioned was bent on one thing: saving Destiny.

Reece felt his whole right side of his body in flames. His left side was numb. He moved his head a bit and saw that he still clutched his hammer in his hands. Looking up, he saw Destiny's bloody leg hanging from the bed. That one glimpse provided a much-needed adrenaline boost.

Reece reached deep inside his core where the spirit of a warrior resided and pulled out strength.

He stood enough to grab Destiny's leg and pull her down to the floor with him. She landed with a smack, in all his blood. Reece felt around for a pulse. A light thump greeted him, which was all the motivation he needed.

Reece began dragging Destiny out of the bunker, drawing inspiration from the countless stories he read of how Africans fought lions to save their loved ones. Reece felt if they could fight lions then he could brave gunshot wounds long enough to save his son's mother. Reece knew he was on borrowed time, but if he could save his son's mother, then he would sacrifice his life gladly. He refused to allow his son to be consigned to the same fate he had been as a child.

Emboldened, Reece managed to make it outside the bunker. The September air provided yet another renewal of energy. He dragged both of them to the Cadillac and managed to pull them up inside the car. He propped Destiny up in the seat be-

side him and fired the engine up. Destiny's arm fell over
Reece, and her cold flesh served as an eerie reminder of the
severity of the situation.

Reece sped down the trail with hazy vision, mercy alone
keeping him from crashing. Before long, he was careening
down a main highway, drifting in and out of consciousness, the
Cadillac swerving dangerously.

"Thank you, Mr. Wahid. If you'll just sign here, your out-
patient services will begin regularly as scheduled. Two days a
week, then less or more if needed."

Qwess took the paper, signed it, and returned it to the
nurse. "Thanks."

"You're welcome."

"Let's go." Qwess motioned to Hulk. Hulk turned the
wheelchair around toward the elevator and started pushing
Qwess toward the door.

"You ready to go shopping?" Qwess asked Prince, who
was right at his side the whole time.

"Yep, is Lisa coming back soon?" Prince asked. "She is
fine!"

Qwess couldn't help but laugh. Five years old and already
ready to be a player.

"She'll be here tonight," Qwess informed his nephew. "She
said she can't wait to see you, either. She has a surprise for you."

"Oooh, is she bringing my mom back? My daddy said my
mom will be home today."

Qwess rubbed his nephew's locks. "We'll see, nephew."

The elevator arrived. Hulk, Qwess, Prince, and a doctor
entered. The moment the elevator started descending an alarm
shrilled to life, followed by buzzers and sirens.

"What's going on?" Qwess asked the doctor.

"This is the emergency protocol," the doctor explained,

answering his phone. He listened to the voice on the other end, and his face turned red.

"What happened?" Qwess repeated.

"A car crashed into the building downstairs! They're evacuating the entire first floor downstairs! We have to go through the auxiliary exit. Come on."

The elevator slid open, and they followed the doctor through the alternate exit. The doctor showed them to the basement where they easily found the Rolls-Royce. Hulk loaded Qwess and Prince in and followed the instructions to the alternate route.

Traffic was backed up from the original parking lot through the alternate route.

When they rounded the corner to where the crash happened, Qwess strained to see because of the crowd of onlookers already cornered around the scene. It was too congested, so Qwess gave up. He reclined back in the chair to play Prince on the PlayStation system attached to the back of the front seat.

Hulk followed the traffic line a little more and was able to receive a clear view of the car smashed into the building. "Damn, that look like Reece's car," Hulk commented. "Whoever it is, they dead. Blood everywhere. I can see it from here."

Hulk wasn't lying. Blood was splattered on the windows so thick it looked like tint.

"Let me see." Qwess lifted up dramatically and froze. "Oh, shit! Not my brother! STOP the car! Stop the fucking car! That's him! That's him!" Qwess saw Reece being hoisted out onto a stretcher drenched in blood. "Let's go, man. Take me over there," ordered Qwess.

Hulk was already jerking the suicide door open and hoisting Qwess on his shoulder. Prince screamed in terror, bringing them back to reality.

"Hold up! He can't see this," Qwess said. "Just take me over there."

Hulk put Qwess back into the car. "I'll go see what's up and let you know," Hulk suggested.

Qwess wasn't too fond of the idea, but thought it best. If it was a dead Reece, Prince definitely didn't need to see him like that. "A'ight, hurry up."

Hulk ran through cars to the scene. He bypassed authorities and was able to see the Cadillac up close and personal. He arrived just in time to witness medics pulling another bloodied body from the car. It was a half-naked female. Upon closer inspection, Hulk realized it was Destiny. She was barely dressed. Her clothes were torn into shreds. *What happened?* thought Hulk.

The Rolls horn blaring snapped Hulk out of his thoughts. He peered over and saw Qwess hanging from the window with his phone smashed to his ear. Hulk ran back to the car.

"Yo, what's up?" demanded Qwess.

"It's him. Some strange shit going on. Ole girl messed up, too. Something happened. Blood is everywhere!"

Qwess covered his face momentarily. "Is he . . . you know?"

"Nah, I don't think so."

"Let's go find out. Doe on his way."

Doe bust through the hospital doors erratically with his wife trailing behind in a funk.

"Where is he!? Where is he?!" Doe demanded to know.

"Who, sir?" an attentive receptionist asked.

"My fuckin' cousin, Reece Kirkson! Where is he?!" Doe repeated. He was on the verge of tears.

"Sir, if you calm down I'll take you where everyone else is, but you must be calm," the attendant pleaded. She knew just who he was talking about. Ever since he and the woman were admitted three hours ago, they'd been the talk of the hospital. Cape Fear Valley Hospital had never seen so much drama.

Doe stepped off the elevator among friends and family. Everyone was present: Qwess, Hulk, Amin, Alysia, Fatimah, Khalid, and Aminah—everyone who meant who meant anything to their circle, including Flame and 8-Ball.

"Yo, what's up?" Doe asked. "How are they?"

Qwess rolled over to Doe in his wheelchair.

"It don't look good, brother," he informed him.

"What happened?"

"Nobody knows for sure, but Reece was shot six times."

"What?"

"Yeah. Shit is baaaad."

"So what happened?"

Qwess shrugged his shoulders.

"Damn."

Qwess looked closely at Doe. "What happened to your face?"

Doe looked away. "Long story."

"Um-hmm."

A doctor emerged from the back with a solemn expression on his face. He wanted to speak to Reece's parents. No one stepped up with that title, which didn't surprise the doctor. Young black men checked in to the hospital every day without parents.

Doe finally came forward. The doctor did a double take at the streaks of blood on his face, but said nothing of it.

"I'm his closest family," Doe said. The doctor nodded and took Doe back.

Upon entering the room, Doe observed two beds with all types of monitors attached to them. On the first bed was Destiny. The second bed contained a bloated man, who looked like Reece in the face, but this man was at least 350–400 pounds. Attached to both Destiny and the bloated man were every medical device possible, it seemed.

"So, you know the young lady also?" Doc asked. Doe nodded. "Son, I'm going to be honest, neither one of them should live another hour."

Doe's knees became weak.

"I'm sorry to sound so harsh, but I must be honest."

Doe nodded. "I understand, but where is my cousin?"

"Who?" The doctor looked at Doe strangely.

"Kirkson. Reece Kirkson."

"That's him right there." The doctor pointed to the second bed. Doe gagged aloud. *That monstrosity is Reece?* "The trauma to the body instigated internal swelling to protect the organs," the doctor explained.

Doe walked over to Reece's bed. He noted the weight gain due to the swelling. Even his lips were swollen and black. Bandages covered his entire middle torso, and his eyes were open in theory only. A glaze that covered his pupils indicated Reece was already gone.

A single tear dropped from Doe's eye.

Destiny began thrashing violently in her bunk, and Doe rushed to her bed. Destiny was conscious, although slightly. She recognized Doe through the drug-induced haze that had become her life.

She attempted to talk. "My son, t-take ca—" She coughed violently. Doe looked away until Destiny gripped his hand, determined to get her point across. She tried to speak again. "Promise me you'll get my son," she wheezed.

"I don't—"

"Promise me!" She repeated with all the strength she could muster. Destiny was determined.

Doe finally relented. "Okay," he whispered.

Destiny nodded weakly. Her eyes rolled back in her head . . .

The machine beeped incessantly as the doctor fiddled with the numerous devices to strive to alleviate the problems. Too bad he didn't realize Destiny had no more problems. Other doctors rushed into the room to help. While they did that,

Doe slipped back over to Reece. Looking at his cousin, Doe felt so many emotions, but one thing he knew for sure and two things for certain. One: Reece wouldn't want to live as a vegetable. Two: Reece wouldn't want pity. So Doe did what he knew Reece would want, if he could he speak. He waited until no one was focused on him and . . . he pulled the plug on the machine.

King Reece was dead within minutes.

Epilogue

One Year Later

Qwess exited the Aston Martin with his cane in one hand and his four-month old son, Reece, in the other. His wife, Lisa Ivory, shut the door, then helped him down the gravel trail.

Up ahead, Qwess could see his destination clearly. The green marble mausoleum shimmered in the September sun. Standing outside the tomb was Doe, who hugged Qwess, and Lisa, who hugged Niya while congratulating her on her pregnancy. She was expected to deliver any day, which was why Qwess and his family were in town.

Qwess had moved to Jamaica and split his time between there and L.A. After Reece's death, he needed to get away for a while, not just to recover physically but mentally as well. Lisa helped him in a big way. It was in Jamaica that she found out she was pregnant. Turned out the very first time they went to Jamaica, Qwess had impregnated her. After finding out about the pregnancy, they arranged to get married. Only immediate family were flown in for the ceremony. Lisa's childhood friend Ruquiya was vexed when she found out. However, when it was explained to her that the marriage wouldn't stop their thing, she fell in line. Qwess never pictured himself in a serious relationship with a bisexual woman, but Lisa possessed so many positive qualities that her lifestyle could be accepted also. Additionally, it kept excitement in the union. A man could tire of the same snatch every night, so with Lisa's "thing" he could have his cake and eat it, too.

"How was the flight?" Doe asked Qwess.

"Cool. It's always uneventful when you use the clear port." Qwess laughed.

"No doubt," Doe cosigned.

They began to talk about Reece, which caused them to reminisce about his and Destiny's funeral.

The funeral was one of the most lavish the Carolinas had ever seen. Destiny and Reece were put to rest in a specially made casket that allowed them to be side by side inside of it. Of course, the entire Crescent Crew was there, except Samson. He was just being extradited back to North Carolina from Georgia to stand charges on the incident he was eventually convicted and sentenced to fifteen years for.

Some of the older members of the crew objected to Destiny being buried with Reece. After all, she was part of the reason Reece fell. The only chink in the armor of the Crescent Crew. However, after Qwess took it back and got real gangsta, they calmed down and let things go unencumbered. One of the most respected gods from up top delivered Reece's eulogy. After Born spoke, Qwess stood to deliver one of Reece's unreleased rhymes. It was then the world knew who Mysterio was. After applause, Qwess stepped down, the funeral closed out, and the funeral procession made its way to the reception (Reece was being entombed so there was no burial). Every car in the procession, including Doe's family and Qwess's family in the Bentley limos, bumped the song "My Life" from Noriega's first solo album. It was the theme song for the funeral because it matched Reece's life perfectly. To commemorate the occasion, Niya and Doe wore orange-and-blue Bo Jacksons that day.

Niya and Doe's marriage was stronger than ever. The day of the hotel incident, Niya was seriously considering walking, but when the phone call came over about Reece, Doe broke down. She couldn't leave her husband at a time like that. He was too vulnerable. Plus she loved him. When he hurt, she hurt. She still had intentions of leaving, but when Reece and Destiny died it put everything in perspective for her. She forgave her husband, and he showed her a love like never before. Now, as a direct result of that (and the tantric sex class they enrolled in) they were about to give Prince a sister. As for Dana, word had it she had another industry bigwig sprung.

"Let's go on inside," suggested Doe. He put his key into the lock and opened the shrine.

The smell of frankincense and myrrh massaged their nostrils. They all stepped inside, besides Prince. He waited cautiously by the door. After much prodding by Doe, he entered.

The mausoleum walls were ivory. On each side of the wall were slats that resembled marble bleachers. They really were small treasure chests. On the left side were all Destiny's jewelry, money, and important personal effects. On the right side were Reece's. Reece had had a jewelry stash that would rival Liberace's.

At the back of the tomb under fluorescent light were the main attractions. Sitting up high and proud on the wall were wax replicas of Reece and Destiny. The statues sat side by side in gold thrones laced with emeralds for Reece and rubies for Destiny. They wore traditional African garb. Reece sported a silk robe with his bejeweled crown necklace draped prominently on his neck, his actual crown on his bald head. Even the diamonds in his teeth could be seen through parted lips. Destiny wore a cream sarong and silk blouse.

All of this had been done just as Reece had requested in his will. Doe had been skeptical, since he definitely didn't believe in building statues for worship or anything near that, but it was Reece's wish and Reece's money. The sculptures were all done that way in Africa. It was a man in Mali who specialized in this type of thing. It took almost a whole year to complete. The mausoleum had been constructed. It was just awaiting its occupants.

This was everyone's first time seeing the finished product.

"Damn, they look so real," everyone commented.

"I feel like that's my nigga right there," Qwess admitted. "This shit is crazy."

Prince peeked from around Doe, saw his mother, and ran to touch her. She was ice cold, which scared him. Doe caught up with Prince at the door, pounding and screaming. Doe kicked himself. He hadn't been sure how Prince would take it. He now had his answer.

"This is too spooky for me," Niya admitted, before leaving.

"Wait up, girl," Lisa said.

Doe opened the door, too. "I'm going to keep them company."

Qwess whispered, "You straight?"

"Yeah."

Doe closed the door, leaving Qwess alone inside the mausoleum.

Qwess slowly walked to the statue of Reece. He inspected it really closely, then he kissed it on the forehead.

"Rest in peace, my brother. Rest in peace."

Before Qwess turned to walk out, he spotted the epitaph over Reece's head. It read just as Reece had recited it to Qwess a hundred times:

> *"Let me be vile and base, only*
> *Let me kiss the hem of the veil*

In which my CREATOR is shrouded.
Though I may be following the devil,
I AM thy son, O Lord, and I
Acknowledge thee, and I feel the joy,
Without which the world cannot stand."

DON'T MISS THE FIRST BOOK IN THE
CRESCENT CREW SERIES

Street Rap

For Reece and Qwess, being rap superstars was the
dream, but in real life, nothing moved without the money.
So they formed the Crescent Crew, an outfit of young,
ruthless hustlers that locked the Southern drug trade in a
stranglehold. They're at the height of their power when
Qwess is offered a record deal from a major label. He accepts
and makes plans for his whole crew to go legit, but Reece
enjoys his position as king of the streets and has no desire to
relinquish his crown . . .

Available wherever books are sold

Enjoy the following excerpt from *Street Rap* . . .

Chapter 1

The black Tahoe crept onto the rooftop of the parking garage overlooking downtown Fayetteville and stopped. The driver lumbered his hefty frame out of the truck and stood to his full six-foot-seven-inch height. He flipped the collar up on his heavy mink coat, readjusted the sawed-off shotgun tucked beneath his arm, and scanned his surroundings for danger. Satisfied that the area was clear, he tapped on the passenger window of the truck. The tinted window eased down halfway, and a cloud of smoke was released into the air.

"It's clear," the giant reported.

"Good. Now go post up over there so you can see the street, make sure no funny biz popping off," the man in the truck instructed.

The giant hesitated a moment. "You sure about this? I mean, I don't trust these dudes like that," he said.

The man smiled. "You worry too much, Samson. Nobody would dare violate this thing of ours again. Look around you, it's just us and them. This is crew business, and this shit has gone on long enough. Tonight, it ends, one way or another."

The window glided up, and the giant assumed his position near the edge of the parking garage.

Behind the dark glass of the Tahoe, two men sat in the back seat sharing a blunt while a brooding hip-hop track thumped through the speakers. The men casually passed the blunt and enjoyed the music as if they were at a party, and not on the precipice of a drug war for control of the city's lucrative narcotics trade. Although partners, each of the men was a boss in his own right. Their leadership styles were different—one was fire, the other was ice—but it was the balance that made their team so strong.

In the back seat of the Tahoe sat Qwess and Reece, leaders of the notorious Crescent Crew.

"Yo, that beat is bananas, son!" Reece remarked to Qwess. "You did that?"

Qwess nodded. "You knowww it," he sang.

"Word. You already wrote to it?"

"I'm writing to it right now," he replied. He pointed to his temple. "Right here."

"I hear ya, Jay-Z," Reece joked. "So, anyway, how you want to handle this when these niggas get here?"

Qwess nodded. "Let me talk some sense into them, let them know they violated."

"Son, they know they violated."

"Still, let me handle it, because you know how you can be."

Reece scowled. "How I can be? Fuck is that supposed to mean?"

"You know how you can be," Qwess insisted.

"What? Efficient?"

"If you want to call it that."

Headlights bent around the corner and a dark gray H2 Hummer came into view. The Hummer drove to the edge of the garage and stopped inches in front of Samson. He spun around to face the truck. The giant, clad in a full-length mink, resembled King Kong in the glow of the xenon headlamps.

Inside the truck, Qwess craned his head over the seat to confirm their guests. "That's them," he noted as he passed Reece the blunt. He climbed from the back of the truck and tossed his partner a smirk. "Stay here, I got it."

Qwess joined Samson while men poured out of the Hummer. When the men stood before Qwess, someone very important was absent.

Qwess raised his palm. "Whoa, whoa, someone's missing from this little shindig," he observed, scanning the faces. "Where is Black Vic?"

One of the minions stepped forward. He wore a bald head and a scowl. "Black Vic couldn't be here tonight. He sends his regards." The man thumbed his chest with authority. "He sent me in his place."

Qwess frowned. "He sent you in his place? Are you kidding me? We asked for a meeting with the boss of your crew, and he sends you?"

The man nodded. "Yep."

Qwess shook his head. "Yo, get Black Vic on the phone and tell him to get his ass down here now."

The minion chuckled. "I see you got things confused, dawg. You run shit over there, not over here. Now are we talking or what?"

Samson took a step forward. The other three men took two steps back. Qwess gently placed a hand on Samson's arm. The giant stood down.

"I need to talk to the man in charge," Qwess insisted. "Because we only going to have this conversation one time."

"Word?"

"Word!"

Suddenly, the back door to the Tahoe was flung open, and all eyes shifted in that direction. Reece stepped out into the night and flung his dreads wildly. Time seemed to slow down as he diddy-bopped over to them, his Cuban link and heavy medallion swinging around his neck. He pulled back the lapels on his jacket and placed his hands on his waist, revealing his Gucci belt and his two .45s.

"Yo, where Victor at?" Reece asked.

Qwess scoffed. "He ain't here. He sent *these* niggas."

Reece looked at each man, slowly nodding his head. "So Victor doesn't respect us enough to show his face and address his violation? He took two kis from my little man, beat him down. My li'l homie from Skibo hit him with consignment, and he decided to keep shit. Now, we trying to resolve this shit 'cause war is bad for business—for everybody, and he wanna say, 'fuck us'?"

"Black Vic said that you said 'fuck us' when you wouldn't show us no flex on the prices," the minion countered.

"Oh, yeah? That what he said?" Reece asked. He shook his head and mocked, "*He said, she said, we said* . . . See, that's that bitch shit. That's why Victor should've came himself. But he sent you to speak for him, right?"

The bald-headed minion puffed out his bird chest. "That's right."

"Okay." Reece nodded his head and looked around the rooftop of the garage. "Well, tell Victor this!"

SMACK!

Without warning, Reece lit the minion's jaws up with an open palm slap. Samson lunged forward and wrapped his huge mittens around the neck of one of the other minions, who wore a skully pulled low over his eyes. Qwess drew his pistol and aimed it at the other minion in a hoodie, while the soldier in the passenger seat of the Tahoe popped out of the roof holding an AK-47.

"Y'all thought it was sweet?" Reece taunted. He smacked the bald-headed minion again, and he crumpled to the floor semiconscious. "I got a message for Victor's ass, though."

Reece dragged the man over to the Hummer and pitched his body to the ground in front of the pulley attached to the front of the truck. He reached inside the Hummer to release the lever for the pulley, then returned to the front of the Hummer. While the spectators watched in horror, Reece pulled bundles of metal rope from the pulley and wrapped it around the man's neck. Qwess came over to help, and when they were done, the two of them hoisted the man up onto the railing.

"Wait, man! Please don't do this!" the minion pleaded. He was fully conscious now, and scrapping for his life. Qwess cracked him in the jaw and knocked the fight right out of him.

Reece fixed him with a cold gaze. "*We* not doing this to you, homie. Your man, Victor, is," he explained. "His ass should've showed up. Now, of course, this means war."

Reece and Qwess flipped the man over the railing. His body sailed through the air, and the pulley whirred to life, guiding his descent. His banshee-like wail echoed through the quiet night as he desperately tugged at the rope around his neck. Then suddenly, the pulley ran out of rope and caught, snapping his neck like a chicken. Both Qwess and Reece spared a look over the edge and saw his lifeless body dangling against the side of the building.

Reece turned to face the others. Slowly, he slid his thumb across his naked throat, and the AK-47 sparked three times. All head shots.

This was crew business.

Connect with 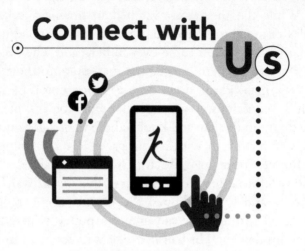Us

Visit us online at
KensingtonBooks.com
to read more from your favorite authors, see books
by series, view reading group guides, and more.

Join us on social media

for sneak peeks, chances to win books and prize packs,
and to share your thoughts with other readers.

facebook.com/kensingtonpublishing
twitter.com/kensingtonbooks

Tell us what you think!

To share your thoughts, submit a review,
or sign up for our eNewsletters, please visit:
KensingtonBooks.com/TellUs.